# *the* secret daughter

# *the* secret daughter

## kelly rimmer

FOREVER

NEW YORK BOSTON

This book is a work of fiction. Names, characters, places, and incidents are the product of the author's imagination or are used fictitiously. Any resemblance to actual events, locales, or persons, living or dead, is coincidental.



Cover design by Emma Graves


Forever
Hachette Book Group
1290 Avenue of the Americas, New York, NY 10104
read-forever.com
twitter.com/readforeverpub

Originally published in 2015 by Bookouture
First U.S. Edition: August 2019

Forever is an imprint of Grand Central Publishing. The Forever name and logo are trademarks of Hachette Book Group, Inc.



Library of Congress Control Number: 2019930105

ISBN: 978-1-5387-3235-9 (trade paperback)

Printed in the United States of America

LSC-C

10 9 8 7 6 5 4 3 2 1

# ACKNOWLEDGMENTS

I have been outrageously lucky to work once again with the team at Bookouture on this book, particularly Oliver Rhodes—I can't thank you enough. Emily Ruston, thank you so much for your patient assistance, particularly when I found myself lost in my ideas. And Jennie Ayers, thank you for the marvellous work you did on the copy edit.

To friends and family who assisted with ideas and feedback on early drafts—Melissa, Tracy, Mum, Aunty Chris and Jodie—thank you. And Sally—thanks for your eagle eye!

To my "Phocas phamily"—particularly Cody, Bill and Val—thanks for all of the support.

I can be obsessive, grumpy and unsociable when I'm caught in the grip of a story—so the biggest thanks of all is reserved for my husband Dan, our amazing children and my ever-patient friends and family—thank you all for putting up with me during the development of this book.

And finally, a note of clarification: although many maternity or "mother and baby" homes existed in Australia until the mid-to-late twentieth century, the setting of this novel (the "Orange Maternity Home") is a fictional institution.

For Maxwell and Violette

# CHAPTER ONE

## Sabina

## March 2012

It's a pretty well established fact in my family that I am not particularly good at keeping secrets. I can think of only two times in my entire life that I have successfully kept something interesting to myself.

The first was when I realised that I had fallen in love with my best friend. We were out at dinner with a group of friends, and over entrées, I caught him staring at me with such love and pride that I could have dissolved into his gaze. I managed to keep my startling realisation to myself for several hours—but as soon everyone else had gone home, I blurted it out in the middle of a totally unrelated conversation. Ted said that I had avoided eye contact with him all night and he'd been wondering why. He says that even when I do hide a secret in my words, my eyes give it away anyway…and that if I'd just looked at him that night, there would have been no need to open my mouth at all.

I suppose my glorious history of failure with secrecy makes it all the more impressive that, when I discovered that I was pregnant, I managed to go a whole two days without telling my mother. Knowing my blabber-mouth tendencies, we took every precaution—I called to invite them around for dinner, and as soon as we'd agreed upon a day and time, Ted took my mobile phone and hid it from me.

Even without such extreme measures, I'm pretty sure that I'd have managed to keep my secret this time. I wanted our announcement to be special; as their only child, I had always felt an inexplicable pressure to make them grandparents. Not once had Mum or Dad said a single thing to me about settling down and having kids, but by the time I reached my late thirties, I'd watched all of their friends acquire a gaggle of noisy grandchildren. Their social set traded proud grandparent stories like kids trade sports cards, and up until that moment, all my parents had to recount were tales of my not particularly impressive teaching career and my adventures travelling with Ted.

It would have been nice to have them share a meal with us and then to tell them in a civilised manner over coffee after, but that was never going to happen. Instead, I greeted them at the door with two perfectly wrapped gift boxes and what must have been a bewilderingly teary grin.

"Sabina, is everything okay? What's this for?" Mum took the box hesitantly. With her spare hand she hooked her handbag onto the coat rack near the door and then carefully unwound her scarf and sat it on top. Dad stepped in behind her and offered his usual cursory kiss to my cheek, then took his gift and shook it curiously.

"Dad! It's fragile!" I laughed, and then I herded them inside with impatient flaps of my hands so that I could close the door behind them. I saw the confused glance they exchanged and I felt the stretch in my cheeks as I grinned hard. "Sit down and open them. Oh, come on you two! Hurry up!"

Ted watched from the little nook in our flat that served as a kitchen. He'd been checking on the elaborate meal I'd half prepared before I got distracted trying to get the ribbons *just right* on the gifts. My husband had been wearing the strangest expression since that moment two mornings earlier, when we stood in the bathroom side by side watching the second line appear on the pregnancy test. Ted was nervous and elated, as I'd expected, but I hadn't anticipated his sudden contentment. We were ready for this, in every sense of the word.

As Mum and Dad took their seats and began to unwind the ribbon around their boxes, Ted leant against the wall beside the stove and wrapped his arms over his chest. He stared at me, and I felt an overwhelming and delicious joy between us. For one final moment, we held a secret in our hearts that no one else knew.

Dad unwrapped his box first.

"A mug?" he said, bewildered. He turned the white mug over and saw the text on the other side. *World's Greatest Granddad.* Dad looked up at me in shock, then he almost dropped the mug as he flew to his feet and scooped me up in a hug. "Sabina! Oh, love!"

It was just as I'd expected, and I was laughing and leaking tears onto his shoulder as he commentated his stream of consciousness about the news.

"When did you find out?"

"A few days ago."

"So when is she due?"

"She?" I laughed. "*It* is due in November."

"Have you two thought about investing in education bonds? It's never too early and the tax incentives are terrific. I'll email you some information next week. Sabina, sit down, you need to rest. Is there champagne? We need champagne, some Moët is in order for an occasion like this. I'll head out and get some."

Dad had gently guided me to the couch and as I sat down, I glanced at Mum for the first time. She had finished unwrapping her gift and was sitting stiffly on the sofa. Her mug was cupped in her overlapping palms and her elbows rested on her lap. There was a flush to her cheeks and a strange intensity in her gaze.

"Megan? Are you okay?" Ted left the kitchen nook and in

just a few steps had crossed the room to sit beside Mum on the sofa. She seemed to shake herself and offered Ted, then I, a bright smile.

"This is wonderful news. I'm so happy for you. I didn't... *we* didn't even realise you two were thinking about children yet."

"Mum, I'm thirty-eight. We're married, our careers are established, we've travelled the world and now we've made a home here in Sydney... what more is there to wait for?"

"You're right. Of course you're right." She looked back at the mug and spoke softly, "But thirty-eight or ninety-eight, you'll always be *my* baby."

"Oh, liven up, Meg." Dad rose and reached into his back pocket for his keys. "You'll have a real baby to play with soon enough. I'm going for champagne. Coming, Ted?"

"Can you keep an eye on the vegetables, Bean?"

I was still watching Mum, who was looking at the mug again. I nodded and smiled at Ted, but as soon as Dad had stepped outside, I motioned towards Mum with my shoulder. Ted shrugged at me, and I returned his confused glance with a grimace.

Once Mum and I were alone, I decided to tackle the tension head-on.

"You don't seem very happy, Mum."

"Of course I'm happy." Mum sat the mug back in its box and rose, crossing the tiny space into our kitchen and dining area in just a few steps. She put the box on the dining room table and stared down at it. "How far along did you say you are?"

"Eight weeks, I think. I have a scan next week to be sure but the doctor thinks I'm due in November."

"Love!" Mum turned back to stare at me. "You shouldn't be telling people yet. Just being eight weeks pregnant now is no guarantee that there's going to be a baby."

I felt my whole body jolt with the brutality of it. For a moment, I couldn't think of a single way to respond. Her words were cruel and her tone was sharp—she was sounding me a warning siren. It hadn't even occurred to me that anything might go wrong with my pregnancy…and why would it? I'd never even been pregnant before, why should I expect the worst?

I'm not sure what the expression on my face was, but I was immediately fighting tears. Mum winced and I saw her clench her fists as she took a deep breath.

"What I mean, Sabina, is that pregnancy… it's just that… it doesn't always…" There was a desperate pleading in her brown gaze. "I just… I don't want you to get hurt. Please don't get your hopes up."

"My hopes *are* up, Mum." I decided to busy myself, to distract myself from how she'd stung me and how disappointing this moment was turning out to be. I'd thought she'd be elated, that she'd immediately be schooling me in the ways of pregnancy and helping me to make plans for motherhood. I stood and moved to walk past her into the kitchen nook, but she caught my elbow and turned me slowly towards her. A single tear slipped onto my cheek and I wiped it away impatiently.

"I'm sorry, Sabina," Mum whispered, then she caught my face in her hands. She wiped at the moisture on my cheek with her thumb and then stared right into my eyes. "Of course you're excited, and so you should be. I just had such a terrible time with my pregnancies. I'm more scared for you than I should be."

"Pregnancies?" I repeated. I was an only child, and this was the first I'd even heard about potential siblings. "But…you never told me you'd had trouble…" I fumbled for a sensitive way to phrase the statement. "I mean, trouble having me."

I watched her for a moment, and noted how distant her gaze was, and the way that her lip quivered just a little as she pulled together a response. The depth of sadness in Mum's eyes was startling, and I suddenly realised that we'd inadvertently opened an old wound for my wonderful mother. I wrapped my arms around her neck and pulled her close for a hug. She was never an overtly affectionate person, but the moment just seemed to demand it. Mum hugged me back, briefly and stiffly, and then stepped away and straightened her blouse.

"We had a terrible time of it. I'm sure things will be much easier for you and Ted."

I felt a heavy, pulsing thud in my ears. I was rapidly processing the implications of this new information and the joy and excitement was entirely gone, replaced with fear and a heightened sense of alertness. Mum had had difficulty carrying a pregnancy? Adrenaline seemed to be pumping through me, as if I was staring down an imminent physical threat to my safety.

"But... I hate to ask you, Mum, but I need to know so I can talk to my doctor about this." It took monumental effort to keep my voice level and my words steady. "Do you know why things were so difficult?"

Mum sighed and shook her head.

"There were lots of theories, but no, we never really knew. We fell pregnant easily enough, for the first few years anyway. I just couldn't seem to carry a baby past the first trimester."

Mum's face was utterly pale now, except for the round apples of the too-pink blush she always wore.

"How many times?" I asked hesitantly.

"A lot," Mum said abruptly. "You really don't need to worry, love, and I'm sorry that I didn't react the way I should have. I was caught off guard. I just didn't realise you and Ted were planning a family."

"Of course I'm worried. I understand that this is hard for you to talk about, but you're going to have to give me some more information here." When the stiffness in her expression did not ease, I resorted to stating the obvious. "Mum...what if your problems are genetic?"

My excitement about the baby had disappeared altogether, at least for the moment. I had just discovered that both my optimism and my pregnancy were fragile things that could be damaged somehow by mere words. I thought about the tiny jumpsuits I'd purchased the morning we'd had the positive test. They were sitting out in the open on the dresser in my room, and I was suddenly embarrassed by my own innocence. I wanted to excuse myself to run into the bedroom and to pack those jumpsuits up and hide them at the top of my wardrobe.

What Mum was telling me meant that there was surely a higher than average chance that I would never get to use those jumpsuits, and that the tiny being I had thought was safe and secure in my womb might not be so safe after all. Was there an inbuilt kill-switch in my genes, inherited from Mum, waiting to stop me reproducing myself?

Mum seemed to be struggling to come up with a way to explain her situation, but I quickly grew impatient.

"I'm sorry to press you, but I need to understand this, Mum."

"It's not genetic."

"You said there was no real explanations, only theories for why...how can you be so sure?"

"I just am."

"But—"

"Sabina! Leave it."

For the second time that night I was shocked speechless, this time left staring at my mother's back as she walked to the stove and began checking on the various pots and pans there. I couldn't miss the way her hands shook as she lifted the lids or the noisy way those lids clattered down as she replaced them.

When I found my voice again, it would have been far too easy to drop the subject. Mum and I were close—closer than any other mother and daughter I knew, and the idea of upsetting her further was beyond upsetting to *me.*

But there was something new at stake, and it was something precious and already loved. A lot had changed in the medical field in the years since Mum had been pregnant, and if my pregnancy *was* at risk, maybe there was something that could be done about it if I had enough information. I decided to try a less direct approach.

"Maybe you can tell me about your pregnancy with me," I suggested softly. "Did you have morning sickness? I've been lucky so far, I didn't even realise I was pregnant."

Mum was still staring at the pots. I had the distinct impression that every single word I was saying now was wounding her, and I had no idea what to do about it. I hesitantly reached to touch her back, just as the front door sprung open and Dad and Ted returned. Their booming voices were jovial and loud, a distinctly uncomfortable contrast to the strained tension in the room with Mum and me. Mum looked across our little living space, straight to Dad at the front door, and I watched the colour fade from his ruddy cheeks.

"Megan...?" Dad's footsteps and his words were suddenly slow and cautious.

"We need to leave," she whispered.

"Hey, no!" Ted held up the icy bottle in his hand. "We're celebrating, remember? What's going on?"

"Mum, no, I'll drop it," I pleaded with her, but she shook her head, and marched past Dad and Ted. I knew she was in a panic when she only scooped her handbag and scarf off the coat rack, neglecting to carefully rewind the scarf on her neck as she would have on any other occasion.

Dad looked at me.

"What did she say?" he asked.

"She just told me n-not to get excited about the baby," I whispered, and at the sound of my stutter, I burst into tears. It had taken years of speech therapy to get my stutter under control, inflicted upon me mostly by my mother and her iron will. I couldn't remember the last time I had tripped up on a word, but then again, I also couldn't remember the last time I'd been this upset.

"She told me you two had lots of miscarriages and that we shouldn't be telling anyone yet. Then I asked her why she'd had problems and if it was genetic and she got really upset. I'm sorry, Dad."

"Is that all she said?"

"What else *is* there?"

Dad made a frustrated sound somewhere between a growl and a sigh.

"I'll take her home, I'm so sorry she's ruined your night." He picked his mug up and made a beeline for our front door. "Let her get used to the news and calm down, and we'll make it up to you both, I promise."

The door slammed behind Dad, and the sobs I'd held back broke free. Ted dumped the champagne on the sofa and pulled me close.

"What the hell just happened?" Ted asked.

"I h-have no idea." I struggled to form the words. "But I think w-we'd better go to the doctor tomorrow."

He gently spun me around, turning my back towards the couches so that we could sit together, and as he did so, I saw Mum's mug still sitting on the dining room table.

# CHAPTER TWO

## Lilly

## June 1973

Dear James,

I'm in so much trouble, James.

I've been keeping a secret from you. I wanted to tell you, but I was so scared. And we only ever speak on the phone and I'm always talking to you within earshot of someone. Then I was going to write it in a letter, but Tata posts my letters to you. And if he read it...

Well, if he read it, I suppose things would have turned out like they have.

I'm pregnant, James. I know this must be a huge shock and I'm so sorry to tell you this way...but to be honest, right now, I'll be lucky if I can even figure out how to get this letter into the post to actually tell you at all.

I don't know when it happened...just before you left for university, I guess. I feel like such an idiot. Did you know that what we were doing was how babies are made? You're so smart, of course you knew. Well, I didn't, and even though you left at the start of January I didn't even realise I was pregnant until April. The nuns at school always talked about sex...but they made it sound so bad and sordid that I didn't actually realise that's what *we* were doing. It just happened so naturally for us, didn't it? We never even decided to be boyfriend and girlfriend, we were just friends and then we were more. I don't even remember our first kiss...do you? It barely seemed important at the time, just another step of this love between us. Every move we took together felt automatic, as if our instincts were guiding us. Not even for a second did I think that we might be doing that thing the nuns had warned us away from.

At first, I thought I was tired because I missed you so much. I wanted to lie in bed and sleep all day, and I didn't much want to eat, which was driving Mama crazy. She kept chastising me, and Henri took to calling me "Lovesick Lilly". Then my appetite came back and my clothes got tighter and tighter, but still I didn't understand. I thought I was just eating too much, making up for lost time during those early months in the year when I lived off scant bites from each meal.

I only realised what was really going on when one of the girls at school was talking about her period and I realised that I hadn't had mine since before Christmas. Even *I* know what *that* means.

At first, I tried to pretend it wasn't happening, and for a while that was easy. The boys teased me for being fat, but I'm pretty used to that. My school uniform got tighter and tighter and no one seemed to notice, and so I didn't think about the baby, or you, or what this would mean for all of us.

Then the baby started kicking me. I figured that sooner or later someone would join the dots and my secret would be out. I used to lie in bed at night, tossing and turning, waiting for the axe to fall. When I felt like the secret I was holding was growing too big to contain . . . and my fears about Tata finding out would grow too strong, I'd close my eyes and imagine the consequences. I had this crazy idea that I could think away the fear if I could just plan it all out.

I'd picture Tata's rage and his shame; I'd imagine Mama's disgust. I wrote a silly movie script in my mind about how things would go—I played around with the story, to see what would happen if Tata found out at night, or in the morning, or while I was at school. I pictured it on rainy days and on sunny days and on the other kids' birthdays or the day I went into labour.

No matter what details I imagined, the story ended the same; I found myself on your front doorstep, sitting my suitcase on the mat beside my feet so that I could knock and call your mum.

I was right about most things. This morning Tata woke me up and told me to pack a suitcase. He lined up the other kids, all seven of them, and he watched while I said goodbye. Kasia and Henri were both crying, and I could see the pity in their eyes. The worst of it was Mama. She wouldn't even look at me—she hid in the kitchen and wept and when I tried to make her turn around to say goodbye, she shook my hand off her shoulder and sobbed even harder.

Then, just like I thought he would, Tata threw me in the car and he ranted. All the way down the long driveway to the end of the farm, he yelled with such fury that spit kept flying out of his mouth and I just sat next to him and tried not to cry.

He said vile things to me, and they were things I deserve, I suppose. He talked a lot about me shaming the Wyzlecki name and letting him down, and the worst part—he called me names that I never realised that *my* Tata actually knew. I knew that I'd make him even angrier if I cried, so I tried to stare at my lap and hold myself together. You know how thick his accent seems when he's angry. Today it really sounded as though he was just roaring at me in Polish. The words were a smooth and endless stream of fury, the gaps between them compressed by his rage.

I held myself together because I told myself that everything would be okay. I thought he'd take me to your Mum and Dad, and they'd be angry at us too but at least they'd let me call you. But Tata didn't take me to your place. My suitcase was in the back of the car, but I never got to feel the sweet relief of sitting it onto your doormat beside my feet.

Instead of turning left at the end of the driveway to your farm, he turned right, and then at the highway turnoff, he turned towards Orange.

I know it's only forty minutes to Orange but without knowing where I was going, it felt like we were driving forever. I begged him to tell me where he was taking me, but all that he would say was that he was "not dumping our family's rubbish" onto yours. I felt like I had been knocked out of orbit and that I was floating through space—all that I knew was that the car was headed *away* from everything I've ever known. I tried to imagine every possibility. Was he sending me to Uncle Adok in Poland, who I've never even met? Were we en route to an abortion clinic—are those places even real?

For a fleeting moment I thought he was taking me to the train station, to send me to you…how wonderful that would have been.

But when he finally stopped the car we were at the big hospital at Orange, and at first that made no sense at all. For a while we sat there. Tata sat with his hands on the steering wheel, staring straight ahead and now I was the one ranting. It was like he couldn't even hear me, then I guess I finally got through to him. For the first time in my life, I cried today and Tata did not dismiss me.

No, today he didn't chastise me for crying, and he didn't remind me of how much easier my life is than his was as a teen back in war-torn Poland. Today, after his rage was all burned up, all that seemed left of him was shame and sadness. Tata told me that we were not going to the hospital, but to the maternity home opposite. He told me that I have to stay here until the baby comes.

We went inside and we met nurses and social workers. They sat me in a cold little room with Tata and he signed pages and pages of paperwork. There were several folders, and by the time we left, each one of them had been marked with black marker the words *Liliana Wyzlecki, BFA*. I think the BFA is a code, maybe it's *my* code in here. I am sure I will find out sooner or later.

I've let everyone down, James. I was so stupid, and now I'm pregnant, and everything is ruined for all of us.

James, I don't know if I'll find a way to post this to you. I don't know what's going to happen, or even how I'm going to cope in this horrible place.

All I know is that the love between you and me was such a miracle that without even meaning to, we made a baby, and I love that baby already just as much as I love you.

I know that you've only just started at university and that you've dreamed of that for years. I know that everything that we planned for our future hangs on you getting your degree. So I know... I really, truly understand that I'm asking a lot of you.

But if you don't come back for me... for *us*... and if we don't find a way to marry before the baby is born... I don't even know what's going to happen. I can't even guess. Tata won't let me go home with a baby in tow, and I have no way to support myself without you.

There's no point calling me here or writing back; they have already told me that they won't let me speak to you. So please just come—get on the next bus and come straight here, so we can tell them that we'll find a judge and find a way to get married right away and then I'm sure they'll let me go.

I love you with all of my heart, James. Please forgive me for keeping this secret and please, oh God please... come and help me and our baby.

Love,

Lilly

# CHAPTER THREE

## Sabina

## March 2012

I had something of an emotional hangover the next day.

Ted and I spoke in hushed tones over breakfast as we made plans to visit the doctor together on our lunchbreaks. Before, our chatter had been upbeat and excited, but now we dared not risk exuberance. The pregnancy suddenly felt too fragile to expose to further loud voices or emotions.

There were times as the morning passed when I'd fully engage with the class I was teaching and for a brief moment the image of my mother's distraught face would fade from the forefront of my mind. I had three individual one-hour classes to get through—including a kindergarten class which was always a challenge, and I was grateful for the distraction. I'd always felt that it was via music that I became fully alive, and that day, even the sounds of five-year-olds drumming against the desks felt like life support.

After I'd finished my last morning class, I went to my desk and withdrew my phone. I fully expected a missed call or voicemail from Mum, and my heart sank when the screen was empty. I opened a blank text message and tapped out a message.

*Mum, I'm so sorry about what happened last night. I know it's hard but please—can we talk, as soon as you're ready? I just want to do whatever I can to protect my pregnancy, if there's anything at all I can do. Love you xo*

—

Our GP suggested we undertake a series of routine tests in lieu of any firm ideas about where to start looking for potential problems.

"Fertility issues aren't always genetic," he assured us. "And even if they are, there's nothing to say you've inherited your mother's issues anyway, or that it's not a problem we've managed to solve in all of those years—medicine has come a really long way since you were born. But I do think we should be smart about this, so we'll send you for a scan next week to see how things are progressing so far, and I'll order a series of blood tests in the meantime so we can look for the common issues."

I didn't feel any better after we'd seen him. I had the blood drawn and then Ted and I went for lunch together, but we sat in near-silence in the café with my still-silent phone on the table between us.

It was going to be a very long week until our first ultrasound. I was confused about which to focus more time worrying about; should I concentrate on Mum's welfare, or on finding out as much as I could about her issues and trying to help the baby?

Ted reached across the table and squeezed my hand.

"Do you want me to call her, Bean?"

"I don't think so," I said. "She was so upset last night, I don't know how to balance finding out all about this stuff with not upsetting her more."

"All of this stress can't be good for you."

I looked down at my plate. The chicken and mushroom pasta I'd ordered was now evenly divided into four quadrants but I'd eaten only a mouthful.

"Are you saying that because I've barely touched my lunch?"

Ted chuckled.

"Well, I've known you for nearly twenty years and I've never seen you too distracted to eat before."

I smiled weakly and stabbed a chunk of chicken, then lifted it to my mouth. The sauce was decadent, laden with cream and cheese and bursting with flavour. I savoured the taste for a moment and felt my appetite kick in.

"If we haven't heard from her in the next few days, I'll give them a call," I said, after a few quick mouthfuls of food. "Maybe Dad can explain it to me so she doesn't have to."

"He seemed pretty spooked last night too. They must've had a nightmare time of it for them both to be so traumatised all of these years later."

"I don't know how people survive losing..." I started to speak, but my voice broke. "I just mean, it's only been a few days, but I already love this baby. If anything happens to it..."

Ted reached across the table and squeezed my hand.

"Let's stay positive, Bean."

—

When the afternoon passed with no response from Mum, I walked home from work and tried to fall into my usual routine. Ted's car was in the driveway, and I immediately headed for the little office opposite our bedroom and planted a kiss on the dark hair on top of his head. He was on a call, a boring one judging by the news article he was reading on his computer screen. He pointed to the clock then held up six fingers, indicating that he wouldn't be finished until 6 p.m.—another half an hour.

I put dinner in the oven, then changed into harem pants and one of Ted's T-shirts, but was very happy to abandon my bra;

my clothes had all become just a little bit too tight and I knew it had nothing to do with pregnancy and everything to do with too much indulgence over the summer.

At that time of the afternoon in autumn, the most comfortable place in our little granny flat was the dining room table. There I could enjoy the warmth of the dying sun and still watch the television all while working, or at least pretending to work. I laid out my lesson plans across the table and hit the power button on the TV remote. The oven timer counted down, but its audible tick was not enough to remind me that a meal was imminent; I opened a packet of chicken biscuits on the table and promised myself *just one more* for at least ten minutes while the game show won the battle for my attention against my lesson planning.

When my doorbell sounded, I glanced at the wall clock: 5:43 p.m.; prime door-to-door sales hour. As I rose and approached the door, I tried to ready myself to be firm, practicing the shape of the words *no thank you* under my breath. I could see silhouettes through the stained glass of the door and I grimaced as I reached for the doorknob. Two doorknockers? More than one usually meant the product on sale was religion, and I always felt particularly guilty cutting off that sales pitch. The motivation seemed so much more innocent.

When I realised that it was actually my parents on my doorstep, my natural reaction was delight and relief. A split second later, my heart sank when I realised that they had both been crying.

"We need to talk to you, Sabina."

There was an unusual defeat in Dad's stance, and as I surveyed the way he held himself, it slowly dawned on me that they weren't there to talk about the events of the previous night or my pregnancy at all. Surely, given the way Dad's shoulders slumped, someone was sick or dying. My mother, standing next to him on the tiny porch to our equally tiny home, was all tension and fight—holding herself bolt upright and stiff, her brown eyes flashing with fire. She looked every bit the part of someone ready to go into battle.

"Oh God. What is it?" I was frozen. Maybe if I didn't let them inside, I wouldn't have to hear whatever it was they'd come to say. Dad motioned towards the cramped living area behind me.

"Can we come in?"

"Ted," I called, as I opened the door to let them inside.

"I'm still on the phone, Bean." The words floated down the hallway at me. Ted was sending me information, not expressing irritation at the interruption.

"Ted," I said again, this time letting the strain and urgency slip into my voice. I saw Dad's broad shoulders rise and fall as he inhaled and sharply exhaled.

"Let's take a seat," he said, and he slid his arms around my shoulders and directed me towards our living area. Dad's scent, of soap and spices and safety, wound its way around me and my eyes watered. As he sat me down on the couch he kissed the side of my head, and with that kiss he knocked the tears onto my cheeks. Mum sat stiffly on the edge of the other couch opposite us, *just* as she'd done the previous night. Ted stepped into the room.

"What's going on?" There was instant alarm in his bright blue eyes. My parents ignored him though, their gazes were locked on me.

"I'm sorry to drop this on you, sweetheart," Dad said. His words were measured and calm, but for the red rims of his eyes this could have been any ordinary conversation. "I know this is going to come as a shock, but you have to believe that we have kept this from you only because we believed it to be for the best."

Mum still hadn't said a word.

"What...what is it?" I felt the anxiety rising as bubbles in my throat and electric shocks down my arms. My thoughts were stumbling into one another. Cancer. It was probably cancer, and if they'd kept it from me for some time, maybe Dad didn't have long left with us.

"Sabina." Dad's whisper was rough, and I felt the trembling of his arm across my shoulders. "You were adopted."

There it was. Three short words, and my life fractured. I didn't realise it yet, but that was the thick black line down the middle of my timeline: there would forever be a *Before* those words, and an *After.*

I really had no concept of that yet though, because my first response was that Dad's statement was nonsense, in fact, it was hilariously far-fetched. I looked straight to Ted. He raised an eyebrow at me, mirroring my own initial reaction—total and utter disbelief.

There was just no way.

No. Freaking. Way.

Surely I'd have known, or at least, suspected. I wouldn't share Mum's brown eyes and Dad's smile. I thought of the interests and habits and traits we shared in common—too many to recount, far too many to be coincidental. What a ridiculous statement. Was this some kind of joke?

I laughed. The sound started as the last burst of confidence from a woman who had known entirely who she was, and then when no one else laughed, it faded away to a confused whimper.

"*Is* it a j-joke?" I glanced at Mum, who was staring at the floorboards and now seemed defeated. The tension had drained from her and she'd visibly slumped. But no, this was not the delivery of a punchline—this was a truth long held behind a wall, and the wall had just collapsed.

I rose, away from my parents as if they were suddenly a threat, but I couldn't take my eyes off them, and so I found myself backing away blindly to find the comfort of my husband. Ted caught me and wrapped his arms around me, anchoring me. So many questions rushed at me at once that I couldn't even organise myself to ask a single one of them.

"Why would—but how—why would—and why—?"

The words wouldn't come. They never flowed when I was distressed; instead they stuck, as if the record of my language soundtrack had been scratched. I'd hit a word or a sound and circle back over it endlessly, until I found a way to still myself and to enforce a rhythm onto my voice. The gentle squeeze of Ted's arm around my waist slowed me enough to finish the sentence, but even when I managed to form it, my words sounded thin and high.

"I don't understand. Why would you keep this from me? *How* could you?" Now the record of my words was playing, but the speed was too fast, and I sounded ridiculous and panicked even to my own ears.

"We thought it was for the best," Dad said. I looked at Mum—my best friend, or so I thought. It suddenly struck me that she hadn't made eye contact since they arrived.

It was no wonder she'd panicked when I asked her about her pregnancy with me. She hadn't actually had one.

"How could it be for the best to lie to her for four decades?" Ted's incredulity hung in the silence that followed his question. Dad pleaded with us for understanding.

"It was a different time, guys. When you came to us, Sabina, we had been told that it would be better if you just never had to deal with it. And by the time society's thinking on that changed, you were old enough that it just seemed too late. We thought..." The sentence faded, and his lip trembled when he finished in a whisper, "...we really thought you'd never need to know."

"So where...where did you get me?" I had visions of being left on a doorstep somewhere, unwanted and unloved. I pictured driving rain and darkness and wailing alone and helpless at the coldness of it all, and the image was so vivid that for a second I wondered if it could be an actual memory.

Was I discovering an origin story for myself that was the polar opposite of the one I'd always known?

"You were adopted from the maternity home where your mother worked."

"She-she worked there?" I was confused. My mother? Who *was* my mother? Was it Megan, sitting in the crumpled heap before me, or the nameless, faceless woman who had given birth to me and then apparently abandoned me?

"Yes. Oh, hang on, you mean—the woman...?" Dad didn't seem to know what words to use either. "No, she was a resident at the home. Mum worked there."

I looked at Mum. Had she really physically shrunk since her arrival last night, or was it a trick of the light? Her face was in her hands now. I wondered what she was thinking, and how this woman who had shared and overshared with me over so many thousands of hours over so many decades, could have decided time and time and time again to not mention this one, vital fact.

I was having an out-of-body moment, floating around on the ceiling while the conversation happened below me. We were no ordinary family—we were an *extra*-ordinary family—close-knit and open and honest and all round healthy. And, it now seemed, liars to our very core.

"Why are you telling me now?"

Even Dad seemed uncomfortable. He didn't generally *do*

uncomfortable, Dad was confident and strong, and he just handled things. Dad could talk to me about periods and boys and sex and which dress I might wear to the party, dealing with the awkward moments of parenthood with ease.

"We knew Megan panicked you last night. She shouldn't have told you about our problems, you didn't need to know. But we understand how worried you must be that you might have inherited the same issues...we couldn't let you spend your pregnancy worrying for nothing or, God forbid, stress yourself about it such that something terrible did happen."

Later, much later, when the shock wore off and the truth sunk in, I'd return to this moment and dissect it from every angle. For now, I just had to cope, and that seemed difficult enough without critically analysing the information I was being drip fed. That was a blessing, because had I really understood that Dad was actually admitting to me that they were only telling me because they felt they had no choice...well, I think I'd have broken into a million pieces, right then and there.

"Why did she give me up?"

Mum finally looked up. There were silent tears drenching her face.

"It was a different time, Sabina. She was sixteen years old. Keeping you was never an option."

"Was this hospital involved in the forced adoption business that's been all over the news?" Ted asked. He always laughed at my lack of interest in news and current affairs—but this was exactly why. This was the first time I'd heard the term *forced adoption,* and I'd rather never have heard those two words together. All of the implications of this rushed at me, but before I had time to untangle the jumbled mess of thoughts, Mum sobbed, and the sound broke me. I slipped from Ted's grasp and sat beside her, wrapping my arms around her slim shoulders. I had just discovered the biggest betrayal of my life, but I couldn't bear to see my betrayer crying.

"Mum..." I didn't know what to say to her, and as strong as the shock and the confusion was, the urge to comfort her was still stronger. I rubbed the space between her shoulder blades, staring at the floor as I tried to wrap my mind around the enormity of the disclosure. The peculiar numbness of physiological shock was settling. I was standing in a glass cage watching a hurricane rage past outside.

Dad rose and crouched beside Mum, his arm meeting mine across her back.

"Keep it together, Meg."

He whispered; his words flat and desperate, but I caught them anyway. In his tone I recognised the one dissonant note that I'd always been aware was sounding in the symphony of our family. Ted could have said that same sentence and sounded both sensitive and sensible, but from Dad, it sounded like a command. Dad was passionate about our family, which was a very good thing nearly all of the time...except for those few moments when the passion went just a little too far, and he seemed controlling and demanding.

It jarred me. It had before, but that night, hearing Dad speak to Mum with such sharpness...it was almost too much—I cringed, averting my gaze to my husband, my anchor. Ted sat down on the sofa opposite us, resting his elbows on his knees, dangling his hands between his legs. He really could be very sensitive when he needed to be, but more than anything, Ted was rational. He would find a way through the mess of this to a truth that I could digest.

"So, who was she?" he asked quietly.

No one answered him, not for a long time. The silence was ragged, then it was awkward. It hadn't occurred to me to ask, but now that the question was out there, I desperately needed it to be answered. When I finally realised that they were just ignoring him, I prompted,

"Mum?"

"We never knew anything about her."

Was she lying? Mum was avoiding my gaze again, but her guilt was palpable. She slumped when she spoke, as if the heaviness of the words was pressing her into the earth. I glanced at Ted, and he raised his eyebrows at me. He saw it too—the hallmarks of a lie.

"Megan, she deserves to know everything you can tell her," Ted spoke softly, reasonably.

Mum shook her head and the tears started again.

"I'm really sorry Sabina, there's nothing I can tell you. I don't know anything else."

"Well, are there records?" Ted said. "Surely there is paperwork. What about Sabina's birth certificate?"

There was the glimmer of hope I'd been holding my breath waiting for. I sat up straight again and turned my attention to Dad.

"It lists your names." I felt washed in relief, too confused to note how ridiculous the notion was—as if, perhaps, they could be mistaken after all. "I've had a copy of it for years, Dad. It lists *your* names."

"Is it not the original?" Ted asked softly, and I slumped again.

"No, it's the original." Mum shook her head. "I told you, it was a different time. We adopted you at birth so we were listed as your parents, and we *are* your parents. Sometimes back then, hospitals didn't even bother to keep records to the contrary."

"So, I can't find her, even if I want to?" I was instantly grieving, feeling an acute loss for something I hadn't even known existed until minutes earlier—something I wasn't even sure that I wanted yet.

"I doubt it very much, love," Dad said quietly.

We sat for a moment, all of us lost together in the mess of it all. No one spoke, but the room was noisy anyway: the television was still on in the background. Someone had won big on the game show, and triumphant music played while rainbow balloons and streamers rained on them from above.

I'd never been diagnosed with anxiety, but I supposed this was probably the best label for the way my fears ran out of control sometimes. When caught off guard, my mind would churn a situation over and over, until I could almost lose myself in the swirling tornado of thoughts. I'd learned, almost by accident over the years, to manage that panic by being mindful of the hard facts about a moment, to ground myself in reality, instead of floating around in my fears.

So yes, the sun *was* still streaming through the window, a patch of bright light reflecting uncomfortably into my face from the polished floorboards in the kitchen—the world had not ended. The oven was still ticking down, and judging by the hearty smell, the lentils and lamb were just about done. Time was marching onward, just as it always had. My bare feet on the floorboards were comfortably cool. I was still me, and I was still here. The red lines on the skin of my stomach caused by my too-small work trousers would have faded now.

And as for that tiny life sprouting deep inside me, I felt a supreme confidence that no circumstance on this earth could inspire me to give it up, and no force in the universe could make me. It was the physical manifestation of the soul-solidifying love I felt for Ted. How could someone ever part with such a thing? An answer came to me almost instantly.

Her story... *my* story... might not be one of love.

A chill came over me. I released Mum, and stood.

"We should go and let you think about this." Dad rose too,

extending his long body to its full height, and I took a moment to think back to the fear I'd had when he first arrived and I thought he might be sick. I'd have preferred that outcome—sickness, we could fight together. Sickness and age were inevitable. Sickness meant there was still some kind of hope, even if it was fragile. *This*... this meant that everything would immediately and forever be topsy-turvy.

"I think that's a good idea." My ever-vigilant husband was staring at my face, and I wondered what he was thinking and if he knew how shaken I was. I could taste panic simmering in my gut. When the shock wore off, I would be wrecked.

"Do you still love us?" Mum asked. While Dad was already making moves towards the door, it was obvious that she didn't want to leave until I promised her that everything was okay. And in any other circumstances I'd have done just that, so she was probably expecting it.

I looked from her gaunt, tear-stained face, to Dad's more subtly pleading gaze, and then to the floor.

"Of course I st-still love you." I was mumbling and stumbling, the words clumping together into a mangled mess. "You just need to let me t-think this through."

—

They left, and after Ted shut the door behind them, we stood in silent confusion side by side at the entrance, almost frozen in time until the oven timer rang. Ted moved first; he turned the oven off, removed the casserole dish onto the top of the stove, and then wordlessly poured me a glass of the ginger beer I'd made several months earlier with Dad. I followed Ted, meandering hopelessly in his general direction, not really cognisant of where I was or what I was doing. After a moment or two of standing near the TV staring at the floor, I took a few further steps to the dining room table and sank into a chair. The upholstered cushion was still warm from when I'd left it only five minutes earlier. How could so much have changed in the time it takes a seat to cool down?

Ted pushed aside my lesson plans to sit beside me. I stared at the bubbles rising through the soft drink he placed before me.

"I wish this was real beer," I whispered.

"I can get you one if you want, Bean. I'm sure one won't hurt."

"No, no."

I took a long, soothing sip of the beer and then turned to him. The evening's normality had shattered, and in its place, I sat in the bubble of a nightmare. I tried again to re-ground myself in the warmth of the fading sunshine, in the glow of the floor lamp between the table and our little kitchen, in the bitterness of the ginger beer, in the closeness of Ted's thigh near to, but not quite touching, mine.

It wasn't working now. What kind of stress relief could I employ in this particular instance? Was there a mindfulness practice big enough?

"Did that really just happen?"

"I can't believe it either." He shook his head slowly. "Did you ever suspect?"

"Of course not." I drank more, until even the creamy bitterness reminded me only of Dad. Mum had the refined palate of a woman who could sip a merlot and comment on the hint of chocolate in its base, but to me, all wine tasted like vinegar. Instead, Dad and I shared a fanatical obsession with beer—all kinds of beer actually; ginger beers and stouts and pilsners and porters. He had a trellis in his backyard where he grew a series of hops varieties, and every few months we'd spend a whole evening cooking from scratch our own elaborate home brew. The last time, just a few weeks earlier, I'd soaked the grain at home during the day while I was at school, and then driven across the suburbs in my little hatchback, the giant pot nestled like a baby beneath a seatbelt. It took us nearly six hours that night to boil and strain the grain to just the right temperature, then to cool it and to apply the yeast, and to transfer it into a vat to ferment.

In another few weeks, it would be ready to bottle, and we'd spend half a day on a weekend chatting while we decanted it into glass bottles with bottle caps pressed on to seal it.

I thought I'd inherited from Dad that love of the intricacies of the craft, not to mention the satisfaction of the yeasty taste at the end of all of the work and waiting.

"But everyone says I look just like them. Don't I have Mum's smile? Don't I have Dad's eyes?"

"I thought so too."

"So everything they've ever said to me is a lie?"

"I can understand why you would say that," Ted said, after a moment. "But it's not true. For all of their faults, you can't deny that your parents have genuinely adored you."

"If they adore me, Ted, why would they lie to me?"

"I have absolutely no idea."

"I'm only thirty-eight. Surely even thirty-eight years ago people understood that denying someone the truth about their birth was not going to be *great* for them."

"Well... I don't know about that, honey. I've seen the news about this forced adoption controversy, it really sounds like young mothers weren't even given a choice about keeping their kids. Hiding the actual adoption from the child is not *much* of a stretch from there."

"But... why, Ted? Why weren't they given a choice?" I'd been stoic until that moment, but the idea suddenly slipped through my shock-cocoon and I felt myself dissolving. This concept was so monstrous and outrageous that I couldn't even stand to think that it had anything to do with me. When I spoke again, my whispered words were uneven, punctuated by the tremors of barely restrained tears. "Are you seriously saying that women's babies were just *taken* from them?"

"Well...as I understand it, yes. I think it was about the shame of babies being born out of marriage," Ted murmured, sliding his arm around me. "We can do some reading...but I am pretty sure that single women, especially young single women who were found to be pregnant were taken to maternity homes, like the one Megan must have worked in. I think the mums were often coerced into signing the paperwork, and the babies were taken after the birth and adopted out from there."

"But I just can't even believe Mum would be a part of such a thing," I whispered. "Surely that must be some mistake, maybe she didn't understand what was happening there. But then, even if that was true—" I was thinking out loud now, and I sat away from Ted so that I could stare at him, searching the blue depths of his eyes, seeking comfort. "Even if she didn't know...she definitely knew about the adoption. And hiding that from me? Mum has always talked to me about everything." I slumped again and leant into him, and a sob escaped. "I thought she did." Ted pressed a soft kiss to the side of my head. "Do I even know them?"

"I guess your parents' role in all of this must be the hardest part to digest," Ted murmured. "The thing is...your parents... well..."

"I know," I said grimly. He seemed uncharacteristically stuck for words but I didn't need him to finish the sentence. I assumed that he was going to refer to how close I was to them, and how invested they were in my life. He'd eventually grown accustomed to us over the years, but in the early days of our friendship, he'd remarked often with suspicion and confusion at how fond I was of my parents. In turn, I'd always thought *his* family was the strange one, with their polite distance, and the convoluted web of ex-spouses and step-siblings and half-siblings that formed their structure. "My parents are just wonderful."

Ted cleared his throat, and shifted just a little. I frowned. "What?"

"Bean, your parents *can* be wonderful…but even so…I really feel like sometimes you look at your family through rose-coloured glasses. This is a really, truly shitty thing they've done to you…and yes it's come out of nowhere, but then again… I totally get that they would be capable of keeping a secret like this."

"What's that supposed to mean?"

"I just mean…honey…they can be manipulative."

"Ted!"

"Remember when we bought the house?"

"They were delighted for us!"

"They *were* delighted for us. The day we exchanged contracts, we went out for dinner and your dad popped open the bubbles just as he always does and we talked with them for hours about our plans for the house, and how we'd rent this granny flat out for a bit of extra income. Remember?" I nodded, but I was on guard.

"So?"

"So the very next day, you went shopping for décor with Megan, and when you came home, you were adamant that it would be foolish for us to move into the big house and rent the flat."

"B-but it didn't make sense. There's only two of us, and the house is huge."

"It was huge when we inspected it, it was huge when we

bought it, and it was huge when we told your parents we'd gone ahead with the sale...and not once did you question the sense of that until they did. It's a large, luxurious house. We went to Dubai and I worked ninety-hour weeks for two years so that we could save up enough to buy that house and set ourselves up. What didn't make sense was for us to buy the house, and then install some other family in it just to maximise our tax deductions. But that's what Graeme thought was most sensible, and so that's what Megan thought was most sensible, and eventually that's what *you* thought was most sensible. And believe me, Sabina, when your parents convince you of something, you are loyal to that idea almost beyond rationality. Look at our situation now—crammed in here like sardines, and now we're going to have to figure out how to break the lease and get the tenants out of the house before the baby comes."

"But *you* agreed to move in here too," I whispered, stung.

"Because..." Ted sighed and entwined my hand on the table with his. "Because one of the things I love most about you is your loyalty, and your optimism, and even those damned rose-coloured glasses. I'm assuming that you use them on me too, given that you put up with me." I smiled weakly, but there were tears in my eyes, because if there was one thing I was still sure of it was that I didn't need rose-coloured glasses for my husband. He was genuinely amazing. "I did try to talk you out of it, but it was obvious to me that pleasing your dad meant a lot to you, and eventually I figured I would just go along with it for a year or two to make you happy. But it was never what *we* wanted. And it wasn't just the house, it was you going to uni, and—"

"I wanted to go to uni, Ted."

"Yes, you did. But you didn't want to study teaching, did you? You wanted to go to the conservatorium to study performance. You told me that the very first time you met me. Your parents convinced you to do the safe course, instead of the brave course. I love your parents. I really do. But I don't think I can listen to you wax lyrical about how wonderful they are any more, not after tonight. What they are, and what they've always been, are two people who love you more than anything else—but to them, love and control are all jumbled up together somehow. I can't help but wonder if a part of your mum's distress last night was because we didn't ask her permission to have a baby of our own."

"You make them sound like monsters."

"No, Bean, I don't mean to. I just want you to look at this rationally. This is a God-awful thing they've done."

"They said they were advised *not* to tell me."

"That's probably part of why they didn't. But surely they questioned that, as you got older and society evolved enough to realise how unfair that is?"

"I have to believe that they kept this from me because they really thought it was in my best interests."

When I glanced at Ted, he sighed and shrugged.

"I hope you're right."

"But you don't think I am."

"I didn't say that."

"Who was it at these maternity homes—I mean, who actually took the babies? Was it doctors?"

"From what I've read, midwives and doctors...and social workers." Ted added the last words very softly, and even though I'd feared as much, I was instantly defensive and surprisingly angry with him for saying the words out loud. I wanted to rage at him, and maybe I would have, but he cut me off with a hasty qualification, "Look, I really don't *know* about any of this—I just skimmed over an article or two in the news over the last few months. And Bean, of course I struggle to see Megan participating in any evil institutional scheme to rob mothers of their babies. But there really were schemes like that and she *was* a social worker and now it seems that she *did* work in a maternity home…I'm just saying that as awful as it is to consider, we're going to have to keep an open mind about her role in all of this until we know just a little bit more."

"Christ, Ted." There was just enough weight in that realisation that my emotions suddenly broke free, and the sobs came in an avalanche. "Please don't say these things. Please, just leave it for tonight now. I don't think I can handle any more than this."

"I'm sorry, honey." I could hear the echoing waterfall of remorse in his tone, just as I'd heard the way his words spilled forward as he talked about my parents manipulating me. He'd been waiting a long, long time to point that out to me, and maybe he'd pushed it farther than he should have given how upsetting the night had already been. "We don't even have to talk about this if you're not ready yet."

"I think…I'm going to have to digest all of this, piece by piece, and it might take a long time."

"Yes…it might."

"When they said they didn't know anything about her…do you think they were lying?"

Ted sighed and nodded.

"Yes. I hate to say it, but they were definitely lying."

"I felt like that too, the way Mum wouldn't look at me. But…the whole conversation happened so quickly, my head was spinning. *Is* still spinning."

"They knew her age, remember? Meg said your birth mother was sixteen, she said that's why she had to give you up. They did try to quickly move the conversation on, but there's no doubt in my mind that they just didn't want to tell you any more."

"So they're *still* lying to me," I whispered thickly. It was a fresh punch to the gut to think that this wasn't something terrible my parents had done, but rather, something terrible that they were continuing to do.

"Maybe they're just going to let you have some time to digest all of this. We can ask them and push the issue a bit more somewhere down the track. It will be much easier to press for those details later on when everyone is calm."

I looked to the television. The evening news was starting. This was the time when I would normally reach for the remote and turn over to a soap or cartoon or just about anything else.

My routine may have changed forever; it seemed that my attempt to avoid the worst of news in the world had failed; the bad news had found *me* and in the most personal way possible.

But the changing of the television programmes was proof that the progression of time continued as it always had—the world had not stopped, although in just a few moments, its axis seemed to have forever shifted.

—

I tried to sleep, after a few hours of sporadic, confused and disjointed analysis with Ted. I repeated myself a lot. We'd start to talk, and then the conversation would become too painful and I'd insist it stop, only to bring the topic up myself again just minutes later. When he suggested we go to bed, I resisted at first, because I still had work to do and I couldn't imagine stilling my racing mind anyway. The deciding factor was that he was going to leave the room and I couldn't bear to be alone.

I lay within the confines of his arms until he was asleep, but I couldn't even bring myself to close my eyes. Every time I did, flashes of my childhood shot past me; the playful holidays we'd regularly taken, the comforting overnight presence of my mother when I was sick, the patient provision of endless speech therapy for all of those years when my stammer seemed like an undefeatable foe. Instead of warmth and a feeling of unbelievable fortune, now those memories inspired a shame at not even *suspecting* the lie—not once.

How could they have kept this from me?

How could I not have known?

I gave up and left the bed when Ted started his deep snoring routine. I made a cup of tea, and sat back down at the table, taking the same seat I'd been sitting in so many hours ago when the doorbell rang. The sun was gone now and it was cold. I pulled my dressing gown tightly around my shoulders. Then I opened the laptop and brought up a search engine, and my fingers hovered over the keyboard.

Where to begin?

I knew that both Mum and Dad had been working at a rural hospital four hours west of Sydney when I was born, in a sleepy rural city named Orange; one which we'd never visited in spite of my curiosity over the years. Every time I had to write a place of birth for an application, I'd wondered about this mysterious place and I'd often asked her if we could go there together, to see the hospital and so she could tell me about my birth and show me the house I first came home to. She always offered the most plausible excuses. I'd never so much as suspected there might be a sinister reason behind her avoidance of that place.

I typed in the word.

*Orange.*

And then my hands froze up as I thought about those strange words Ted had introduced me to; *maternity home*. I closed my eyes and pictured a prison-like structure with bars on the windows and faces of pregnant teenagers peering helplessly from between them.

My fingers went to work again.

*Maternity.*

*Home.*

I clicked search.

There was recent news coverage—lots of it. I clicked on the top link.

*Pressure is mounting on the Australian government to apologise to families impacted by the government's forced adoption policies in the 1960s, '70s and '80s in Australia... Although exact numbers are unknown as records were often destroyed or not kept at all, it is believed that up to 150,000 babies were taken from their mothers during the period, with some commentators calling this an epidemic of unimaginable proportions. Midwives, doctors and social workers—*

As soon as my eyes hit the words *social worker*, I hit the back button with a little too much force.

I turned to Wikipedia.

*Orange and District Maternity Home.*

There were a few pictures of a nondescript red brick building; no bars on the window, no signs out the front. It could have been any post World War Two office block. I skimmed the brief text.

*Operating from 1954 until 1982, the Orange and District Maternity Home was a Salvation Army sponsored home for unmarried mothers. It is believed to have housed more than 1,000 young women during their pregnancies, although record keeping practices were notoriously poor. The home is believed to have been a participant in government sanctioned forced adoption practices.*

*In 1982 the Maternity Home was closed, and the building was repurposed as a ward of the Orange Base Hospital until its move to the new Bloomfield Campus in 2012. The building is currently vacant.*

I stared at the photos. The building seemed far too ordinary to have housed such an evil scheme.

Eventually, I closed my laptop and rested my head in my hands. I thought of the first time I left home, when I graduated from uni and decided to take a job singing on a cruise ship. It had been an adventure that I'd loved every second of—after the first night.

But that first night, docked in Sydney in my tiny, windowless berth, I'd felt more alone than I ever had in my life, and it had been terrifying. The enormity of the ship, of the Harbour, of the journey ahead and of the world itself had dwarfed me and I'd allowed myself to become overwhelmed and lost.

It had been a long, cold night of regret and anxiety and fear.

But then, of course, I had left my berth as the sun rose and at breakfast made friends and spent the next few years in one endless party here and there all over the planet.

From the fear had grown courage, and from the courage had grown confidence, and now the stint at sea was a part of the fabric of my character.

I wanted to believe that this long, cold night would grow something beautiful in me too, but I couldn't even imagine how that could ever happen.

# CHAPTER FOUR

## Lilly

### June 1973

Dear James,

I miss you so much. There's almost nothing in the world I wouldn't give just to see you today. This is just a horrible place. It's cold and it's miserable and I'm lonely and scared. Yesterday was the worst day of my life... until today, anyway.

I learned today that the social worker who admitted me is named Mrs. Sullivan and I am pretty sure she's in charge. She is awful, James. The way she speaks to me... the things she's said to me... just the sight of her gives me chills already.

There is, thank goodness, another social worker. Her name is Mrs. Baxter and in that whole day of tears and confusion yesterday, she was the only person who showed me anything like kindness. She actually hugged me when she was showing me around the place, and she told me that things will be okay. She told me that I just need to keep my chin up.

I'm trying James. God, I'm trying.

They don't call me Lilly in here. They call me Liliana W. At first, I thought it was because they couldn't pronounce Wyzlecki, but then I realised that they do this to all of the girls. I'm not sure why they do that, but I do know that I don't like it. It makes me feel uncomfortable somehow—I mean, even at school, we at least got to keep our last names. Here, there are no uniforms, but other than that one small thing it's just like

I imagine a prison would be... so many rules and restrictions, and no one wants to be here.

There are twenty-seven of us confined in the home and we all share a room with at least one other resident. I think I must have lost the room-mate lottery. I'm sharing a room with an aboriginal girl and she's awful. Her name is Tania J., and although we've only had two conversations so far, she's already made fun of me for my stutter and teased me in front of everyone at dinner. I cried and I ran back to my room, but it was only half an hour later that she joined me, and when she did, she just turned the light off as if I wasn't even there.

Tania works in the kitchen—she's actually in charge of the team who cooks our meals. We all have to work. I got assigned to the laundry team, which didn't sound so bad at first because it meant I'd be away from Tania all day. The thing is, this isn't a laundry like we had at home; this is a commercial laundry that services the hospital. I could barely bring myself to step inside the room when Mrs. Baxter first took me there. Right at the door, I could taste and feel the detergent in the air; it was like a wall of heat and humidity and smell. It's my job to load and unload the dryers, which I know doesn't sound all that hard, but they are *huge*. The wet laundry is so heavy, and then the loads of dry laundry are unbelievably hot but I have to empty them as soon as they finish—there's no time to let the linen cool down. So I was hot all day, like summer on the farm, on those cloudless days when the air is too still and you dream of even a whisper of a breeze just to take the edge off. The scorching wet air that the dryers blast out is what makes the entire room so uncomfortable and it's my job to work *right there* in front of them. In the first few hours, every time I'd bend to pick up a load of washing and strain to raise it high enough for the dryer's mouth, dots would swim before my eyes and I'd be sure I was going to faint.

I got used to it a little by the end of the day, although I saw myself in the mirror tonight and my face has never been so shiny or so red.

I don't mean to complain... I mean, I *can* do the work... and of course, I will do it, because I don't really have a choice anyway. And at least it gives me something to do while I wait for you to come. I could almost distract myself with the endless loads of washing and wish away the time until you arrive.

I keep thinking about what Mrs. Baxter said, and trying to keep my chin up. It is already really hard to do that, because when I see the residents I can tell that they feel lost too. I wonder where their boyfriends are, and why they didn't just get married. They can't all have found themselves caught with bad timing like we did.

Are all of these girls waiting for someone to come get them, like I'm waiting for you?

I can't wait until you see the way my belly moves. You'll feel the baby from the outside now, its kicks are so strong, its jabs determined and constant. Today was the first day I really thought about what it all means, and I know that's silly, but until the secret was out I really was very busy pretending this wasn't happening at all. As awful as it is here, at least I can start to get used to the fact that I'm about to become a mother. Those bumps and kicks and punches inside me aren't gas or my imagination—there's really a whole other person in there. I'll bet our baby is going to be so cute. How could he not be, with you for his father? I hope he gets your brain and your eyes and your smile. Actually, I hope our baby is just like you, except maybe with my hair because yours is always messy, and mine seems to manage itself just fine.

I love this baby, James. We're going to make a wonderful family together, you know. Can't you just see it? We'll move into one of those little houses on your farm, the ones the shearers usually stay in when they come through. I'll try to decorate it and set it up for us—as well as I can, anyway. I know we won't have much money, but we will have each other, and isn't that all that really matters? I won't finish high school or make it to university now, but I'll see our baby's first smile, and first steps. Isn't that so much more important than any degree or job?

I can always borrow books from the library and read while our baby sleeps. I can still learn, and now, instead of just teaching children facts and inputting information to their minds, I can mould an entire little person by being a good . . . no, a great mother.

I never really understood what it would be like to be pregnant. I saw Mama have the younger kids, and I watched her grow fat and uncomfortable and cranky. I didn't realise that she would be feeling a devotion bigger and bolder than anything else in the world. No wonder she was so angry with me yesterday when she found out what we've done. She had such big plans for my life; I was going to be the first member of our family to go to university . . . the first of us to get a profession. She must be so disappointed. But you know what, James, as much as I'm starting to get that, I'm equally sure that Mama will come around. Nothing this baby could ever do could make me love it less. And that's how I know that Mama will eventually see that somehow, this baby will be the best thing that could have happened to me.

I hope I find a way to reach you soon, James. I'm hoping I can get Mrs. Baxter alone at some point to ask her if she could post these letters for me, she seems like my best shot at contacting you.

I love you, always and forever.

Lilly

# CHAPTER FIVE

## Sabina

### March 2012

I was still sitting at my dining table when the sun came up. I had tumbled headfirst into the trap of believing that if I turned the situation over in my mind enough times, it would suddenly swim into focus and make sense. When Ted woke just after 6 a.m., and placed a gentle kiss on my head, I realised that all I had actually done was to exhaust myself into a state of utter fragility. The sight of my husband; the way his gaze searched and assessed the shadows on my face, was enough to bring me to tears again.

"Are you okay?" he asked, but I could see that he knew that I wasn't.

"I called in sick," I said. I'd sent the text at 4 a.m., so that my boss would find it as soon as she woke and have time to make other plans. I loved my job and hated to miss a day, but trying to wrangle classrooms full of primary school children into something like musical harmony was difficult enough on an average day. Attempting that feat on no sleep was a recipe for disaster.

"Do you want me to stay home with you?" Ted suggested. "We can sit under a doona and drink hot chocolate and watch movies?"

"No, no." I shook my head. "I just need..." I looked back to the laptop. The internet held somewhere just about every secret in the world, almost every piece of information the human race had ever discovered. Surely sooner or later I'd stumble upon just the right search to make it all make sense. "I think I just need some time to think."

"The last few days have been so full on." Ted turned the coffee grinder on and the sound was jarring, but the reward soon came as the scent of fresh coffee filled the air. He waited until it had finished before he spoke again. "Did you sleep at all?"

"No."

"Tired now?"

"Exhausted."

"What are you thinking?" He busied himself packing the coffee into the machine, and the simple act of that was a strange comfort to me. Everything was upside down, but there was still a world waking up. Ted was making himself a long black, just like he did every morning, and soon he'd dress and go into work as if nothing had changed. I couldn't even imagine how I would ever do the same.

"I think I relived every moment of my life through the night, from my first memory to now, wondering how they could have kept this from me, wondering how I didn't know. And it makes even less sense than it did last night when they told me."

"Do you want to talk to them? We could ask them to come round again tonight?"

"No." The very thought made me shudder. "*God* no, I don't want to see them yet."

"You're angry?"

"No . . . not angry. Not yet, anyway . . . I'm still too shocked and confused for anger. I keep thinking this is some strange nightmare and I'll soon wake up."

"You look like shit." Ted flashed me an affectionate smile, and I couldn't help but smile back.

"I feel like shit."

"Go to bed?"

"I will when you go to work," I promised. "Let's have breakfast first and make small talk about the boring engineering jobs you're going to suffer through today."

—

I slept the morning away. When I woke up, I was disoriented and confused at the blaring midday sun, and at first I thought I'd had a feverish dream. I stared at the ceiling for a while, facing properly this time the full barrage of the hurt and confusion. Even after a little sleep, the shock had eased just enough that I could think the words and understand their full implications.

I was adopted.

I knew a lot of things about myself. I was a teacher—but a singer and a musician at heart. I knew jazz better than almost anyone I knew. I could take a ratty seven-year-old and transform him just by giving him a triangle. I was petrified of crowds, unless I had a microphone in my hand and a band behind me. I preferred to wear bold colours, and I was taking my first baby steps towards motherhood. I loved my husband with a strength and a passion that seemed almost other-worldly. I hated the taste of cinnamon, and with an equally strong preference, enjoyed any form of basil. I had never had a piercing, or a tattoo, or even dyed my hair. I had always been overweight, and in recent years, I'd finally accepted that I always would be. I had a very happy, uneventful childhood. I had scraped through school and university, just by the skin of my teeth and the strength of my results in my music classes.

And now, I had new facts to add to my internal dossier on Sabina Lilly Wilson.

I was adopted. I was a victim of a life-long lie. I had been betrayed.

I had five missed calls on my phone and a bunch of text messages. Mum and Dad had both phoned me twice, and there had been a call from Ted. I drafted a quick message to Ted to let him know that I'd slept and that I was "doing ok," whatever the hell that meant. And then I turned the phone off.

After a shower, I made myself a decaf coffee and sat back at the laptop. I opened the browser and brought up the Wikipedia page again, and this time I read all the way through it, right to the end.

I let the picture form in my mind. I stared at the photo of the maternity home and I imagined in sepia a young woman standing out in front of it holding an old style vinyl suitcase. Mum had said she was sixteen—less than half my age. In my mind, my biological mother looked exactly like me, and was lost like me, but she was about a million times more terrified.

And then I imagined her looking down at her stomach and I wondered what she was thinking of me, nestled in her womb. I imagined her looking to the front doors of the maternity home and being nervous to step inside, but believing she had no choice. I imagined that she thought it was for the best, but maybe she was really not sure. I could only assume she wanted the best for me.

I wondered if she wanted to keep me.

I wondered if she had made something of her life.

I wondered if she still thought about me.

And then I wondered if I should try to find her.

—

I took a second day off work, and I went to visit my parents.

I didn't tell them I was coming, just as I didn't tell Ted that I was going. I was nervous about the discussion, and I thought

I might back out at the last minute, so I didn't want to have to deal with any expectations or concerns.

As I stood on their doorstep, I wondered if, on some level, I was looking for revenge. Here I was, turning up unannounced, demanding answers and information—just as they had turned up unannounced and tipped my life on its head. I hesitated at the double oak front doors, my hand on the ornate gold knocker. My parents were not wealthy, but they were definitely well-off. I'd grown up in a large home in the pricey suburb of Balmain, only a few kilometres from the Sydney CBD. My parents always had new cars, I'd attended prestigious private schools, and we'd holidayed overseas almost every year.

I'd led a charmed life, or so it seemed.

I slammed the knocker into the door with too much force. When the door opened a moment later, my mother gasped as she recognised me.

"Love, you know you don't have to knock—why didn't you just let yourself in?"

I thought of the keys in my bag and the countless times I'd let myself into this very house. That seemed like the action of another person in another life. Physically, I knew every inch of this house, I knew its cracks and its crannies and the secrets within every crevice. I'd hidden cigarettes here during my *very* brief smoking phase at age fifteen, I'd snuck a boyfriend in via that window over there when I was seventeen, and more than once I'd caught Mum crying on this very step after a disagreement with Dad.

This was my home, and I knew it like a fourth family member. But emotionally... spiritually... I was visiting this place for the very first time, and I didn't know a single one of its rules.

"I don't know," I admitted. My voice was small. Mum stepped aside and motioned for me to enter, but I hesitated.

"Mum, I just don't know what to think about anything any more. Can we talk, please?"

"Of course," she said, and she brushed the hair back from my face and then framed my cheeks with her hands, just as she'd done the night that I'd told her about the baby. Mum's eyes, close to and locked with mine, were concerned and sad and relieved all at once. She didn't often touch me now that I was an adult, not that we weren't close; she just had never been the physically affectionate type. The very fact that she was making physical contact with me so much these days told me that she was as scared as I was.

How could I navigate this and come out the other side? How could I understand this lie, and hold onto the truth that even when we had clashed over my lifetime, I'd *never* doubted the ferocity of her love for me?

"Of course we can talk," she said, "Dad's just coming back from golf. But let's make some tea and sit down and I will tell you whatever I can."

"Thank you," I said, and I was suddenly teary and *so* glad that I'd come. Everything had changed, but Mum's presence still meant comfort to me. She slipped her arm through mine as she led me into the kitchen, and didn't release me until the very moment when she had to use both of her hands to open the fresh box of tea. After she'd handed me my cup, she opened the cupboard and withdrew a packet of low calorie fruit biscuits, then at my incredulous expression, sighed and put them back in the cupboard. When her hand emerged again she was holding Dad's not-so-secret stash of triple chocolate cookies, just as I knew she would be.

"That's more like it," I muttered. I took the packet from her and helped myself to one as we walked through to her sitting room. Awash in the sun at this time of day, the room was an explosion of pastel floral fabrics and throw cushions. This room was my mother's favourite, and maybe it was mine too, because it was so uniquely *her*—stylish and neat and impeccably decorated, but comfortable and familiar. That same insanely expensive lavender room spray she'd splurged on for years lingered, dragging me back to a time when I lived under this roof. Way back then, my incessant nagging meant that Mum had tolerated a television in one of the few spaces not taken up by burgeoning bookshelves.

The television was long gone now, upgraded and shifted out of sight—Dad had turned the second office into a media room, although they rarely used it. Most of their leisure time was spent here, in the carefully styled sitting room overlooking the cottage garden that Mum maintained with military precision.

It was only once we were seated, and I'd taken a gulp of the hot tea, that I realised that the easy silence that had once characterised my relationship with my parents was gone, and in its place was a tension and awkwardness. I tried to find the words to put together an intelligent question, then failed, and my bewilderment and hurt came out as a hopeless sigh.

"Mum, what the hell?"

She nursed her tea and stared at me.

"Where do you want me to start?"

"How about at the beginning? There is so much I don't understand. Can you just tell me the whole story? Tell me more about the problems you had having kids of your own?"

"You *are* my own," Mum said, and her gaze flashed with a fierceness that startled me a little. I cleared my throat impatiently.

"You know what I mean."

"I didn't give birth to you. But I was there for you from then on, from the beginning right up until now. And you are *my* daughter."

"Okay. I get it." I sat the tea down on a coaster on the rattan coffee table and rubbed my forehead, then offered her a helpless shrug. "I'm sorry, Mum. I don't even know what words to use here."

"Dad and I tried for years to have a baby. We just couldn't. When we were first married I seemed to fall pregnant easily enough, but the pregnancies never lasted." Mum nursed her tea in both hands, up close to her face as if she needed the warmth. "After a while, we stopped falling pregnant at all, but there was nothing available to us like IVF, not back then... it was still years away. We saw a bunch of different doctors and they tried a lot of different things but..." She sighed and shook her head. "It just never happened for us."

I heard the front door open and close, and Dad called out,

"Sabina?"

He would have seen my hatch in the drive, and I could hear urgency and desperation in the way he called my name.

"In the sitting room, Dad," I called back, and I listened to his heavy footsteps as he rushed through the house towards us. I rose and reached onto my tippy-toes to brush a kiss onto his cheek.

"It's so good to see you," he said, then surprised me by adding a slightly-too-tight bear hug to our usual polite kiss.

"You too, Dad."

"You're having a chat, then?" He released me, and I saw the warning in his gaze as he looked to Mum. She shook her head, just a little, and I frowned.

"I came to chat to you guys about..." There was another strange pause while I figured out if saying the word "adoption" was going to be like dropping an awkward-bomb into the conversation, "...things," I said eventually. "Can you sit and talk with us, Dad?"

"Of course," he said, and he sat right beside me and leant back, as if he was open to my questioning. "What can we tell you? Where were you up to?"

"Mum was just explaining to me about the issues you had with pregnancies. So, I take it you decided to adopt?" This question was almost rhetorical, but neither one of my parents seemed to know how to answer it. The pause stretched until it was uncomfortable and I prompted, "Mum? Dad? Obviously you decided to adopt?"

"Yes," Dad said suddenly. "We tried for a long time, then decided to adopt."

"And this maternity home? How did you end up there, Mum?"

"We wanted a change. I think you'd call it a tree change these days; we just packed up and we moved to Orange for a fresh start. But the job at the maternity home just wasn't what we'd thought it would be, and... well, I hadn't dealt with our own fertility issues properly, so it was a very bad situation for me to be in. I didn't last long there."

I pictured the building I'd seen online, and now when I formed the mental image, the scared young woman who looked like me, was also somehow half my Mum too.

"So, what was it like?"

"It was the worst experience of my life," Mum whispered, then cleared her throat. When she spoke again, her voice was clear and proud. "Sabina, I really don't like talking about that time. I was only there for a few months. Even now I don't really like to revisit the memories."

"Okay," I said. That seemed reasonable. And she'd lasted only a few months? That was surely a good sign—she would hardly have become a kingpin of the forced adoption industry in such a short period of time. I looked to Dad.

"What did you think of all of this?"

"It was a difficult situation," Dad agreed slowly. "But nothing in life is clear cut, Sabina. Mum just was not a good fit for that place. It was probably the most difficult period of our entire marriage, to be honest with you."

Mum nodded, but I watched her eyes drift downwards to the table between us. She seemed drenched in sadness just reliving the time she'd spent there. Once again I found myself in the strange position of being forced to ask her questions about something which was clearly very painful for her.

"So... *did* you know her?" I asked softly.

Mum looked at her cup now, as if the answer to my questions could be found in the thin liquid.

"I suppose I probably knew her," she whispered.

"But there were a lot of women in the home," Dad added. The words were measured but he spoke far too quickly, cutting off the natural pause after Mum's admission. "Mum wouldn't have known all of them."

"A *lot* of women?" I repeated. "That's not what I read online. How many women are we talking about here? Hundreds?"

"No, dozens," Mum admitted. "Somewhere between twenty and thirty, most probably."

"And you really have no idea which one she was? Did they all give birth on the same day or something?"

"Of course not." Dad was impatient. "Look, it was always the same story. These girls were sixteen or seventeen, they got themselves pregnant, and their families dropped them at the home until the baby came."

"Always the same *story*? Jesus, Dad, you make it sound like they were disposable baby incubators."

"No, God no—" Mum said, shaking her head. "They were wonderful girls, they really were." She was pinched and pale at Dad's careless phrasing. I waited, as I always did, for her to shoot him a glance that put him in his place, just as she'd have done with me if I ever said something so offensive. Mum did not shoot Dad those glances, though. They were reserved; for me, for my teachers, for my friends and our extended family, and even for strangers on the street...but never for Dad. He was, and always had been, off limits somehow. "Dad just meant that I really only dealt with the other side of things, Sabina... the actual adoptions."

"Well, what was it about me that made you keep me? Was I especially cute or something?" I tried for a joke and it fell heavily flat. Dad half-smiled and shrugged at me, Mum didn't even acknowledge my attempt at humour.

"You were a beautiful baby...perfect, actually. Things just worked out; you needed a home and we needed a family."

"*Tell* me about it, Mum. Where did the idea to keep me come from?"

"I told you, you needed a home and we—"

"Mum, *listen* to me," I interrupted her, but I was calm. "I want you to tell me *about* it. I need the detail...some context. Surely you must remember—were you walking down the corridor and you saw me in the nursery? Did someone tell you about me? Was there a memo on the noticeboard that a 'perfect' new baby needed parents? You must have seen a lot of adoptions, so why did you keep *me*?"

"You would have gone to the orphanage," Mum said stiffly. "We didn't have a family for you yet, and I was worried that if you went to the orphanage, you'd stay there. That happened sometimes and it wasn't a good outcome for anyone."

"Why wasn't it a good outcome?"

"No one wanted to adopt the older children. Babies who weren't placed quickly tended to go into the orphanage and then stay there for a long time. A child needs parents and stability."

"So had you decided to adopt and you were just waiting for a baby to be available?"

"No, not really," Mum admitted. "It was a little impulsive—things happened very fast. I heard that a girl had been born and there were no families ready to place her with. Then I went and saw you and I suggested to Dad that we take you."

"But once we saw you, we knew that this was just meant to be," Dad added. "So we made it work."

"So... you weren't—" I stopped and frowned, trying to understand. "Are you telling me that you weren't even going to adopt until I came along?"

Mum and Dad stared at each other. I could see that they were communicating with their gazes, but it was like the meaning was encrypted somehow—I had no idea how to interpret their expressions.

"We would have, eventually," Dad said slowly. "We were still coming to terms with our infertility. You brought healing to us. You were *ours* from the first moment you entered our lives, and we never, ever looked back."

There was something almost romantic about it. I could easily picture my parents in their youth, feeling the ache of loss at the family they would be unable to have. And then, just like that, I was there, alone too, and as soon as they saw me they realised I could be theirs. I felt a warm glow start to grow inside me after the confusion and ache of the previous days. Just as I let the beginnings of a smile creep toward my face, Dad glanced my way and I saw the shutters come down in his gaze. "Okay, Sabina? That's pretty much the whole story. I hope that helps."

And there it was, the finality again, and in spite of the more complete picture they'd just given me, I still had a million questions that he was trying to prevent me from even asking. My father still thought he could just cut this chat off with a shrug and wave of a hand. I'd seen him do this a million times when he and Mum were disagreeing about something. When I was very young, I'd thought of it as his way of preventing me from seeing or overhearing their arguments—I'd somehow assumed that the discussions had continued at a later time, when I wasn't around to witness the tension.

But Dad had no intention of continuing this chat with me later. This was not a break in the conversation to cool our heads or to give me time to process what they'd told me; it was an attempt at an enforced end to the discussion. I thought about Ted's comments about my parents being controlling. It was as if the rose-coloured lenses he'd accused me of wearing shattered in an instant.

"You are *not* getting off that easily. Those breadcrumbs give me an idea of the first part of the story. But what about the rest of it? What right did you have to hide this from me?"

"We honestly believed that it was best that we never told you. Wouldn't you rather have never had to feel like you're feeling right now? All of this confusion and turmoil?" Dad said. I heard the rising frustration in his voice, and I could see it in his posture. He always sat up straight and tall, but in that moment, there was a visible tension in the way he held his hands against his thighs and in the set of his jaw.

The simplicity of his view was astounding.

"But Dad . . . I don't know who I *am* now!"

"You're the same person you were before we told you."

"But my heritage—"

"Your heritage is *us*." Mum's voice broke, and her eyes were filled with tears. "Sabina, you are *my* daughter."

I loved my mother, with the passionate zeal that comes from having fought a long-term battle of wills and walking out the other side feeling that we understood one another. Things had been simpler with Dad; in spite of his flaws, he had always been a hero to me. But Mum and I had worked out our relationship by grinding one another down, often in all-out brawls as she forced me to attend speech therapy or do my school work. We had worked damned hard for the close bond we shared.

I knew that I had every right to insist that they tell me more about my own past, and I had no intention of backing down—but it was utterly heartbreaking to see Mum so hurt and to know that *I* was the one forcing the discussion.

"Mum, of course I'm your daughter." I reached for her hand and held it tightly within mine. Her hands were bony, even her skin was thin. For the first time, I thought about my mother's tiny, rake-thin build and my curves, the ones that I'd never quite curtailed. I had assumed that this was a failure in my character somehow, a lack of self-discipline. Could it have been simple genetics all along? "I *love* you guys. I appreciate the wonderful upbringing you gave me. But surely you can understand that now that I know this much, I need to know more."

"Well, I'm very sorry to tell you, but you just aren't going to be able to find anything out. That's not how things worked back then," Dad said tightly.

"Surely there are *some* records—"

"There just *aren't.*"

There was a flat finality in Dad's words. I released Mum's hand slowly, then sat back in my chair and took a deep breath. Once I'd inhaled and exhaled again, and I felt like my temper was back under control, I met Mum's gaze.

"Are you really telling me that you could just decide to take a baby home and make it yours?" I couldn't fathom any hospital in the world just letting a random staff member help herself to some woman's baby.

"Our adoption criteria was pretty simple. All we were really concerned about was that we were placing babies with married white couples. It was brutally cruel, and brutally unfair, and racist and sexist and you *can't even imagine* how awful it was." Mum's words wavered around the edges. "But at the time, no one else—well, no one thought twice about it. That was just how things were." She slumped again. "When we told you it was a different time, I wasn't kidding, love."

"Did you take me the day I was born?"

"The day after."

I was suddenly deflated, thinking about the speed of that and the implications of the timing.

"So…she relinquished me within a day of my birth?" I whispered. "She must really not have wanted me at all."

"That's not really how it worked, Sabina," Mum said.

"Well, explain it to me, Mum. How did it work?"

"She was a minor, so her parents would have made the decision for her. A long time before you were even born—when she was first admitted to the home."

"So *did* she want me?"

I wasn't sure what was worse; the idea that my birth mother might not have wanted to keep me at all, or that she might have *wanted* to keep me very desperately indeed, but had no way to achieve that.

"We told you," Dad interrupted suddenly, but I saw his warning glance to Mum. "We don't even know *who* she was, let alone what her private thoughts about the matter were. Mum is talking in generalisations."

I turned my gaze to Mum but she was staring at the damned tea cup again.

Dad was lying to me? Still?

"They don't sound like generalisations."

"No, Dad is telling the truth," Mum whispered. "We had no idea which resident gave birth to you."

"So how do you know she was sixteen?" I asked Mum softly.

"That was a guess," Dad answered for her. "Most of the girls were teenagers."

"So why did you say *six*teen?" I kept my gaze on Mum.

"It was just a general—"

"Dad!" I turned to him, impatient with the game. "You can't seriously expect me to buy that!"

"You're focusing on the wrong things here, Sabina," he said, with barely restrained impatience of his own. "Sixteen, eighteen, twenty—what does that minor detail even matter? What matters is that you had a home to go to and you weren't lost to the system. God only knows what would have become of you if we'd allowed that to happen."

I laughed then—a cynical, derisive snort that instantly drew narrowed gazes from both of my parents.

"So what you're saying is, you're the heroes in this story, and I'm being an ungrateful brat?"

"You know life isn't black and white like that. It was a complicated situation and we found an outcome that worked for everyone. For you *and* for us." Dad was becoming increasingly impatient. He was tapping his forefinger against his thigh, and his foot against the floor. He had no sense of rhythm at all and the fact that he couldn't even manage to tap nervously in time was suddenly incredibly irritating. I glared back at him. The tension in the room was mounting very quickly now, almost beyond what I could bear.

"But what about *her*, Dad? What about my..." I stopped. The words "birth mother" were on my lips, but I couldn't bring myself to say them. Mum tensed, and I knew she was thinking the words too. She didn't want me to call this other woman "mother," and I didn't want to assign that term to someone other than Mum, but there was no other way to say it. I tried desperately to find other words, *any* other terms. I resolutely promised myself that I would go home and Google search the language of adoption, to somehow arm myself with the vocabulary of this horrible new world. But for now, this other woman, the invisible party in the room, deserved a name and she deserved to be acknowledged. And maybe Mum had hurt her, and maybe—just *maybe*—my Mum deserved to be hurt anyway. I stiffened my back and I fixed my gaze on her, focusing past the plea in her eyes. "You say you found an outcome that worked for everyone. But what about my birth mother? What became of her?"

"We just don't know, Sabina." Mum was defeated again, just like she'd been at my house. She pushed a lock of hair back from her face and sat the teacup on the table opposite mine, her hands trembling. "I wish I could take you back there, so that you'd understand what it was like. But I can't. You just have to trust me that we really had no choice."

"Trust you? No choice?" I couldn't hide my incredulity. "*She's* the one who had no *choice*, Mum!"

"Sabina, it was 1973." Dad was outright snapping at me now, unable to hide his irritation at my questions. "Doctors smoked *in* the hospital for God's sake. The single mother's pension seemed like a pipedream, especially out there in the country. Suppose she *had* taken you home with her, what then? No one would have employed her, or given her housing. The stigma attached to being an unwed mother would have ruined her life. Society offered those girls *no* positive alternative. This was for the best."

I was still staring at Mum. She had been the one *in* the system. If anyone had answers, it would be her.

"And you, Mum?" I murmured.

"And *me,* what?" She was on guard, and she glanced to Dad. Was there some magic question they didn't want me to ask, something I could say that would bring the house of cards crashing down? Why were they so on edge?

"Did *you* offer her a *positive alternative*?"

"That wasn't my job, Sabina."

"What *was* your job?"

"I told you, I found families for the babies."

"So you played no part in forcing these young women to give their children up?"

"Why would you think that I did?"

"Because I know how to read, Mum. This is all over the news and the internet, and every article I see mentions social workers."

Mum lifted the tea cup to her mouth. She took a slow, civilised sip, swallowed it, then lowered her cup again. I saw her lips twitch, as if the words were *right there*, like they were for me sometimes, but she just couldn't form them. Then I saw the tears well, and trickle down her cheeks, and she met my gaze again.

"Sometimes... helping that decision along was a part of my job."

The admission landed heavily. My throat felt tight. We stared, neither one of us willing to look away. I felt that if I let myself break the eye contact I'd never stand to look at her again.

"That's enough, Sabina," Dad said, and he rose, as if he was going to escort me to the door. I saw him only out of the corner of my eye, though, because I still did not look away from Mum.

"Mum... did you... did you take me away from her?" It took me several breaths to get the entire sentence out, and then once I'd said it, I held my breath. Another tear ran down Mum's cheek, and I heard the sob that she tried to muffle.

"It wasn't like that," she whispered.

"Well, what *was* it like?"

"No, I did *not* take you, or force her to give you up. But yes,

Sabina, I was a part of the system that did. Is that what you wanted to hear me to say?"

"I want you to be honest about all of this, Mum," I was pleading now. "How can you not know what her name was? Do you really expect me to believe that you have no further information, other than her age? That I can never know *anything* about the woman who carried and gave birth to me?"

"We'd just love to tell you who she was, or how to find her, and to help you facilitate a beautiful reunion where you could lament all of the things that were lacking in your upbringing." Dad's words were delivered with that strange, stiff awkwardness that seemed to linger around this subject. The song of our family conversation was now entirely staccato, jarring and abrupt, and I desperately missed the rhythm we'd once shared. "We just can't."

"Is that what you think this is about?" Now I looked to him, incredulity colouring my tone. Dad was insecure, about me? The thought was mindboggling, and I didn't know how to begin to tell him how crazy he was being. "The only thing lacking in my upbringing, Dad, was honesty. I'm not looking to replace you or even to supplement you—I just need to understand. If you could give me her name, or something about her circumstance, or if you could *really* tell me why you kept this a secret for so long... it would just help me so much."

"We've told you everything we know, Sabina. We've explained this as well as we can." Dad's words were calm now, but he was still standing by the door, and as he spoke he offered me a heavy shrug. "Beyond that, we can't tell you anything further."

I sighed and rose, and Mum shot me a panicked glance and reached to catch my hand.

"Where are you going?"

"I can't sit here and talk around in circles with you. You're either ready to tell me the truth, or you aren't."

"That *is* the truth, Sabina. There's really nothing more to say. Please, stay and we can talk about something else."

"I-I'm *pregnant*, Mum," I whispered, and I was so frustrated that I clenched my fists in her vague direction. "I'm about to become a mother. I'm going to spend the next seven months carrying this baby, getting ready to bring it into the world. I don't want to spend that time wondering about the woman who carried me, and what became of her. I want to deal with this and process it and get on with the business of being happy before my own baby comes. Can't you understand that? We *can't* talk about something else. If you guys can't talk to me openly about this, I don't think I want to talk to you at all right now."

I waited a moment, and when neither of my parents spoke, walked from the room and down the long hallway back to the front door. Mum was silent, although she followed me all the way, hanging a few steps behind. I paused at the doorstep.

"Please, Mum. Think about it. I'm not even sure I want to track her down. I just want the chance to decide for myself."

She was staring at the floor in her lobby.

Again I waited, and again she failed to be moved even a little by my pleading and so I left. As I drove home, I thought about the values they'd raised me to be loyal to. Truth, integrity, honesty—honesty almost above all else, to the point that I struggled to keep secrets even as an adult.

Clearly those things had meant nothing to Mum and Dad, or perhaps they'd been overcompensating because of the dark history of our family which they were so desperately trying to hide.

In any case . . . there was a particular bitterness to the irony that I had struggled to keep my pregnancy a secret for even two days, only to have it bring all of *their* lies out into the open.

—

I knew I would have to go back to work some time. As I lay in bed the next morning, I toyed with the idea of a third day at home, but the endless emptiness of unfilled time seemed a curse. So I dressed, and I returned to my classroom, and I threw myself into my lessons with over-the-top enthusiasm. We played music games and I took one class out to the oval and had them form an orchestra of shouting. I revelled in the children's laughter and the sunshine on our faces, and in the perfect distraction of the scent of freshly cut grass in the air.

When lunchtime came and I checked my phone, I was rewarded by a voicemail from our doctor. My blood tests had all been clear, my hormone levels were absolutely perfect. It was somewhat less surprising now, but still a relief.

It was a good day, in the end, and as I packed up to leave I was so glad I'd convinced myself to get out of bed that morning. It was only as I walked home that my mind wandered back to the mess of my family life. I dawdled—I'm no speed walker at the best of times, but that day, my thoughts drifted so far away that I was barely strolling. I pushed earbuds into my ears and turned on my *manic jazz* playlist on my phone, inviting the perfectly ordered chaos of Miles Davis and John Coltrane to keep me company.

For a while, I let myself daydream. I thought about how one single piece of information had changed the way I viewed my past and my future. I had been so proud of the life I'd built and my personal series of humble achievements; I had a wonderful marriage, we had paid off our house, we were going to build a family. I'd travelled the world, and although it was by the skin of my teeth, I'd finished a university degree.

But now, now that I knew, I wondered: who else could I have been? Would that *other* Sabina have been raised with siblings, and if so, would that have changed her attitude when it came to friendship? I'd lunged from one extreme to another even as an adult. At uni and in my cruise years, life was one endless party. For a while, I'd even shared a berth on the cruise ship—there were months where I had no private space at all, and it didn't bother me one bit. I made friends easily and I could have them live in my back pocket, back then.

Until, I suppose, I reached saturation point with that lifestyle and I moved back to dry land. As I'd put down roots, I'd naturally retreated into myself. In recent years, my social activities revolved around music. Most nights, I wanted to be at home, in my little nest with Ted. He really was enough for me, I never tired of his company at all.

There were times, at least in recent years, when we'd get around to organising that dinner party we always talked about, and 9 p.m. would come, and I'd run out of energy for entertaining. Ted could tell hilarious anecdotes for hours and our guests would settle in for a late one, but I'd gradually fall quiet and then fade to silence. I'd learned to quietly exit, to apologise as politely as I could, and to take myself off to bed, recognising that I had nothing more to contribute to the conversation, and no more energy to maintain my part in it.

I knew this was rude. I knew that it was confusing for our guests, and it was probably lazy and selfish too. Ted hated it when I did it. Would that *other* Sabina have been more consistent with other people? Would she have been kinder, or gentler, less self-centred?

Would she even have liked music?

Would *she* still have struggled to keep her curves under control? Had my biological family figured out the magic way to regulate their calorie intake and keep these food-loving genes in check?

Would she still have worn her hair long, or would she have dared to cut it short? I loved my hair, but I'd always taken the safe road with how I styled it, I'd never even coloured it, or worn a dramatic cut. I knew it was my best feature. Glossy and healthy, a beautiful shade of warm brown, my hair was straight and thick and bouncy, even if it was humid or if I'd washed it in terrible shampoo or on the very rare occasion that I had been exercising.

Mum's hair was dark brown too, but beneath the dye it had long since turned grey. Her hair was wiry and untamed. At some point I'd assumed that the difference between my bouncy hair and Mum's frizzy hair was the dyes she used for so many decades, and I'd shied away.

Would a Sabina raised with people who looked more like her have made bolder stylistic choices?

My voice was spectacular. Teachers had told me since I was a child that I was one of the most naturally gifted vocalists they'd ever taught. But I cruised through high school and university, putting in the minimum level of effort possible to gain a pass, and then I'd maintained that attitude throughout my career. Would that other Sabina have had more ambition, more drive? I had always been so content, there was no burning need within me to become more famous or to make lots of money, but maybe if I *had* possessed such a drive, the world would have been my oyster. I would surely have gone to another school, and what difference would that have made? Would I have gone to the same uni? Would I have gone to uni at all?

Would I have met Ted?

Would I still have loved him, even if I did?

Would we be pregnant now? Would we be pregnant with *this* child?

Or...would I have a brood of children already? I felt I'd left it late in life to start my family, but that had come not from some drive to build a career or wait for the perfect time, more a spoilt assumption of good fortune. My life had long since taught me that things would just work out for me, one way or another; why rush to have a baby?

Of course, the other possibility was that my childhood would have been awful, and that I'd have been damaged beyond repair if I'd not been relinquished. Would I have fallen into addiction? Would I have been depressive? Would I have made terrible choices with relationships?

And what about my stutter? I'd mastered it, but the truth was, *Mum* had mastered it. It had taken years for me to get to the point that I could confidently communicate, and I distinctly remembered fighting my mother through every step of that journey. I had wanted so badly to just give up; very willing to accept that I'd never speak clearly and to find other ways to live my life. As a child, usually sulking after Mum had physically locked me in the car to force me go to speech therapy, I'd imagine easier ways to solve the problem of my stutter. I'd just sing instead—all of the time. Or I'd write people notes, or I'd just find a way to avoid communicating with people altogether. Usually I imagined myself living isolated forever.

Would that other me, with that other mother, have ever crawled out from beneath the shadow of her stutter? Would she have even discovered that she could sing, fluently and with faultless perfection, every single time?

The thought of living with the choking unpredictability of the jerking speech I'd struggled through as a child was unbearable.

If *that* would have been my fate, I doubted that I'd have survived it intact.

It is a strange thing to know yourself, and to realise at the same time that you are merely the product of the nest within which you are raised—and that a different nest might easily have produced a different *you*. As I walked that day, I grieved and worried for that *other* me, and I missed and regretted not knowing her. She might have been a miserable failure. Equally though, she could have been fabulous, she might have been amazing, she might have overcome all of the flaws that I felt had held me back at one time or another.

I was about to turn into our driveway, to walk past the beautiful home of our future to the cramped reality of our present, when I stopped. Once I was inside, I would sit and ponder, and there was a long afternoon left to fill.

I spun back out into the street, and for a while, I let my feet wander like my mind. I looked forward to the day that I'd feel peace again, and until then, I'd need to give myself space like this...time to just feel the chaos of it all. I was already becoming used to the idea that I was adopted, but I knew instinctively that this phase of questioning was there to stay, at least in part because there were no answers to any of my questions.

This was the beginning of grief for me. I was grieving a version of myself I could never know, because she had never had a chance to *be*.

—

Sunday was a weekly punctuation point for my family. We stopped, we rested and we spent time with each other. When I lived at home, we'd often go bushwalking on Sunday. Maybe it was Mum's not so subtle attempt at getting me to exercise, but I'd loved those long Sundays far away from the city. They were all about connection, stopping together to smell the proverbial flowers, or at least the eucalypts. In my two long stints overseas,

Sunday was the day when I'd called home one way or another. I had never missed connecting with my family on a Sunday.

Our commitment to Family Sunday was one of the things Ted had found so startling when we first met. It was one of those key components which had defined my life to that point.

The sparks of anxiety I'd been conscious of all week mounted to a fever pitch as the weekend arrived. It was almost a relief, to stop thinking about what the whole adoption reality actually meant. Now all I could think about was that I didn't particularly want to see Mum and Dad, but at the same time, I didn't know how to avoid them. Family Sunday was more than a habit. It was a compulsion, and apparently that was the case for all of us, because Mum phoned our house on Saturday night.

"Oh hey, Megan," Ted said, and we shared one of those meaning-laden glances that spouses sometimes share. She would be calling for me, of *course* she'd be calling for me. I could tell, just by how late in the day it was that she was nervous about speaking with me too, and I pictured her sitting in the lamp-lit sitting room playing one of those stupid puzzle games on her mobile phone, hoping the whole time that I'd call her and save her having to be the one to reach out.

I shook my head at Ted, then, just to be sure he'd read my meaning correctly, drew a slow line across my neck, shaking my head again. He gave me a helpless shrug and said, "Yes, she's here. Just a second."

I narrowed my gaze so much that I could barely see him as I took the receiver into my hand. Then, I cupped the mouthpiece with my other hand, so that I could hiss at him,

"Why did you do that?"

"You have to speak to her eventually."

"Shouldn't *I* get to decide when that is?"

"Bean, just talk to her. You have to decide now anyway, are

we going to meet with them tomorrow, or not?" He was whispering more than hissing. Damn Ted and his calm reasonableness. I groaned softly and lifted the phone to my ear. Just as the cold plastic hit my skin, I heard the softest of whimpers and my stomach sank.

*Be angry, Sabina, you have every bloody right to be angry. Be strong.*

"Mum," I said, and I sounded mean and cold. Ted winced and I immediately felt ashamed.

"Hello, Sabina. Dad and I were wondering...we were just wondering if you were going to join us tomorrow for a meal."

Right up until that moment, I hadn't made up my mind. If it wasn't for the tremor in her voice, I think I'd have said no, and hung up the phone. I was so torn. Did I persist with things the way they were? Did I meet with them, carry on as if nothing had happened? Or did I take some time—the time I damn well deserved to take?

I closed my eyes and saw her patiently putting up with my adolescent angst, sitting in the front row weeping through her pride when I first performed in public, travelling halfway across the world to surprise me when I was particularly homesick on the cruise ship, and then taking a second trip for the same reason when Ted and I did our stint in Dubai.

"How about brunch?" I heard myself suggest.

"At the café," Ted interrupted me suddenly. "Let's go to the café."

"Yes, we were thinking the café." I said, as if we'd discussed it, which we most definitely had not.

"Oh. How lovely, yes," my mother said, and the relief in her voice was palpable. "Dad and I will be there. Is 10.30 a.m. okay?"

"Yes, that's fine. See you then." I hung up, then slammed the phone onto the bed. "God, Ted. Why didn't you just tell her I was busy?"

"I panicked," he admitted, and at least he had the grace to seem sheepish. "Sorry, Bean. So, we're brunching then?"

"I can always call and say I'm sick," I muttered, but we both knew I wouldn't. "Shit."

"I thought the café might be better because you'll be in public. Your family would *never* squabble in public." He was trying to mock me, but I glared at him again.

"Too soon, Ted."

He rubbed my shoulders.

"I know, Bean. But you won't. You guys are so polite and civilised, I'm sure it will be a perfectly comfortable brunch and you'll probably feel better about things after."

"I'm scared they'll never really open up to me about this," I said suddenly. "It's like they pulled the earth out from under me and they're just going to leave me floating around in space forever. Do they really think things will just go back to normal? That we'll carry on with Sunday brunches as if nothing has changed? I wonder if they have any idea how maddening it is that they refuse to just address this directly?"

"They must still be getting used to you knowing too. They're probably petrified that you'll never forgive them, or that you will track your birth family down and replace them somehow. I think you just need to give them some time too."

"I don't want to give this time," I whispered. "I want to understand it all *now*."

"I get that, Bean. I really do. And maybe they've had the past few days to do some thinking. Who knows, maybe tomorrow they'll come more prepared for a frank chat with you."

# CHAPTER SIX

## Lily

### July 1973

Dear James,

It's been a few weeks since I last wrote. I've been trying to adjust to the routine here.

It starts before dawn—well, it's supposed to, but I often sleep in and I'm usually late before the day even begins. I'm *so* tired, but I find it so hard to sleep here. The mattress is old and uncomfortable and I'm so heavy now. And although I feel hot, so *very* hot all day, at night the rooms aren't heated and I have only one blanket. I seem to fall asleep most often in the early hours of the morning and then I struggle to get out of bed when the others do, but even the few extra minutes of sleep I've been taking end up costing me my shower. That is a price I can't really afford, because I desperately need one after spending all day in the heat.

Breakfast is at 6.30 a.m. sharp. We start by bowing our heads to say grace, although we aren't allowed to actually *say* it, we just listen while the nurse on duty does the talking. She thanks God for the day, then usually she spends a little while telling God how lucky we are to be in the home, with a roof over our heads and food in our stomachs in spite of our sinfulness. At first, I thought about this a lot. It doesn't make any sense, does it? Doesn't God already know? Isn't He the reason we're in so much trouble…that what we've done has so offended him? Why remind Him *every single day?*

I've realised now though that this whole ritual is not for God...it is most definitely for us, to make sure that thoughts of our transgressions are never far from our minds. The nurses always finish the prayer by almost begging God—and us—that we will *do the right thing* for our babies; that we will find a way to be selfless, and to make amends for what we've done to our families and our community.

I am sure that the nurses just love that our first thoughts for the day are of shame, but whenever I hear them praying for us to *do the right thing* for our babies, I wrap my arms around our baby and I agree with all of my heart.

I'll find a way to do the right thing for him, James. I haven't figured it out yet, but I'll get these letters to you sooner or later so that you can come and take us home. There is not a single ounce of doubt in my mind; *that* is the right thing for our baby.

After breakfast we go to work, and I've already told you what that's like. Some days we work in silence, but some days there's quiet chatter between the other girls. I haven't really talked to them much yet, except for a few words as we walk to the laundry or as we sit to eat our dinner. At work, it's just too hard to raise my voice loud enough to be heard over the machinery. When I try, I stutter so badly that I may as well not have bothered.

While I work now, I try to cast myself forward to the time after the baby is born, when we can all be together. My mind is back at the farm setting up our home in the cottage and raising our baby with you. That's how I'm keeping myself sane.

I miss home, James. I miss it so much and that surprises me. You know how busy and chaotic my family is, and how frustrated I get with the younger kids. All I ever wanted was peace and quiet to read and study in, and now I'd give anything to hear the bustle of it all again. I even miss the way Kasia snores at night...it's such a gentle little sound, compared to the way

Tania's snores echo around our room and keep me awake. I miss the scent of garlic and butter in the air whenever Mama is cooking. I even miss Tata. I miss the way he made *right* and *wrong* so crystal clear, and how safe I felt living under his roof. I miss that sense of Wyzlecki *common-ness*. Whatever that thing is that makes a group of people a family—and I feel it with you too, so I'm certain it's more than just blood and genes—I'm missing it desperately now. Sometimes these days I wonder if the opposite of "home" isn't actually "away", but "*alone*".

That's why I spend so much time thinking myself away from here. I'll be back in the embrace of my people when you come for me. I'm sure I'll still miss the Wyzleckis, but you and our baby will be my family soon enough.

Love,
Lilly

# CHAPTER SEVEN

Sabina

March 2012

"How do you think I should play this?"

We were sitting in the car outside the café. Ted was in the driver's seat, waiting patiently for me to make the first move and leave the car. *I* was waiting for some miracle burst of courage.

"I think," he said quietly, "we should go in, just like we would any other day, and let the conversation take us wherever it goes. If it feels natural and things aren't awkward, maybe you can ask again. But I don't think they'll bring it up if you don't."

"Okay. So if it's awkward, I'll just stick to the safe topics—politics, religion, ethics."

Ted barked a laugh.

"Oh dear."

"You know how they love their opinions, Ted. I'll just ask some meaty topical questions and let them fill the awkward space up with their arrogance."

I thought Ted would laugh again, but instead, he turned to me with a very serious frown on his face.

"Bean...I know that I made you talk to Meg last night so it's probably my fault we're even here, but we can go home if you want to."

"No, you were right last night. I can't avoid them forever," I sighed, then glanced at him. "Can I?"

He shrugged.

"I guess you probably could, if you really wanted to."

I shook my head, and at last stepped from the car. I waited at my door until Ted walked around to take my hand. I let him lead the way, through the café into the courtyard behind—a path we'd walked dozens of times. I even knew exactly where we'd find my parents. We always sat in the courtyard in nice weather, often at the same circular wrought-iron table in the centre of the paved space.

A gentle breeze was blowing, and a few random leaves from a potted ash tree swirled around my feet. Mum and Dad were seated at our table. When I saw them, I felt a tension ripple down my body, a wave of nerves that surged from my head to my toes. Ted gave my hand a gentle squeeze. I took a deep breath and pushed down the feeling, focusing only on keeping my thoughts rational.

*We will get through this. They will get used to me knowing, and they will come clean with the details. I will learn to understand, and to forgive. I will come to terms with this.*

I took a few steps forward and was actually almost calm, until Mum seemed to panic and rose and then Dad rose too, as if I was a stranger and this was a formal meeting.

Only then, and maybe too late, did I realise just how angry I was at them. It wasn't a deep-seated resentment, it was right there near the surface, ready to break through my skin and unleash itself on them. In an instant I was out of control—furious that they could be so arrogant as to assume that they could break this news to me, now, at the happiest point of my life, and just deliver it without any warning and without even having the decency to come absolutely clean about the whole story.

"I can't do this." I blurted the words far too loudly; they represented a near-shriek of panic.

"Sabina, please." Dad held out his hand towards a chair. "Please sit down. We can have a nice brunch, just like we always do."

People were staring. All over the courtyard, customers had

fallen silent, and out of the corner of my eye I saw a waiter approaching us slowly. Ted released my hand at last, but immediately slid his arm around my lower back.

"Honey, maybe we *should* go and do this another time." His words were gentle against my ear, although they were peppered with hushed urgency.

"Sit down, and we'll talk," Dad said, a quiet determination in his voice. Once upon a time, I might have interpreted that as strength but here I recognised it as control. Dad was corralling me. I looked at Mum, and tears were rolling down her face again. She was more vulnerable than she'd ever been with me before, because now I knew her secret. She pointed to the chair and begged me with her miserable eyes to stay.

I sat heavily and Ted pulled his chair right up close to mine before he sat beside me. Looking around, I realised that the waiter was Owen, one of the regulars who knew us by name. He breeched the last few steps across the courtyard to join the awkward circle of my life, standing in the oddly distant gap between Dad and Ted. He cleared his throat and said,

"Is everything all right, Graeme?"

*No, nothing is all right*, I wanted to say. *Everything is wrong, actually.*

"Everything is fine thanks," Dad said, but the stiffness of his voice betrayed him. "Can we please order some coffees? Sabina, flat white? Make that decaf please, Owen. Ted, long black?"

Usually when we met for brunch, we sat and read the newspaper. Often Dad would start with the broadsheet and Ted would read the tabloid, while Mum and I rotated through the inserts. We'd take turns pointing out interesting movies or books, or the ludicrousness of world events, or discuss the movements of financial markets. Dad, ever the accountant, loved to talk money. Today, we all dove into the newspapers for refuge, before we even ordered our meals. Ted actually lifted his in front of his face. No one spoke, and while the others may have been reading, I was staring at a page blurred by my tears. This was the very thing I'd feared when Mum had called the previous night. Here we were, hiding behind our newspapers, pretending that nothing at all had changed. The forced normality was an insult to me, offensive, as if Dad and Mum were telling me that I didn't deserve the truth about my own birth. My hands clenched into fists around the edges of the paper.

I looked to Dad, and found him staring at me. For a moment, we locked eyes, and I knew that he could see how upset and frustrated I was, which made it all the more frustrating when he quietly lowered his newspaper and pointed calmly to an article.

"Have you heard about this project, Ted?" he said. Ted peeked over the top of his own newspaper and glanced at the hotel Dad was referring to.

"Oh yes, fascinating, so many challenges—inbuilt desalination, and the whole structure will be solar and wind powered. A first wave of Dubai sustainability, they say. It certainly wasn't that way on my projects there, unfortunately."

"How is work going, anyway, Ted?" my mother asked. Dad had broken the ice and she had apparently been waiting to strike up a conversation.

"It's steady," Ted said. "I have a manageable project load these days, much better than when we were living over there, isn't it, honey?"

I nodded silently. We'd moved to Dubai shortly after our wedding, lured by Ted's lucrative job offer. It was like a long-term honeymoon, isolated in the bubble of Ted's company compound. In the first year, that had been marvellous, but by the third, we'd earned enough money to buy a house back in Sydney and Ted's manic work schedule had long since worn thin.

So, we'd bought that house in Sydney—a huge, beautiful home in Leichardt, just a few suburbs from Mum and Dad's house, and then apparently Dad had convinced me to switch our plans and move some strange family into it. It hadn't felt like that at the time. It'd felt like we'd made a foolish decision and I had suddenly seen the light.

"And you, Sabina?" Mum asked, "How was your week?"

"I wouldn't exactly call it the best week of my life," I said, intending it as a light-hearted joke, but when the words left my mouth they were dripping with bitterness. The awkwardness rushed back in at us like a tide, and Mum shifted in her seat then cleared her throat.

"Are you talking things over with someone, Sabina?" she asked, and suddenly I felt like one of the patients she'd worked with in hospitals over the years. I could see her regarding me curiously, momentarily detached from the problem behaviour, conveniently forgetting that she herself was actually the cause of it.

"I'd *like* to talk it over with *you*."

"Of course," Mum said, but then she looked back to her paper, as if she couldn't bear the pressure of looking at me for a second longer. Ted squeezed my knee under the table, a subtly supportive gesture, and I caught his hand and entwined our fingers together tightly. Mum cleared her throat and added quietly, "Although maybe in this case, a professional would be able to offer you better support."

"I don't need a therapist, Mum. I need my family."

"And you've got us," Dad said firmly. "That's why we're here, isn't it? To spend time together, as a family?"

Owen returned with the tray of coffees, and silently slid them around to their owners by memory. When he'd finished, we immediately ordered—no need to look at the menu because we'd all been there so many times that we knew our favourites off by heart. I always ordered the bircher muesli with low fat yoghurt, but that day, I ordered the double chocolate pancakes with ice cream *and* cream. I knew it would drive my mother crazy, especially if I ate the lot right there in front of her, which I absolutely intended to do. She didn't say anything, but I saw her eyebrows rise, and I chuckled inwardly like a rebellious teen.

Then the waiter was gone and we were back to our newspapers. The elephant in the room sat quietly on the table and we all leaned this way and that to talk around it, discussing world events and the theatre, but every now and again I felt like the elephant might have just trumpeted a reminder to us that he was in fact there, and awaiting our attention. The trumpets were disguised as inexplicably tense statements and guilty glances, but *I* recognised them for what they were. Still, I forced myself to stay on topic, to avoid that nasty *a*-word, and most importantly to avoid another scene. When our orders arrived, I ate my pancakes; every last mouthful.

When I was a child, Mum had drilled into me that restaurants always serve too much food, and that it is proper manners to leave something on your plate. I looked over to see a perfect quarter of her egg white omelette resting on her plate beside her carefully aligned knife and fork. There was something so enraging about that—the healthy, pleasure-free choice of breakfast food, the sharp edges of her leftovers, and the cleanness of her plate around them. How many times had I felt the stab of shame when we ate out—that I wanted to eat my entire serving, and that she never even seemed tempted to? How many times had I stared at my body in the mirror and wished that I'd inherited her lightning-fast metabolism, or even wondered if I actually *had* inherited her blessed genes, but my weight loss efforts were hampered by a disgusting lack of self-control?

I stared right at my mother's face, and without breaking that gaze I reached over to pick up Ted's leftover toast, and then I took a determined, satisfying and unnecessarily noisy crunch of it. I've always been an emotional eater, and it was inevitable that I'd gorge myself that day, when it felt like my emotions were so out of control that they'd never be sated again.

We'd ordered a second round of coffees and swapped the papers all the way around the table when I felt it was time to push the issue again. I felt I'd done some kind of penance, some pretence of happy family time just as my parents wanted, but it was nearly time to go home anyway and if things became awkward again, *so be it.*

"I know this is really difficult for everyone, and I'm trying to be mature about it, but I just want to understand. You seem so sure that I won't be able to find her, but surely you have *some* idea..."

"I don't know what else you want from us, Sabina. I don't know what else you think we can tell you," Dad said. I tried not to glare at him.

"Well, I want you to know that I've decided to try to track her down anyway."

"Why can't you just trust us when we tell you that is not going to be possible?" Dad was frustrated, but calm. I hated the steely quality to his voice, the flat finality in the way he politely enunciated a question, but intended a statement to wrap up the conversation.

"I just *need* to try."

"Then, by all means, try, but you won't get anywhere. We've told you, there are no records. Megan worked in the home; if there was anything recorded, we'd know about it. And if we knew who she was, we'd tell you. From your birth you've been *ours*, and there's nothing more to add to that."

"I'm going to contact an organisation that helps adoptees

find their families," I said, hesitantly, and Dad's hand shot out as if he was stopping traffic.

"*We* are your family, Sabina."

"Dad!" I groaned in frustration. "Of course you are. But I probably have another family out there, I just want to see if I can find out some further information about them. I was actually hoping, Mum, that you might come with me to meet with the social workers there."

I hadn't been hoping that at all. It was an impulsive test, to see if she'd support me.

"*No*," Dad said, and I raised my eyebrows at him.

"Mum can speak for herself, Dad." I tried to say the words gently, but as soon as I opened my mouth he gave a fierce shake of his head.

"No, Sabina, I won't allow it. Megan won't be coming with you. We think this is a terrible idea, and we won't be a part of it."

"Don't *speak* for her, Dad!" My voice was rising again, this time with a new kind of frustration. I'd been aware of Dad's arrogance, but I'd never noticed how deeply it defined their interactions. His halo had slipped, and suddenly my wonderful, strong father looked a whole lot like a bully. Mum sitting beside him looked almost like a stranger too, someone who lacked even the spine to assert her own will.

I'd thought of her as uniquely beautiful, now I realised that those wide eyes, brimming with sadness and confusion, were just a little *too* big. Above the downturned corners of her thin lips, her cheekbones were so prominent that the skin there seemed stretched. Mum had an unusual face, and I saw her as if for the first time and acknowledged with some shock that she was an ordinary, flawed human after all—they *both* were, and this realisation was almost as devastating as the discovery of the adoption had been.

I could suddenly see with vivid clarity every single one of

my mother's flaws. She was too reserved, and her life sometimes seemed too staged—everything looked perfect, but was there any substance to it? She could be so pushy when it came to my decisions. I'd always seen her as stable and reliably concerned, but maybe that was naïve, maybe my Mum was actually overbearing, and staid.

Was that the kind of mother that *I* would be?

I rose now and flicked towards Ted a split second glance which he instantly understood. He rose too.

"I think we'd better go," I murmured. Mum and Dad both stared at me; Mum's eyes pleading, Dad's gaze hard and emotionless. "Maybe we need some space while I get used to this."

"What does that even mean?" Dad asked.

"You know what it *means*, Dad," I whispered now. "It means I can't carry on as if this never happened. I know now, and I can't pretend that I *don't* know. I don't want to have a pretend polite brunch with you as if nothing has changed. I want to have a tear-filled, raw discussion where you open up your hearts and your memories to me and tell me *who I am*."

He sighed impatiently, and that was so maddening that I could suddenly hear my own pulse in my ears. I turned away from them, and without a farewell, walked from the café—under a veil of tears all the way back to the car. When I tugged at the door handle, I realised with some frustration that Ted had the car keys but had remained inside to pay the bill. So I leant against the car and stared at the entrance to the café. I was torn right down the middle—wanting desperately for my parents to stay in the café and give me the space I needed, and at the same time mentally pleading with them to follow me; to come and invite me back for a more open discussion.

They didn't come, but after a moment, Ted did. He approached me quickly, and pulled me immediately into his shoulder.

"How can they not understand how this is hurting me?"

"I have no idea," he exhaled as he shook his head, apparently as confused as I was. After a moment, he shifted my position in his arms so that he could survey my face. "Did you mean what you said, about tracking her down?"

"Well, I actually said it for a reaction," I muttered, thinking of how successful that particular plan had been. I'd intended to drag a rise out of them—instead I'd succeeded only in enraging myself.

"So you don't want to do it?"

"No, I didn't mean that. I mean... I don't even know where to start, but... I want to. She might have been looking for me, or she might be wondering why I never sought her out. And maybe she didn't want to give me up at all, and maybe she's been waiting for me to come find her for nearly four decades. Can you imagine if someone took our baby and then for nearly forty years we were waiting to find out if it was o-okay?" Even the thought of that had me choking on sobs and stumbling on my words. "What a ni-nightmare, Ted. I have to try to find her."

"You won't be able to plan for this, honey," Ted said softly. "Whatever you decide, I'm right behind you... but you'll need to go into this with your eyes open. You could find anything, and you won't necessarily be able to prepare yourself before you do."

"I know," I said, but the very thought of that made my stomach lurch. "But... I don't think I can avoid this. I think it's the only way forward."

I was positively shaking with the frustration of it all, but beneath the loudness of that emotion, I became aware for the first time of a quiet resolve. I'd press on towards the truth, and I'd do it on my own. Mum and Dad were apparently so desperate to keep their secrets that they would maintain the ridiculous lies even when my hurt and pain was right there on display in front of them.

I owed it to myself to at least *try* to find out the truth about my own life. I'd never defied them before, but this thing that they had dumped into my lap was just big enough that I would have to take my life into my own hands for the very first time.

And as hurtful as it was, and as difficult as it all seemed, I had to be brave. I knew instinctively that leaving all of these issues about my origin unanswered would mean that I began my own journey as a mother with baggage that would cripple me.

I wanted to be a fun mum, a supportive mum, a secure mum.

I had to find some sense of closure and resolution. And I would; if not for myself, then for my baby.

# CHAPTER EIGHT

## Lilly

### July 1973

Dear James,

I saw a doctor a few days ago so at last I know when our baby is coming. They didn't give me a date, or talk *to* me at all, actually. But I heard the doctor tell Mrs. Sullivan that if he or she hasn't arrived by September, they will go right ahead and induce the labour.

It seems far too soon to me...to think that in just two months our baby will be born! I feel like I have only just found out that I am going to be a mother, because I spent so long trying to pretend this wasn't happening. I've really only had these last few weeks to properly think about it and to figure out my own feelings. And the date does make sense, doesn't it? I mean, after all, we saw each other last after the new year.

All is well with the baby and with me, so you don't need to worry James, but the examination was very difficult. The doctor did the check-up right there in front of Mrs. Sullivan, without even a privacy screen, just a flimsy gown that was too small anyway...it feels like everything is too small for me these days. And having myself on show like that was humiliating enough, but the worst came when he announced the due date. Mrs. Sullivan said she was surprised how far along I was, and amazed that no one had noticed my pregnancy until now...then the doctor made jokes about how difficult it was to tell a *cake belly* from a *baby belly* in big girls like me.

And they laughed at me; they laughed with this filthy pleasure at their own superiority, as if I wasn't even in the room or... I don't know... it's awful to even think it but maybe they laughed like that *because* I was in the room. I wanted to cry, but I also *really* did not want to be weak, and besides which I was scared that they'd be even more amused if I did show how upset I was. Instead, I just looked down at my bare naked belly and pictured our baby tucked up safe in there. After a while, the doctor used an ultrasound machine, and while I didn't get to see very much because they wouldn't let me see the screen, I heard him explaining it to Mrs. Sullivan and so I know that our baby is healthy and strong and with all of the right body parts.

When I have let myself think of our baby, I have always thought of it as a boy... until I heard the thumping rhythm of its heartbeat during that ultrasound. I can't explain why, but I somehow feel now that our baby is a girl—a daughter.

Can you imagine it? I can see her little ponytails flying in the wind when she runs out to the driveway to meet you as you're coming home from a day's work in the paddocks. You'll scoop her up in your arms and she will giggle and squeal with excitement, then she will tell you about the day she's had with me. We'll have read books and played games and she'll have helped me around the house, and probably have driven me half-crazy with her questions and her chatter.

I can see it, James, as clearly in my mind as if it's happening now. I live in my mind maybe too much at the moment, thinking about the way that we will all be together and how happy we will be.

I try very hard not to think about the sad things. It has taken me a few days to stop the rush of tension and anger in my chest when I think about that examination. Its taken time for me to feel calm enough about it to even sit down and write this to you.

It felt like a violation somehow. I know they are trying to help me, and they are looking after me while I am pregnant, and Tata obviously entrusted them to provide care for me... but I don't understand why they think it is okay to talk about me like that, or to deny me even the dignity of privacy. Even though I'm to be an unwed mother, am I not also just a mother? If I actually had a voice here, I'd ask Mrs. Sullivan that. Didn't she grow up under the care of someone's nurturing embrace? How would she feel if her mother was treated that way?

But I don't have a voice here. I am just here to kill time—until you come for us.

And now that I have started to think about the awful things, I will tell you one more miserable story. On Sundays, we have to go to church, but it's the strangest church you've ever seen—no crucifixes or stained glass like at the chapel at school. The minister is called "Captain", and he wears a military uniform. I learned that they are called Salvation Army and they give the money to run this home, so we have to attend the services.

At first, I really thought this was lovely. The walk is awful, but the church is warm, and the music is different to mass; there's a guitar and brass instruments, so the hymns sound full and alive. I actually thought it might even make a nice change from spending all day in the laundry.

It was only after the service, when the minister invited the congregation to have tea or coffee and some biscuits, that I really understood that we are not there as guests at all. We were told to stay in our seats until everyone else had had their fill of morning tea, and then we were allowed a cup of tea and one of the wheat biscuits. Not the cream biscuits, mind you, because they were all well and truly gone by the time we were allowed near to the plate.

The rest of the congregation watched us, as if we were a television show; some scandalous drama performed for their amusement. Can you imagine what a spectacle we must have made, twenty-seven heavily pregnant girls, all lining up to take our morning tea, while the respectable people all stared on at us in silence?

If they left me to my own devices, I'd never be embarrassed to be carrying your baby. I am full up—full of love, and baby, and new life and the beauty of the family we will be.

But put me on parade in front of those people and their condemning eyes and I shrivel inside. I want to curl up around this baby and protect it from their scorn. I can see what they are thinking, as clearly as if they were holding placards. *Scarlet woman! Whore! Sinful child, to be born out of wedlock! Unfit mother!*

I've been to the church several times now, and I have noticed that even the chattiest of the residents walk home in silence after the service. Maybe we are all fighting the same battle internally; the fight between what our instincts tell us about our children, and what those sharp gazes in the church would have us believe about ourselves.

There is one final, awful thing about our visit to the church on Sunday, James. We walk right past the post office, but even though I have asked, I am not allowed to slip these letters into the letter box. I begged Mrs. Baxter last week and she has told me to give her some time and she will see what she can organise. I don't know if I am foolish to pin my hopes on her. She is so nice, but...she *works* here, and there are so many rules. I am sure she would lose her job if she posted letters for me and was found out.

But I will keep writing to you. I will always keep writing. This pen and paper seems like my only way out of here, and I don't let myself think for more than a second at a time about what will happen if I can't reach you.

I'll never stop trying. I love you. Come for us soon,

Lilly

# CHAPTER NINE

## Sabina

### April 2012

Almost twenty-four hours after the low of the scene in the café, I rode the high of seeing my baby for the first time.

We'd booked into a private clinic in the city, a few suburbs east of our house, and I'd taken the morning off. Ted had done the same, and we travelled in together, conversation coming in jolts and starts as we swung between nerves and excitement.

The sonographer introduced herself, and led the way into a darkened room with several large television screens around the walls. She left so that I could change into a gown, and instructed us to ring a bell when I was on the bed and ready for her to return. When we were alone and I was changing, neither Ted nor I spoke. The excitement was on hold for now, and hopefully just for a moment, we were too nervous to make small talk or jokes.

Ted rang the bell once I was comfortable and covered on the bed, and then sat beside me and held my hand while the sonographer prepared the wand and covered my belly in pre-warmed gel. On the large screen angled towards me on the roof above, I watched the static on the screen blur in and out while she sought a good angle. My throat ached and my eyes were burning, and I realised that I was holding my breath. What if there was nothing to see? What if there was a baby there, but it wasn't healthy? I felt my heart start to race, and now the television screen blurred through my tears, until Ted squeezed my hand. I looked to him, almost frantic, and he nodded back towards the screen.

The image was in focus now, and I immediately recognised the flickering pixels that represented the blossoming of a new life within me.

My baby was at that fragile stage between blob and recognisable human form. I could see the buds of its arms and legs, its tiny hands waving around as if it was sending us a greeting. There was a tremor in Ted's arm, and I glanced back over at him to see a single tear running down his face. Unashamed, he beamed at me, and if there was any space of my heart that wasn't already full of love for Ted Wilson, it would have been swallowed up by sheer emotion at the sight of the pride on his face.

This was *our* moment, and it was big and heavy enough that it pushed every other thought to the back of my mind. For the first time in nearly a week I actually felt the joy of our situation. It bubbled up inside me and suddenly I was crying too, leaking sheer happiness down my cheeks and onto the bed. The era of waiting for the right time and saving money and clamping down on every urge for motherhood was over. We had not left it too late, we were apparently, blessedly fertile. We really were about to become a family of our own, and regardless of anything else going on in my life or even my mind, that was beyond wonderful.

Once the sonographer had finished, and after Ted and I both had tucked our blurry little prints into our wallets for safe keeping, we stood at the front of the sonography clinic beaming at each other like fools.

"I don't want to go to work today," Ted said, and he laughed. "I want to go shopping for cots and prams and…whatever else babies need."

"I think we had better do some reading first and figure out *what* babies need," I said, but I was laughing too. The joy and relief was intoxicating. I felt light inside, as if my troubles were momentarily removed, although as tempting as the idea of skipping work was, neither one of us really had the option to. I was back in front of a classroom within the hour, my class of seven-year-olds resting their heads on their desks with their eyes closed while an orchestral recording played.

My lesson plan had us playing recorders that day, but there was no way I was going to spoil my buzz with that particular form of musical torture. Instead, I let the music wash over me and my mind wandered. I thought back to the fear I'd felt pulsing through me, right up until I heard the baby's steady heartbeat. As the music faded, and the children raised their heads, I almost forgot to direct them onto their next activity.

There was a terror that came from the instinctual protectiveness I already felt for my child; the same child whose picture was resting in my wallet and whose future resided in my heart. My baby was within me, but invisible to me, and although I controlled my body and my body was nurturing it, I had no control over its welfare at all. I suddenly understood that the other side to the attachment I was increasingly feeling for my baby was risk—the harder I loved, the more I had to lose. Just nine weeks into my pregnancy, motherhood had already taught me new heights and depths of emotion. I'd felt almost overwhelming relief when I saw that he or she was healthy and growing as they should.

As soon as I could put words to my own thoughts on the matter, I made the connection to the other storm swirling in my life. Had my birth mother known all of those same fears? Had she felt the same anxiety once upon a time, but instead of feeling the sweet relief of knowing that her child really was okay, faced only the vast emptiness of thirty-eight years with no knowledge of my welfare? I couldn't begin to imagine how a person could ever live with such a depth of fear for so many years without completely losing their mind.

Suddenly I wanted to believe that she had managed to carry and birth me without ever feeling that same attachment. I wanted to discover that she'd calmly, rationally decided to relinquish me, truly believing it to be for the best. I almost wanted to believe that she'd abandoned me at the hospital and never, ever looked back.

But that would mean that her pregnancy had only ever been a burden, and my existence only ever a thing of shame. What if my parents' bewildering secrecy was hiding not *their* dark secrets, but *hers*?

What was worse?

Just thinking about the parallels between her situation and mine triggered some kind of crazy empathy in me, and by the end of the day, I was feeling a desperate compulsion to drop absolutely everything else in my life and figure out some way to find her—and to find the answers. I was surely just projecting my own feelings onto her, or perhaps the impulse and the urgency was some manifestation of the stress I was under... but by the time I went to bed that night, I felt like I was trying to tune out a desperate cry for help. It was as if she had always been calling to me, her voice echoing across the decades, waiting for a response that had never come.

But now that I could hear her... I could no more ignore it than I could undo the hurt of the years of silence.

I had to find her. I had to give her the chance for that same moment of relief that I felt when I saw my baby's heartbeat on the screen.

There had to be a way.

# CHAPTER TEN

## Lilly

## July 1973

Dear James,

I have some good news at last.

A whole series of small things happened that have made life in here just a little better. The first wonderful thing that happened was that I got some clothes that actually fit me properly, and even some new blankets for my bed. Mrs. Baxter was showing a new girl around the home one day when she saw me struggling with my too-tight trousers, and she asked me about it. I explained the situation, and then the next day, like magic, there was a bunch of new clothing in my locker with a little note asking me not to mention it to anyone. I haven't, of course, but every time I saw her after that I flashed her my brightest smile. She is so very kind, but she does not seem very happy, and I really hoped that seeing how happy she had made me would cheer her up somehow.

A few days later, I came into my room from dinner one night and there on my bed was a new blanket. No note this time, but I know who arranged it—there's no one else here who could or even would, other than Mrs. Baxter.

Just being warm at night has helped me a lot with my sleep. I am getting up on time, getting my shower, and sometimes even have time for a quick chat with the girls from the laundry before we go to work. I wouldn't say I've made friends... but I'm not the newest girl now, and I feel a bit less an outsider.

Then, yesterday, out of the blue, Mrs. Baxter came to take

me from the laundry in the middle of the morning. She suggested we take a walk around the block, out in the sunshine. I know you're probably thinking that I might not find that idea appealing, given that I'm heavily pregnant and hardly interested in walking at the best of times. But things are different here, we are not allowed outside except to walk across the road to work or to church... and even then we do it in a group and under supervision. There is no outside leisure time allowed, I guess because they are trying to hide us away in here. So yesterday, I felt like Mrs. Baxter was offering to bust me out of prison for an hour.

We walked very slowly around the hospital block. There was ice and snow in the gutters, and the wind was so bitter that my lips were stiff and it was hard to talk—yes, even harder than it usually is. But I talked anyway because Mrs. Baxter had a million questions for me and she seemed like she really wanted to hear the answers even if it took me a while to get them out. She asked me all about my family, and school, and then we talked about you and me.

I loved telling her about us. When I talk about you... when I write to you... when I think about your baby inside me... those things make me feel warm, even if I'm freezing like I was on that walk. And Mrs. Baxter... well, she really seems to understand about us. I feel like everyone else might think we're just stupid kids, but she told me that she knows teenagers can love as deeply as adults.

We talked a lot about the future. I told her about how I had always wanted to study history, and she told me not to let go of that dream as it might still be possible. I think she's a little naïve, to be honest... I mean, I obviously can't go to university now that we are having a baby! But then again, Mrs. Baxter told me that she does not have children of her own, so I guess she might not understand how impossible it would be to study with kids.

I explained to her about your course, and how you're learning about technological farming, so that we can have an easier life than our parents...and how guilty I feel that you're not going to get to live that dream now. Mrs. Baxter told me a little bit about herself too; that she is new in town, and her husband is an accountant over at the hospital. I think that maybe she loves him like I love you. Her voice changes when she talks about him—it gets softer and higher, as if she still thinks he's perfectly dreamy even after years of marriage.

I can tell that Mrs. Baxter does not like her job here very much and that makes me like her even more. I asked her why they don't have kids, and she said that they are finding it difficult to have their family, but that she is still hopeful for the future. It's so unfair that such a nice lady is struggling to have children of her own but has to work around us pregnant girls all day. It must be hard for her to be kind, but it doesn't *seem* hard for her...she genuinely seems nice.

When we'd finished our very slow walk around the block and it was time for me to go back into the laundry, Mrs. Baxter asked me to think about what I'll do if you don't come for us. I can understand why she'd ask that. I know that not all boys are like you.

But I know that you *will* come for us. I'm as sure about that as I am that the sun will rise tomorrow morning.

I actually know you'll read this letter too, and it makes it so much easier to write. The very last thing Mrs. Baxter said to me today was that if I can sneak my letters into my clothes tomorrow, she will come and take me for another walk, and we will find a way to post them to you.

I'll see you soon, James. You're all but on your way to come get us and I can't wait to see you.

Love,

Lilly

# CHAPTER ELEVEN

## Sabina

### April 2012

I didn't realise how difficult it would be to make the first steps past my clumsy Google search; *how do you find your birth parents?* It was simple to find an agency who might help, but making the actual call was infinitely more difficult than I'd anticipated.

"Hello, Adoption Information Registry, you're speaking with Hilary."

I really did intend speaking each time, right up until I heard the greeting. Then, without consciously deciding to, I would panic and jab at the "end" button on my phone. I'd waste minutes giving myself a pep talk, or making a cup of tea or hanging out the washing or rearranging furniture, until I suddenly felt brave and capable again. I was surprised every single time that the cowardice returned and I backed out of the call by some instinctual reflex.

With the business day drawing to a close, I sat with the handset in my hand for a few minutes, trying to really understand why this phone call was so difficult. I'd always hated the phone. In person, if I stuttered and couldn't finish a word, the other party to the conversation would see the panic in my eyes and realise that I was trying. On the phone, it was like shooting words out into a black hole.

So, the phone always made me anxious to a degree, but not like *that* phone call. There were just too many unknowns. What if I rang, and they found her quickly, and I had to actually meet her before I was ready? Or what if I rang, and they found her, and she didn't want to meet me? Or if I rang, and they couldn't find her at all, and there was nothing anyone could do—we were just lost to each other? Or if I rang, and they found her, and she was awful or the story of my conception was violent or—

It was all just a little bit too much. And yet, in spite of all of the potential horrors and the sheer unpredictability of it all, was *not* knowing somehow even worse? Could I even live with the not-knowing? After all, wasn't it worth the chance that we'd reunite somehow...eventually...and have at least *something* in common? I'd had a great relationship with Mum and Dad, surely I could also build bonds with the woman—and maybe even the man—who actually created me?

I dialled a final time; and faster, my fingers stabbing at the numbers with focussed intent.

"Hello, Adoption Information Registry, you're speaking with Hilary." The voice that greeted me was weary. I felt myself flush.

"G-good afternoon, Hilary." My stutter nearly tripped me up, and if I'd stuck on the sound even a split second longer, I'd have just hung up again. But having now managed the greeting, I suddenly found the confidence to continue. "My name is Sabina. I've recently discovered that I was adopted and I'd like to get some information about tracking down my biological parents."

"Hello there, Sabina. I'm so glad you've contacted us, that's exactly the kind of thing we do here." Something about her tone suggested she knew I'd called and hung up on her a number of times. Then again, my understanding of her tone might well have been tainted by the guilt of knowing that I'd essentially prank called her several times over the past few hours. "We usually find the easiest way to begin this process is to set up an appointment and meet with you face-to-face, does that sound okay?"

"Okay," I said, and then all of the air I hadn't realised I was holding onto rushed out of my mouth as I relaxed.

When I hung up the phone a few minutes later, an appointment time scrawled on the back of my hand, I felt as though I'd climbed some tremendous summit. I knew this was ridiculous, and that all I had done was to take the first baby step onto what might be a very long journey, but I was proud of myself for at least doing *that*.

And I was hopeful—that somehow I might find a way through the maze of my adoption without Mum and Dad. If the agency could help me find answers, there was a chance I might preserve my relationship with them after all.

—

Hilary Stephens was a lot younger than I'd imagined—and I spent a lot of time imagining her in the four days between making my appointment and actually meeting her. I had pictured her as my mother's age, with a maternal expression of concern and a big notepad to scribble details on. I even went so far as to imagine the moment when she told me my birth mother's name and how I might feel hearing it, and what Hilary Stephens would do when I cried. She'd come around her heavy oak desk and rub my shoulders, and then when she told me that my birth mother had been desperately wanting to meet me and couldn't wait to make contact, we'd actually embrace.

But in the real world, Hilary Stephens was only in her early twenties, and she was not very motherly at all. She was concerned and empathetic, but clearly very professional. I couldn't imagine her hugging any client, not even if they were weeping buckets of tears. I was irrationally disappointed when she shook my hand, then shook Ted's hand, and pointed us towards a partition. She didn't even have an office. Instead of the heavy oak desk I'd been picturing, we sat on cheap plastic chairs while she took out an iPad and began my file.

"So, Sabina, tell me about yourself. What's your date of birth?"

"10th October 1973."

"That's what's on your birth certificate?" When I nodded, she made a note then glanced at me. "Do you happen to know if it's your actual birth date?"

The question was more startling than it should have been. I felt my jaw slacken, and I stared at her, as if she'd said something offensive. Ted reached over to take my hand.

"Well, yes. I think it's both." But how did I know? I slumped. "I mean, I assume it is."

"And do you know your place of birth?"

"Orange. There was a maternity home."

"Yes…I know it." Her tone was grim, and she made some notes on the iPad.

"Is that bad?" Ted asked.

"Sometimes, the paper trail can be difficult to follow, especially at these rural maternity homes. But not always—so we'll cross that bridge when we get to it. Is this the first time you've tried to find your first family?"

"I only found out about this a few weeks ago."

Hilary glanced up at me, assessing my expression.

"So, still coming to terms with the adoption? Was it a shock?"

I laughed.

"That's an understatement."

"And how are you handling it?"

"I don't know. I'm really hoping that finding them, or finding out who they are, might help me to understand it."

"There are a lot of ways this can play out, Sabina. Sometimes,

I meet people like yourself, people who discover late that they were adopted and immediately come looking for answers about their past, and they have expectations about a reunion which are just not fair to anyone. It doesn't always go smoothly, and it's rarely a fast process. Rural births during that era can be very difficult to trace, and even if I *can* find your first mother or your father...well, they don't always want to be known. There are a lot of careful steps between here and any reunion, and the reunion is the beginning of a journey, not the end of one."

"I understand," I said, but I was already disappointed, and feeling so fragile and on edge that even her very reasonable warning made me want to get up and leave. I looked at the floor and started counting the loops of carpet near my feet.

I got to seventeen loops of the blue-grey carpet, one slightly longer than the others, before she spoke again. The room smelt faintly of coffee. Had Hilary Stephens had a coffee just before we arrived? How many other men and women had sat in this chair and prepared themselves for this journey? How many had waited decades to hear about their own origins? How many times had it ended in tears—and not happy ones?

"Is this always the right thing to do?" I asked.

"I don't think there are right or wrong ways to process what you've learned. I think you can only go with your gut, and your gut has brought you here, so I'm very happy to help you start if you chose to. But if at any time, you decide you don't want to proceed, or you don't want to proceed just yet...just say the word, okay?"

"That sounds like a great plan," Ted said softly. I glanced towards him, drew comfort from the steady gaze he maintained on me, and turned back to Hilary.

"Okay. Yes, let's do it."

"Do you have your birth certificate?"

I reached into my bag and withdrew the faded copy I'd had for years, since my very first job at a music store when I was fifteen. Hilary took it and reviewed it carefully.

"Did they tell you anything about the adoption?"

"No, not really... Mum was a social worker at the maternity home... but she told me that she never knew who my birth mother was."

"But..." Ted interrupted me, although I could see he was hesitant. "I mean, they say they don't know who she was... but it's pretty obvious that they're lying. They knew how old she was, and they're very defensive when we ask any other questions."

"I traced a birth at the Orange home a year or so ago," Hilary murmured, "from just a few years before you were born, actually. The home wasn't all that large, no more than forty women even at its height, and by the seventies, it was on the downhill slide—it closed in the early eighties from memory. I'd be surprised if she really didn't know who gave birth and when, especially given that it sounds like she adopted you quite quickly after you arrived. But look, we'll track back through the records and see what we can find."

It had been easy to focus my anger on Dad until that moment. His abrasive manner had been drawing my ire like a magnet. I could blame him, because he seemed to want to control the situation, and surely that meant it was all his fault.

But Hilary Stephens was twisting the kaleidoscope again, and shifting my perspective with it. The situation swam in and out of focus and suddenly I realised that it was *Mum* in the system, *Mum* in the home, *Mum* who had somehow mysteriously been able to take me home from the hospital.

Mum was where this whole lie started, and if Hilary was right and Mum really did know who my birth mother was, then Mum had the power to end it.

I could not think of a single acceptable reason for my mother to keep that secret and to keep me in this anguish. I'd assumed that we'd get past this. I'd assumed that we'd have a difficult few weeks or months but eventually they'd open up and I'd forgive them and we'd all move on.

Suddenly though, I realised that there was a possibility that I'd face my future without my parents. My first thought was to my pregnancy and the challenges of parenthood ahead—how would I ever cope without Mum's guidance and advice, or Dad's support?

But, I told myself, I'd managed just fine in the last week, and I'd continue to do so. I was beyond angry; my rage dialled all the way up toward hatred, and I wasn't sure that I even wanted to get "past this" at all.

"I've read a little about forced adoption," I said. My voice was strangled and strained. Ted gave another gentle squeeze of my hand. "I just can't understand—it sounds like something out of the dark ages."

"The thing to keep in mind is that being pregnant and unmarried was a huge deal when you were born—especially in rural areas. Here in the city, attitudes were starting to shift, but in the country—well, the idea that an unmarried woman might raise a child alone was unthinkable."

"Mum did tell me that her parents probably gave consent on her behalf to the adoption. That she might not even have had the right to give consent because of her age, I mean."

"Yes if she was a minor that's probably how it worked. But something to keep in mind is that consent is a very loaded word when we talk about adoption. Particularly during the era of your birth, and even more so in these little rural maternity homes. There really was no such thing as *informed* consent. In a maternity home like the one you were adopted from, even if a woman did sign the right paperwork—even if she was an adult and had the right to—it was usually after months of coercion. If we find that your first mother did 'consent' to the adoption, that doesn't mean that she *wanted* it to happen."

"I'd run away," I whispered, sliding my hands over my belly. I had a fierce confidence in the protectiveness I felt for our child. "I'd find a way to escape. *No way* would they take my baby."

"That wasn't really an option, Sabina," Hilary said gently. "These were highly regimented places, attendance rolls marked at regular intervals and doors physically locked at times to keep the women inside. Not to mention serious punishments where the rules were broken. When women did escape, they were often returned by the police—remember that the law was *on the side* of the maternity home."

"It just seems crazy now, doesn't it?" Ted murmured. "If this was happening today, there'd be an uproar."

"The uproar is finally starting now," Hilary said. "The problem at the time was that the government didn't see what was happening as an injustice, if anything it saw the whole adoption industry as a way to deal with the moral failure of the mothers. At the heart of all of this was a sick kind of misogyny, the belief that women who fell pregnant outside of marriage were fundamentally sinful and undeserving of their babies. A lot of maternity homes were run or sponsored by religious institutions. Orange was sponsored by the local Salvation Army, from memory."

"Did they really think they were *helping* anyone?" I murmured, shaking my head.

"I am sure that most involved in the system thought they were doing the right thing," Hilary said quietly. Ted and I glanced at each other, and I knew we were both thinking about Mum.

"What is the process from here?" Ted asked quietly.

"Sometimes, it's a long one." Hilary sat the iPad on her

lap. "I do have the bulk of the Orange records already, so that may speed it up a little. But basically I need to look to find an exact match for the details provided. If I can be sure who your first mother was, then I can search to see if she's already registered with us. Sometimes, the end of this journey comes that quickly—either *yes*, she's registered with us looking for a reunion, or *maybe*, if she hasn't registered at all, and we have to then try to track her down…or *no*. It's a *no* if she's registered with us to put a veto on contact."

"Does that happen often? The veto, I mean." My mouth was dry.

"More often than you'd think. Sometimes a first mother really does want to carry on as if the pregnancy never happened, and we have to respect that. Often it's that the mother has gone on to have a family later in life and has never told anyone about the pregnancy. If there's a contact block, there is *nothing* I can do. And if I can't be sure who your first mother was, there's usually nothing I can do. That scenario can happen if the paperwork was forged, which happened sometimes too… often where the first mother entirely refused consent."

"Refused consent? So—even if the women didn't agree, the babies were taken sometimes?"

Hilary hugged the iPad against her stomach and nodded slowly.

"In most cases, Sabina, it didn't matter what the mothers did. If they weren't minors and they were even entitled to a say in their child's future, and they did somehow resist the coercion and the pressure, then 'consent' was achieved via drugging the mothers, or even brute force, and sometimes when all of that failed, staff resorted to fraud."

Brute force. Forced adoption. Fraud. The language of this new world was so violent.

"Do you think…do you think Mum—my adoptive Mum, Megan—would she have been involved in those things? As a social worker?"

I think she was trying to maintain a poker face, but I saw that slight compression to Hilary's lips and the minute narrowing of her eyes. The hint of disdain told me everything I needed to know.

"It's possible," was all that she said.

When we left her office, I slipped into a daydream, and I didn't really emerge until later that night. I thought about the woman who had given birth to me, and what it would be like if I could reunite with her. I thought of how wonderful it would be to look into a face that mirrored mine, and I wondered if, on some level, I had actually missed that for my entire life. I thought only about the future, because every time I wondered about the past, I'd feel my heart rate start to race and the simmering anger in my gut would threaten to rise.

Mum shattered my daydream and triggered the explosion. She sent me a text, a sweet and somewhat innocent text, but it enraged me such that I nearly threw the phone.

> *Sabina, are you okay? Please just let me know that you're okay, I am very worried about you.*

How dare she enquire after my welfare? How dare she check in on me, as if I was walking through some unpredictable, unavoidable turmoil…as if she hadn't caused the whole damn thing?

My hands were shaking as I replied.

> *I am not okay, Mum. You're still lying to me. I won't be okay until you tell me the truth. What is it you're trying to hide?*

I let the phone rest in my palm while I waited for a response, but I stared down at the screen with such a desperate fury that my eyes began to ache. After a few minutes I realised that she wasn't going to reply.

"I am starting to hate them," I whispered to Ted.

He looked at me in surprise.

"I've never heard you say that about anyone."

"I want to hurt them. I want revenge. I want to break them into a thousand tiny pieces and rebuild them as the people they were supposed to be all along." I was typing on my phone again as I spoke, but Ted suddenly caught my hands.

"I know you're angry, and you have every right to be," he whispered. "But don't do anything you'll regret, Bean."

I snatched the phone away from him and finished my text message with violent jabs of my fingertips. When I was satisfied with the message, I added Dad to the recipient list and held the phone up for Ted to read.

> *I don't want to hear from either of you, not ever again if you can't even bring yourself to be honest with me. Don't contact me until you are ready to tell me everything.*

"Are you sure that's what you want, Bean?" I heard Ted's hesitation, but I ignored it. I hit the "send" button and tossed my phone onto the coffee table.

"No," I said flatly. "But I *am* sure it's what I need."

# CHAPTER TWELVE

## Lilly

### July 1973

Dear James,

I am watching the door all day and night, waiting for you to burst inside and run to me. I have thought long and hard about how everyone else will watch us, wishing it was their boyfriend coming to take them home. Will you catch the bus from Armidale, and come straight here? Or will you go home first, and break the news to your parents?

Any day now. You'll come, and take me home.

The truth is, I have been trying to stay positive, especially in my letters to you, because I really don't want you to think badly of me. I want you to be proud of how well I cope with everything, but...it is beyond awful. I am getting worn down by the sadness, the endless hard work, the constant reminders of how much I've ruined my life. Don't worry, James, of course I do not believe the things they say—of course I am fit to mother this child, and of course it would never be better off being raised by someone else. How could I ever believe those lies? Her heart beats within my body. I am growing her. I am nurturing her already. She is me and you, and she needs us. It makes me angry to hear them say that handing her over to strangers would be for the best.

But James...that *is* what they say. They say it at grace at breakfast, they say it when they mark the roll of names at the laundry, they say it when they think we aren't listening, they say it even louder when they know we are. It is the nurses, it is Mrs. Sullivan, it is the doctors—this is their mantra; that we must relinquish, that it would be selfish to entertain any other possibility. They want us to believe that we can and must redeem ourselves and that the only way to do that is to hand over our children to a family constructed with better moral fabric.

It is an endless, repetitive theme of life here. The pressure to plan for adoption is constant, even from Mrs. Baxter, although of course it's delivered in her gentler way. She asks me almost every time we see each other what I will do if you do not come, and as much as I like her, I am starting to think that this is her more subtle way of trying to convince me to prepare for an outcome I know with all of my heart that I need not worry about.

I have heard the chatter among the other girls, and I know that most of them believe the lies. I wish I was braver, so that I could beg them to reconsider. I understand why it's called brain*washing* now. We are bathed and basted in the negativity, every moment of every day.

I feel a love for this baby already, a bond with it that is stronger than anything else I've experienced, except perhaps for the love that I feel for you. I wonder...is this common to all women? If it is, then surely those who do sign away their children must miss them forever. Tonight, I heard Mrs. Sullivan telling Tania that it will be as if the baby never happened and that after the birth she will be able to move on with her life as if she never made this mistake. That is insanity. It's disgusting to even suggest such a thing. How could someone create a life and then forget it existed?

That's what's made me so upset tonight, actually. I was so confused by what Mrs. Sullivan had said. To suggest that it would be as though we were never pregnant...well, that's just idiotic. Don't they know that our hearts and minds expand, just as our bodies do? I know that the babies will be born and the physical changes will mostly disappear with time, but no one could ever convince me that I could forget this child. She's tattooed herself onto my spirit.

So when Tania came to bed, I actually tried to talk to her. Usually, I feel invisible to Tania—she doesn't acknowledge me unless she absolutely has to, and so I've never tried to start a conversation. Tonight though, I desperately wanted to believe that someone else can see through the lies, and so I asked Tania what she thought about those things Mrs. Sullivan had said.

Tania gave me that derisive eye roll that I know so well now, made some unkind comments about my naïveté, and then she told me the story of her baby's conception. She didn't love the man who got her pregnant. She has no interest in a future with him, and she really does believe that her baby will be better off without her. After that, Tania shut the conversation down with a few curse words and a tone that would terrify anyone. She is just so mean and so hardened.

I was too upset to sleep so here I am hiding in the toilet at midnight, breaking the rules in so many ways...writing a letter to you because again and as always, you're my only comfort.

If I was in her situation...I mean, I would never be in her situation because I'd never be doing those things with someone I didn't love.

Oh, James. As soon as I wrote that I felt sick with guilt, because I realised that I just did to Tania exactly what they are *all* doing to me. What right does anyone have to be so superior, heaping judgement here and there, as if any one of us is better than any other? That's at the heart of all of the misery in this place, and maybe I am just as prone to it as anyone.

Is what she has done so different to what we have done? The only distinction is that you and I love each other, and apparently to the people who matter here in the home, that means absolutely nothing.

And I keep trying not to think about it, because I still am so sure that I don't need to...but the truth is, James, I just don't know what I'd do if you did *not* come for me. I would surely find some way to keep my baby, but if I were in Tania's shoes, and there was no knight in shining armour on his way...

Well, I can almost understand it. Without you, I'd leave the home with the baby in tow, and I'd have nowhere to go. And even if I did find a house, I'd have no way to pay for it, let alone buy food. And if I found a job, who would look after our baby? Who would hire me, anyway—a woman with a baby but no husband? And how would I shield our baby from the whispers and the comments as she grew? Everyone would know that she was illegitimate, it would be her undoing before she learned to speak a single word.

I kind of get it...at least on a practical level...but the thing is, I love her, already, so much. *Too* much to just pass her over as if she was an unwanted thing. In spite of Tania's anger, surely it's the same for her, and for everyone else? This love I have for our baby is immense—so strong already that it makes me feel sick to even think about parting with her. I could just never do it. No one could ever convince me to. Never.

I'm getting upset again, so I'll stop writing now because I know it's all for nothing. I'm so glad I don't have to worry about being left alone here. I know you'll come—you're probably already on your way, even while I'm writing this.

See you soon, my love.

Lilly

# CHAPTER THIRTEEN

## Sabina

## April 2012

Ted and I were seated beside one another on the sofa, watching a movie on the television late on Saturday night. I had a crocheted blanket over my lap, and I was trying to remember where it came from. I'd had it for a long time. Had Mum made it for me? I couldn't remember her giving it to me, but she must have—why else would I have carted it onto the cruise ship, to Dubai, and back to Sydney twice? I felt a strange ambiguity enjoying the warmth of the blanket. I was furious with Mum, enough that if she had made me the blanket, I wanted to hide it away or throw it straight into the bin. At the same time, I already missed Mum terribly, and I was strangely comforted by the thought that the blanket might have been handcrafted by her.

The ads came on. Ted, as he always did, reached for the remote and flicked the channel over a few times, searching for something to distract us until the ad break ended. He stopped on a wildlife documentary. A turtle laid eggs on a beach and swam away, and the scene faded to black, then faded back in to show the turtle eggs hatching and the baby turtles stumbling around on their uninitiated legs.

"...the babies are self-sufficient from birth, by the time the eggs have hatched, the mother is long gone..." The commentator seemed to find this an unremarkable fact, but I was transfixed. I watched the tiny turtles stumble their way into the ocean. Maybe in the natural world it was an ordinary thing for a mother to leave her child behind sometimes.

I shivered, returning to that vision I'd had the first time I realised I was adopted, of myself abandoned on a doorstep in the pouring rain and driving wind. I knew it hadn't been like that, of course, although I didn't have an alternative picture for my overactive imagination as yet. The one thing that was most definitely accurate was that, in some way or shape or form, my biological mother had at some point left the hospital without me. I knew almost nothing about her, but that simple fact was heartbreaking enough.

I paused on that thought, and Ted flicked back to the movie, unaware that I was yet again having some kind of minor breakdown, right there in his arms. We were sitting in darkness but for the TV, our faces illuminated by the flickering light of the imagery. I had disconnected from the movie now. It seemed to take so little to trigger a return to thoughts of the adoption.

I reached my hand down to my stomach and rested it there, a flesh and bone protective shield over my own pregnancy. No matter where my thoughts on my parents wandered to, they always returned to my baby. I wanted to believe that my love for my own child was going to be big enough to protect it from any threat, but I was slowly, reluctantly realising that sometimes even the greatest love a person could feel would not be enough to outweigh the bad in the world.

I reached for Ted, pressed my face into his upper arm, and started to cry.

"Hey! What's this?" he asked, automatically turning to me and pulling me fully into his arms.

"Do you think those turtles miss their mother?"

"What turtles?"

"On the nature documentary."

"Oh, the eggs? Miss their mother? No, of course not. They're born self-sufficient, that's what the narrator said."

"I wonder why I didn't miss my mother. Would our baby even miss me, if it wasn't with me?"

"We're talking about babies, Bean. You don't remember, maybe you *did* miss her. Maybe you fretted horribly and Megan just did a wonderful job of helping you to adjust. And you don't need to worry about our baby missing you because you'll be right here with it."

"But what if something happens to me? What if I couldn't be with our baby?"

"Sabina, where is this coming from?"

"If we ever find my mother, I'll bet she's hurt that I didn't miss her," I whispered.

"Or, she'll be delighted that you found a happy family, and grew up to be well adjusted and content." He was so patient with me, always the voice of reason. I extracted myself from his arms and he protested, "Where are you going?"

"I think I'll just go to bed."

"Bean..."

"I'm sorry," I said. "I know I'm c-crying because a turtle never knew its mother and that's insane." I laughed, then sobbed again. "Ted, it's just too horrible. It's just too unfair, and too confusing. I can't bear it."

Ted sighed and flicked the television off.

"You don't have to c-come to bed with me," I said, through another sob that I could neither understand nor prevent.

"Yes I do." Ted sighed, and pulled me close. "Because what you're going through is awful, and the timing is awful, and it's not fair so it doesn't have to make sense. If you need to go to bed and cry over that poor lonely turtle, then I need to be right there with you."

—

Less than a week after we met Hilary, she called me with an update. I know that a week doesn't seem like a long time to wait, but the days had stretched and I'd thought about little else but that search for the whole time. I was walking home from school when the number flashed up on the display on my phone, and an instant adrenaline-high kicked in. I was shaking with equal parts fear and excitement.

"I have some news," Hilary said, after she greeted me. I could hear the hesitation in her voice, and my mood sank with her tone as she added, "It's not great."

My footsteps slowed and then stopped.

"Okay," I said.

Hilary started talking, but she was giving me too much information about legislation and too little information about my actual situation. Eventually, I wrapped my brain around the basic idea—her hands were tied.

"...so you see, I can only release to you information which I'm sure is about your own birth. And I have reviewed the records from the hospital for the date on your birth certificate and there's just no one to match you to. Whatever happened, it didn't happen by the usual procedures."

"What does that even mean?"

"There were two components to birth registration; each individual birth certificate which was submitted to the federal authorities, and then the hospital kept a record of actual birth. So, I can see on your official birth certificate that you were born on the 10th of October at the Orange hospital, but when I reviewed the files for all of the women in the maternity home at the time you were born, none of them gave birth on

10th October. So either your birth mother wasn't confined in the home, or more likely, the date on your certificate is wrong."

On the road beside me a push-bike rider raced past a tiny hatchback. They were going so fast—was that even safe? I breathed in the scent of exhaust fumes and tried to hold myself stiff against the coming pain. It didn't work—the disappointment hit me. It slammed at my gut, the very same sensation a passenger feels when a plane hits unexpected turbulence.

"Even my birthday is a lie."

"It does seem as if that's the case. And look...it's not common, but this isn't the first time I've come across this scenario. It was unfortunately not unheard of for the birth registration paperwork to be entirely forged to neglect the birth mother's role altogether. For the right adoptive parents, sometimes staff would arrange this kind of thing...it kind of makes sense, given that Megan worked at the home." I was clutching the phone so hard that my fingers were aching. "It's a complex puzzle, and there are too many pieces missing for us to really proceed anywhere at this point. I'm so sorry."

The words swirled around and echoed in the sudden emptiness of my mind. All of my daydreams about finding *Her*, and feeling some cosmic connection to her, and learning and knowing *Her*...they disappeared in a single conversation.

"So that's it, then. I'll never know?"

"Not necessarily..." I felt as if Hilary was with me one moment, and then gone the next. The professional tone was shifting, as if the sadness was overwhelming her too. I felt the extraordinary pity she felt for me. "But, well...from a *paperwork* standpoint...it really is like the adoption part of your birth never happened at all."

Which, I suddenly understood, was exactly what my parents

had wanted. They wanted to pretend I was really theirs, and then they did, for nearly four decades.

"I can't believe I hit a dead end already."

"It's *almost* a dead end," Hilary confirmed softly. "But it's not *the* end. It just means you have to take a different route to find your answer."

I laughed bitterly.

"Mum?"

"Well, there are DNA registries I can connect you with too. We take a swab from your cheek and it's processed and compared with swabs from people all over the world, so it's a possible route." I sighed impatiently, and heard Hilary's answering sigh. "Yes, I know… it's a long shot. But the other possibility is… if your adoptive mother would tell you even a first name or a real date of birth, I could probably take it from there. I just need some reliable link."

"Are you sure she even knows my birth mother's name? She says she doesn't."

"Look, maybe she's telling the truth. Maybe someone played intercessor, and maybe she really had nothing to do with your birth mother. But even if she could give us the name of the person who facilitated the adoption… we could potentially find a way to proceed."

"I just know sh-she's not going to help," I whispered. My throat was tight and my words were jumpy. Disappointment sat like a heavy weight on my chest.

"I'm really sorry, Sabina. I'll keep digging, of course. But I wanted to let you know that at this stage, I just don't know if we'll find her."

"Thanks anyway, Hilary." The sinking disappointment in my stomach was there to stay, then. "Thanks for your call."

I stood there for a while, beneath the canopy of oak trees

that I passed through every day on my way to and from work. I realised that this closed door was probably the end of my search, and that simply could not be—I couldn't allow it. I was overtaken by an urgency and desperation to *do* something, *anything*. I turned back towards school, then I changed my mind and turned towards home, and then I stopped completely and had to lean against a tree to hold myself upright.

Clarity came as suddenly as the phone call. I left the support of the tree and headed towards my house, my steps furious and fast, fuelled by a determination to force some justice for myself.

—

I thumped on my parent's door with the metal knocker again. This time, I wasn't unsure, this time I was there on a mission, and now letting myself in was actually a warning salvo. Dad answered the door, and I saw the joy that transformed his face when he saw me there. Even his affection infuriated me.

"I need to speak to you both," I said. He sighed, as if I was already being unreasonable, and now I barged past him into the house. "Mum? Where are you?"

"Sabina—hello, love! I'm in the bedroom," she called from up the stairs. I turned back to Dad.

"Come with me."

Dad followed me, but I could see that he was uncomfortable. When I stepped into the bedroom, Mum was carefully placing folded clothes into their chest of drawers. The happiness on her face when she saw me faded into the same wary confusion that Dad now wore on his.

I didn't sit down. I stepped into the room and waited for Dad to join us. Then I broadened my hands and I said as calmly as I could,

"I am *going* to find her. And if you won't help me, you are going to lose me, and Ted, and your grandchild."

"Sabina, please—"

"I'm *not* here to discuss this. I'm here to give you an ultimatum. I think you both love me; very, very much. But ever since you told me about this I've had a desperate, burning n-need inside myself to find her. It's like she's *calling* me and she has been the whole time, but I've only just realised. Do you understand how hard it is going to be for me to live with that?"

My parents looked shell-shocked. Mum was still holding a pair of Dad's briefs. They stared at me in silence, even though my voice was wavering now and there were tears on my cheeks.

"You won't see me again, or hear from me, and I don't want you to contact us; not if you're sick, not when my baby comes. *Never*. I want her name, and I want my real date of birth, and until you give me those things, I don't want *anything*—at all—to do with either of you."

Finally, Dad cleared his throat.

"You don't mean this."

"That's the best you've got, Dad?" I hadn't expected them to suddenly soften and help me, but Dad's ability to resist being moved *at all* was shocking.

"We've raised you better than this, Sabina. We don't deserve this." Dad genuinely seemed to think that I was being unfair. I laughed, but it was a sound of disbelief and of outrage.

"Neither did *she*, Dad. I know that the maternity home forced those girls to give up their babies, and no matter who she was, or how I was conceived, or how this all happened, there's no way she could have deserved *that*."

I stared at Mum but I felt Dad's eyes on me—they both stared at me. There was so much I wanted to say, so much I needed to get off my chest, so much fury and confusion and heartache swirling around in my brain that I felt I had no chance at all of explaining myself. I started to cry, and Mum dropped the briefs and took a step towards me. I held my hand up towards her and forced myself to make one last attempt to speak my mind.

"I can only assume there are ghosts buried in my adoption that you don't want me to uncover. I know the paperwork was dodgy—I assume there's more. I can't think of any other explanation for why you would withhold the truth from me when I so desperately need it. Let's imagine that I find her, and I discover all of your nasty secrets—ask yourself this question, are you any worse off than you are now? At this point, it looks to me like you lied to me for my entire life and you're both still too cowardly to face the truth of what you've done." Mum was staring at me with visible distress, her hands clenching and unclenching at her sides. I still did not bother to look towards Dad. "Prove me wrong, Mum," I whispered. "I can't forgive what I don't know. Please help me find her. I'm *begging* you. This is the end of our family if you don't."

Once again I stormed away from them, and once again they did not follow me.

This time, it felt like the closing of a book.

I truly thought it would be the end of the first part of my life, and that I was walking into a second half—where Megan and Graeme Baxter were no longer my parents.

# CHAPTER FOURTEEN

## Lilly

## August 1973

James,

I don't understand why you haven't come yet. You have to come *now*, do you understand me? This cannot wait—you must get in a car, or a bus, or start walking and you *have to do it now*. If you need to, borrow money off someone, or even—just this one time—*steal* it. You can't wait any longer. I don't know if you have exams or assessments due or you're finishing out the semester, but whatever it is that's holding you up, put it aside and *get here*.

It is worse than I thought, James—it is so much worse than I thought.

I have realised something today, and it's not even an easy thing to write, so you're going to have to bear with me. There was a girl on my laundry team, her name is Anita. She disappeared today. That's nothing new, because girls go to maternity all of the time to have their babies... but this was the first girl from my work team, and I was anxious to hear how she went. As the day went on, I was confused—I just didn't understand why everyone was so quiet and sad. I figured that something terrible had happened to her, and I was waiting for a chance to ask someone at work, but we were so busy, and before I knew it we were back at dinner. When we all sat down, Tania told us all that she'd had her baby. That's all that she said, and no one was celebrating; in fact, they were all even sadder than they had been all day and I was just so confused. Was Anita unwell? Had the baby died? Had something gone wrong?

After a while, after we all ate dinner in silence and no one so much as made eye contact with anyone else, I finally asked what sex her baby was. No one answered me, so I pushed a little harder, asking whether it was okay, whether Anita was okay.

I felt like Tania's anger came out of nowhere. I just wanted to see if our friend was all right. But Tania stood, and she waved her arms, and she screamed at me and she called me stupid—and God, I *am* stupid, because in all of these weeks here I just didn't understand how much trouble we are in.

The thing is, James...we don't know what sex Anita's baby is. We don't know if the baby is okay. *Anita* doesn't even know those things. They might have given her medicine so that she slept through the labour, or they might have held her down, or they might have just have put a pillow over her face so that she couldn't even *see* the baby.

She will never know anything at all about her child—not even if the baby lives, or if it dies.

It is the policy of the maternity home that when we give birth, our babies are taken immediately, and if what Tania told me tonight is true, there's no point even fighting—they will take our babies anyway. Pregnancy makes me feel strong, like a superhero, but the truth is, even the strongest of us is weak against the system.

The only thing that we actually *do* know is that Anita would not have had the chance to hold her baby to even say hello, let alone to weep her goodbye. She would never have had the chance to look down to find out its gender, or to count its tiny little fingers and toes, and inhale its sweet new scent.

And as unthinkable as all of that is, there is worse; because it doesn't matter what Anita wants for herself and for her baby.

This routine of taking babies away from their mothers doesn't just happen to the girls who consent to relinquish. Tonight when I told Tania that I would never give my consent to such a monstrosity, one of the other girls quietly took my hand and led me from the room. I was raging—breathing so hard and fast that the cold air was like fire into my lungs—and she whispered to me that even if I want to take our baby home, and that even if I fight and kick and scream, I will *never* be allowed to.

That is not what this place is about. All of this pressure to relinquish our babies is like a formality…or maybe some added penance—just a way to increase our pain while we wait. In the end, it doesn't really matter what we decide or what we want for ourselves. The social workers are not here to help us make a choice, they are here to find a way to take the choice from us, and to place our babies with more deserving families.

I hope you can read this. I know that my handwriting is bad tonight and I'm sorry. I am so upset that even hours after all of this happened, I am still shaking like a leaf. I am too upset to sleep. I can't even sit still. I want nothing more than to sob and scream and rail against the unfairness of it all, but if anyone hears me awake at this hour, there'd be hell to pay.

Do you remember that hot summer day when we were maybe ten or eleven, and we wandered too far from the houses, even after Mama told us not to, and there were snakes *everywhere* in the long yellow grass? Do you remember how you sat me up on that rock, and you took both of my hands and promised me that everything was going to be okay because you would take care of me?

Until today, that was the loudest fear I'd ever felt. For years after I had nightmares about those snakes. If I woke up too early from the dreams I'd be drenched in sweat, my heart racing, convinced that I was going to die then and there.

But if I stayed asleep just a little longer, you did in my dream what you did that day in the paddock. You'd hold tight to my hand and lead me back through the grass, comforting me… promising me that we just had to keep moving.

I feel just like that again today, James…even worse, actually. This is a nightmare; the serpents are coming for our baby this time, and I'm trapped if you don't come to take my hand. This is a different fear—it's bigger and blacker, and I don't even know how to deal with it.

I am looking back at these past weeks through sharper eyes tonight, and I finally realise that I am not only in the worst trouble imaginable, but that there really is *no* escape without you. There is nothing *at all* that I can do, James. I know you are probably wondering why I don't just run away and find my own way to you, but it really is impossible. Not only do I not have a single dollar, but the doors are locked at night. There are rumours that when girls have broken out in the past, the police have been sent after them. What is happening here is not some under-cover baby-stealing operation…it is *organised* by the authorities, and if I did run away, *I* would be the one in the wrong.

I was in such a panic when I realised that Tania was telling the truth. I ran from the dining room and all the way to our bedroom, but then I was scared that she would follow me and mock me for being stupid, so I ran back down the stairs and out into the out-of-bounds stairwell behind the home.

All that I wanted was to be alone. It is such a basic dignity to have enough privacy to cry. But even there, in the one place in the home no one is supposed to go, Mrs. Baxter was waiting. As soon as I stepped onto the landing I saw her, sitting on the cement stairs one level up.

At first I did not actually register that *she* was crying, all I knew was that I had believed her to be a friend, but now I realise that she *works here* and it's actually her job to figure out how to take my baby. I was so angry with her that I could have hurt her, if I'd had the presence about me to coordinate any physical action. You know I'm not one to yell, but in this situation, I think I might actually be capable of anything—I've never felt so outraged before. But when she finally realised I was there too and looked down at me I swear to God that looking into those red eyes of hers was like staring at a corpse.

I feel no shame about my situation, but you know what, in that regard I think maybe I am actually better off than Mrs. Baxter. There was no denying the pain she's in. She doesn't want to be here anymore than I do, and I can't even begin to guess why she stays. Seeing how upset she was shocked some sense into me and I climbed the stairs and sat beside her. For a while we sat in silence, and then she suddenly wrapped her arms around me and all of our tears started all over again.

After a while, she pointed out that I had to go to bed, or I'd be missed by the night nurse and Mrs. Sullivan would be informed. I was still crying, and Mrs. Baxter wiped away the tears on my cheeks with the pads of her thumbs and told me that I have to be brave for the baby. Beneath the dull resignation and the self-loathing in her brown eyes, there is still kindness there. I begged her to help me. There has to be a way, surely, and if anyone could do it... well, maybe *she* could.

She promised to think about it, and she told me to do this; to go somewhere when I could, and quickly write another letter to you, to make as blunt as I could the desperation in my situation.

So here I am, James. I am laying it all out before you. There is no "brave face" over these words this time, just in case my brave face until now has fooled you somehow into thinking that I am okay.

I am *not* okay, James. *We* are not okay. Our family is in terrible danger, and there isn't much time. This just isn't right. We can't let it happen, can we? We won't, will we?

James, if you really can't get away, and I can't think why you wouldn't but... if that's the case, then please just contact your parents. I know they will help.

Please, James.

Lilly

# CHAPTER FIFTEEN

## Sabina

### April 2012

I was still in bed the next morning when Ted went to leave for work. He had been in to kiss me to say goodbye and I was lying semi-awake in a tangle of sheets and blankets, wondering at the slight curve to my tummy.

It was easy to forget that something quite miraculous was happening while we rushed about our lives, distracted by all of the drama with my parents. I slid my hands over my lower belly several times, trying to measure the angle of any potential bump that might be emerging. I wondered if the baby was moving around beneath my hand, and if it was bothered at all by the stress hormones that had no doubt been pumping through my body lately. Would it look like me? I hoped it inherited Ted's metabolism and my voice. We hadn't talked about it, but I had a feeling that Ted was hoping for a son. I was starting to form a mental list of potential boy's names when I heard Ted open the front door, and I paused, waiting for the sound of it locking behind him. When I didn't hear the slam, I rose reluctantly and pulled on a gown over my night shirt, thinking he'd left it open.

I found him sitting on the step beside my mother, his arm around her thin shoulders. For a moment, he didn't realise that I was behind them, and the expression on his face was pure agony. I stopped and watched them, thinking about how quickly the landscape of my family life had changed. I'd been doing a lot of talking since my parents had told me the truth about my birth.

I hadn't thought nearly enough about the impact all of this was having on my husband.

"Come inside, Mum," I said softly. Ted glanced up at me.

"I can't," she whispered. I had startled her, and now she pulled away from Ted and rose. "I don't deserve your hospitality... and I don't deserve your forgiveness, Sabina. I'll never even ask you for it. I wanted to do this weeks ago, but we were so scared, and Dad..."

There was an aching sadness in her smile but she held out her hand, and I reached for it automatically. I felt the tremors running through her, transmitted to my skin via the piece of paper she clutched, now sandwiched between our fingers. There were thirty-eight years of guilt in her red-rimmed eyes.

"We so loved pretending that you were really ours, Sabina. It was like a wonderful game, and after a while, we forgot that we were only ever playing. Dad doesn't want to let that go, but I know that you need us to."

She withdrew her hand from mine, leaving the paper behind.

"C-come in," I pleaded. "Come in and talk to me."

"No, Dad will be upset if he wakes up before I get home."

"*Don't worry* about Dad! *I* need you!"

The last of my sleepiness had disappeared. My hands shook when I looked down at the paper. Mum's handwriting was uneven. I could see that she'd been shaking when she wrote.

*Liliana Wyzlecki*

*3rd September 1973*

My breath caught.

"This is her? This is *me*?"

Mum nodded.

"Mum, t-thank you." A sob overcame me and I pressed my hands against my mouth to stop myself dissolving completely.

"I..." Mum tried to speak, but couldn't quite form the

words. She looked to Ted helplessly, and he pointed to a box on the ground beside our door.

"Megan brought some photo albums for you. So that if you can find her, you can show her what your life has been like."

I stared at the box. It contained a collection of mismatched photo albums that I'd never seen before.

"Where did these come from?"

"I made them for her," Mum choked. She took a step backwards and away from us. "Good luck, Sabina. I really...I really wish you luck, love."

She turned away and started to walk towards her car. Ted caught my arm as I moved to give chase.

"Bean, let her go."

I thought about it. After all, I had in my hand the thing that I needed most from her.

I didn't have what I *wanted* though. I wanted comfort and assurance. I wanted an open chat, and some easy answers.

"I *can't* let her go, Ted."

I shook his arm away and took off at a half-jog towards my mother's car. She was fumbling with the key button to open the door. Her brave face was gone now; she was a mess of ugly tears.

I snatched the keys from her hand and then we stared at each other in the early light. I was furious and I was grateful and I was devastated and relieved. I didn't know where to start explaining all that—my emotions were running so high and fast that words barely seemed big enough to funnel them out.

"You did know her."

Mum nodded, and wiped at her eyes. God, she looked so old—painfully thin, drowning in her own tears. I felt like Mum had undergone a physical metamorphosis in the weeks since she'd told me the truth.

"She wanted to keep me, didn't she? That's why you never told me."

"Sabina, I told you, it wasn't as simple as that—"

"I know, Mum. I just need to hear it. She wanted to keep me. You wouldn't let her. You took me yourself. That's what happened, wasn't it?"

"If you need to simplify things that much, Sabina, you will never understand this."

"I would *hate* anyone that took my baby from me," I whispered, thinking of the blissfully calm moment I'd just abandoned, lying in my bed thinking about my pregnancy. I hadn't intended cruelty and hadn't realised how hurtful my words had been until I heard Ted's stifled gasp behind me. Mum suddenly met my gaze again.

"And you'd have every right to," she said flatly.

"I almost get Dad's part in this—I can imagine him deciding what was best for everyone and then pulling all of the strings like some sick puppet master. But *you*? You were the one who taught me that every person matters. You taught me to always tell the truth. *You* were apparently even keeping these photo albums for her—you obviously knew that I'd have to find out about this one day, but you kept it from me for my whole life anyway? None of this makes sense, Mum, and now you're leaving me to deal with it all on my own and it's just not fair!"

Mum reached towards me, and for a moment, I thought she was going to take my hand. I read this as an act of contrition or a softening of sorts and almost whimpered in relief, but froze again when I realised that she was only reaching for her keys. She was still crying silently, her face still a crumpled, blotchy mess, but there was a determination in her gaze.

"I need to go home now, Sabina."

"The worst part of all of this isn't that I'm adopted," I spoke in desperation, and the words sounded much harsher than I'd intended them to be. "It's not even that you hid it from me. It's that I've realised that you were never the person I thought you were."

Mum snatched the keys from my hand.

"I'm sorry that you feel like that," she whispered. "I know that I've let you down. I know that what we've done is unforgivable. I only hope you can move on and build a new future, now that you have some answers." She sat quickly in the car, then put the keys into the ignition and started the engine, staring ahead at the road instead of me. "Take care, my love."

Ted slipped his arms around my waist and rested his cheek against mine, and we watched her car pull away.

"At least you have her name now, Bean."

"I know," I whispered. I watched until Mum's car was out of sight then turned to him and returned his embrace. "At least now I have her name—and I am going to find her, Ted. It's too late to make things right, but maybe at least I can find some closure—for us *all*."

# CHAPTER SIXTEEN

## Lilly

## August 1973

Dear James

You won't believe this, but lately, I haven't felt like eating. I am watching the calendar and the days are disappearing. It feels like the clock is ticking faster and faster, and while I can't wait to get out of here, I also can't bear to think what's coming and so I feel trapped and on edge and scared all of the time. The fear takes up all of my energy, and I can't concentrate. I try to eat for the baby, but I don't even want to. For the first time in my life, it is too much effort to open my mouth and put food in there.

I just want to go home.

So, I have been going to the meal times to have my name marked off by the nurse, and sometimes I sit and pick at my food, but mostly when I am not at work, I sit alone in my room and stare out the window at the road. I've imagined you getting out of a car at that kerb so many times that I feel like I can remember it happening for real.

Tania has made some mean comments about me not eating, and tonight while dinner was on, she actually followed me to our room. At first I thought she was going to demand I return for dinner—that perhaps she was taking my lack of appetite as a personal insult against her cooking. Instead, she withdrew a small black canvas bag from the very back of her locker and told me that I must come for a walk with her.

I tried to resist, but Tania is a very forceful girl. I am a little scared of her, to be honest. In the end, I followed her only because I thought it might be quicker to just do whatever she wanted to do than to argue with her against it.

She took me to Eliza's room. Eliza works in the kitchen, and I don't know her very well, but we all heard the commotion from her room in the small hours last night. Her quiet moans became grunts and screams, and a nurse came to check on her and found her in the late stages of labour. The ward men came and took her away and after she was gone, the home seemed too still.

Poor, shrunken Eliza came back to the home this morning. Her belly is deflated, and the rest of her with it. She has spent the day in her room alone. At least she does not have to work now—she is only here for a few days until her parents arrive to take her home.

I have gone out of my way to avoid Eliza in the hallways because I don't have a clue what to say to her. She is spending all of her time grieving her loss, I am spending all of *my* energy *resisting* mine.

Tania explained what we were doing as Eliza and I followed her towards the front door. The three of us were going to the maternity ward in the hospital across the road. If there were kind midwives on, they would allow us to spend a few minutes with Eliza's baby. This is apparently something that Tania does whenever she can for the girls, and although it's totally against the rules, Mrs. Baxter must know that she does it. The black canvas bag houses a Polaroid camera that Mrs. Baxter gave us, so that if we have the chance to say goodbye to our babies, we can at least take home a small memento of that moment.

I asked Tania why *I* had to come. It seemed an intensely personal journey, and I felt awkward tagging along. I thought maybe she was being cruel, just trying to ensure that I really understood the true horror of what was about to happen to me.

But Tania explained that not all of the midwives are kind enough to allow this mercy mission. She would go inside the maternity ward first, and look into the staff room to determine who was on duty. If the awful midwives are there, or if for some reason Mrs. Sullivan was in the office, I would need to feign an emergency to distract them so that she could sneak Eliza in. Tania suggested I groan and moan as if labour pains had started, generally to make as much noise and fuss as I could to get the attention of all of the staff.

You know how I hate trouble, James. You know how hard I worked at school to avoid confrontation with the teachers. It seems that I'm not that girl anymore. I didn't really want to do what Tania proposed, but how could I not? There was such desperation in the way Eliza held my hand that it would have been inhumane to refuse to help her.

In the end, I didn't need to do anything, because the kindly midwives waved us in and one even allowed Eliza the chance to hold her son. Oh, how beautiful that little boy was, with his mop of fine blonde hair and his squished up button nose. Tania took a photo of Eliza with him in her arms. It was a beautiful moment, the best one I've had since I came here—actually, the best by far. For just a few minutes, she was any new mum, getting to know her babe. I could see what Eliza was doing—she was staring at him, almost unblinking, and touching every part of him with her fingertips, and even breathing in deeply again and again, trying to soak the essence of her baby through her senses... to steal it away with her.

But when the time came to leave, the bliss of those moments was gone. Eliza just wouldn't give her son back. Eventually I had to hold her arms while Tania and the nurse worked to get the baby away from her and back into its cot. Eliza begged and wept and tried to bargain with us for just a second more and we all wanted to give it to her, but we really had to be back before 10 p.m. As it was we only made it by a minute or two before the nurses locked the front door and came past to do a head count.

I can still feel the way her body shook when she fought to get out of my arms and get back to her baby. I can still hear the way she screamed, the sound is bouncing around in my ears—burned into me like some kind of audio tattoo. I don't think I've ever been so close to someone in so much pain before. I could feel her agony just as if it was my own—maybe because I am so terrified that it will *be* my own.

When we got Eliza back to her room, Tania handed her the Polaroid, and Eliza clutched it to her chest and collapsed onto her bed. We left her alone then, because we had to run back to our rooms, and because even though I wished with all of my heart that I could do something more for her... anything more for her... there was nothing more that we could do for Eliza H.

She's one of the lucky ones, you know. Lots of the girls never even get those moments with their babies. It seems like such a small thing to ask for—after all, we're talking about one single cuddle here. It's nothing at all in the scheme of things and it's *everything in the world* to the girl who misses out.

My heart and mind are racing tonight. I feel trapped and desperate because I really am just a caged animal with everything on the line. I was so sure that you'd be here by now. Why *aren't* you here, James? I turn it over in my mind day and night, trying to find the missing piece of the puzzle that would explain why you haven't come. I am so distracted by your absence that I don't even want to eat and I can't sleep.

You must by now have received these letters and you must know how utterly, hopelessly desperate I am for you to come.

What possible excuse could you have for not being here now?

I don't even want to write this in case writing it down makes it real, but I really am starting to wonder...did you ever love me? How could you have loved me, if you leave me here to face this alone?

Could I have misjudged you so badly? Did I know you at all? You've been part of my life forever, how could I have been so wrong?

I am sorry for the handwriting, and for the mess of these words. I keep thinking of Eliza, and me, and our baby, and you—and I am all over the place.

If it is true that you don't love me and that you are just going to leave me here, then please at least send your parents to let me know. I will find a way to extinguish the love I have for you too. Maybe if I do that, I will feel less, and maybe that will make me numb so that I can survive what's coming.

Lilly

# CHAPTER SEVENTEEN

Sabina

April 2012

Ted and I both called in sick from work. We sat at the dining table with the piece of paper, watching it, like it was a newborn child.

"Wyz-lecki?" I read awkwardly, after a while. "German?"

"Polish. It sounds Polish to me. But so does Sabina, now that I really think about it. And Liliana . . . Lilly . . . do you think—"

"They named me after her?" I picked the paper up again, and stared at the name, then sat it down as if it might bite me. "That's ridiculous. Why would they give me her *name* but keep her from me for half of my life?"

"Unless she was the one to name you?" Ted suggested.

This was startling. I had always loved my name. There had never been another Sabina in my classes at school, and I often revelled in comments on its uniqueness when I was growing up. I remember once asking Mum where the inspiration had come from and her shrugging and telling me she "just liked it."

There was something disconcerting about Liliana's potential involvement in the selection of my name. If I hadn't already been wondering who I was, this revelation would have really raised the stakes around that question. That Liliana might have chosen my name made me feel as though she really had made an impact on me beyond just genetics. A person is known by their name—in every circle of their life, in every context, in every situation.

I had been Sabina Lilly for my entire life, but maybe without Liliana's input into my label, I'd have been someone else entirely.

I picked up the paper again and stared at the date, then did the calculations in my mind.

"There's more than a month between this date, and the date on the birth certificate," I whispered.

"Maybe she cared for you for a month *then* had to relinquish you for some reason? Maybe she didn't cope with motherhood, or something terrible happened," he sighed, and shook his head. "This just gets more and more confusing, doesn't it?"

"But...if it was really as simple as that, wouldn't Mum just tell me?"

"True," Ted conceded. "And...I'm not sure we can believe her, but Megan *did* say they had you from the day after you were born."

"There are photos, too. In my albums at her house. Photos of me with Mum and Dad as a very new baby."

We both stared back at the paper.

"Polish," I whispered. Random memories were connecting in my mind, I was joining the dots with perfect hindsight. "But...maybe some of it makes *perfect* sense. Remember, Mum took me to Europe when I finished high school, and we spent nearly half the trip in Poland?"

"Didn't that seem strange?"

I shrugged.

"We were having the trip of a lifetime, and she'd been fascinated with Polish history for a while. I had no reason to suspect she was secretly trying to connect me with my roots."

"Do you remember when she went through that phase of trying to cook those Polish dumpling things...what are they called?"

"Pierogis, I think," I grimaced, and then Ted did too.

"That's right. God, they were disgusting."

"She said she'd read about them in a cooking magazine."

Our eyes met, and we shared the sadness of the moment. Poor, misguided Mum had apparently made at least some kind of effort to expose me to the culture of my birth mother.

"Could I just look Liliana up on Google?" I asked, and the idea was so exciting that I warmed to it immediately. "Maybe she has Facebook—"

"I don't think so, honey. I think we need to do this via Hilary, in case there's a veto."

"Oh yeah." I slumped, then glanced at the clock. "We can call Hilary in an hour or so."

After a while, Ted went out to get us coffee and croissants for breakfast. Alone and impatient, I paced the house for a while, until the photo albums caught my eye

I couldn't imagine how many hours of careful attention had been invested in these albums. There were hundreds of photos of me, but not a single one included Mum or Dad. I could see from some of the odd shapes of the photos that Mum had cut them down with scissors sometimes to remove their image. There were photos of so many milestones when I was an infant; *Sabina, trying to roll over, January 1974. Sabina, sitting up, April 1974. Sabina, eating pears, April 1974.* There were photos of me at preschool, and some of my early paintings and drawings, and merit certificates from primary school and even a ribbon I won for a novelty race at an athletics carnival. Every single school report was included, carefully labelled with a date. I read through the comments and grimaced. *Sabina needs to apply herself. Sabina is managing her stutter much better but still will not speak or read in front of the class. Sabina is a nice girl with a good heart but needs to put more effort into her classwork.*

There was a photo of me at every birthday, and photos of me

in the car sleeping or listening to music when we went on holiday, or at the airport sulking while we waited for a flight. There were photos I remembered Mum taking—like the one she took of me the day we moved into the house at Balmain, standing in my bedroom grinning my gappy grin and pointing with delight at the brightly coloured walls. I'd chosen the gaudy shade of my pink myself, and although she and Dad must have cringed, they'd let me have my way. There were also photos I had no recollection of—my first singing performance in Year Seven, me holding the microphone at the wrong angle and looking like a rabbit caught in headlights. She had included a photo of me with my first boyfriend, and underneath *that* snapshot of teen awkwardness and embarrassment had been written *Sabina and Robert—true love forever, at least for a few weeks.*

It was miserable to look back through my life like that—I felt like a spoilt brat, because here was photographic proof that I'd experienced every opportunity and privilege that a child could want for, and I still felt cheated. Where was the truth? How could my mother be so thoughtful as to collect these mementos, but so selfish as to keep them to herself for all of this time?

I had always known that Mum kept detailed photo albums; she had a whole wall of her own in the family room at her house, but I had never seen these before, and I couldn't imagine where she could have hidden them or when she would have found the time to maintain them. She'd obviously been meticulous about it. This was no last minute after-thought.

When Ted returned, he handed me breakfast and motioned towards the albums.

"Did she just do this in the last few weeks?"

"No, it looks like she's been keeping these pretty much since I was born. The photos are all old, and I can see how her handwriting has changed over the years."

"That's *so* sad."

"It really is," I murmured, shaking my head. "It's bloody tragic. I don't even know what to make of it. Why go to all of this effort, but miss the step of actually telling me to *look* for the woman she made the albums for?"

Ted picked up an album and laughed at a particularly unflattering photo of me as a toddler, my face covered in birthday cake. I was mid-tantrum, "*protesting our refusal to sing 'Happy Birthday' for an eleventh time,*" according to the caption.

"Apparently you loved music even as a two-year-old."

"You've heard Mum and Dad sing. I was probably c-crying *because* they sang me 'Happy Birthday' ten times," I muttered, but I wanted to cry again. I couldn't remember, of course, but I could very easily imagine the scene around this photo—Mum and Dad had put such work into my birthday each year. There would have been a terrible, hand-made cake that Mum would have invested hours in creating, and at the party there would have been loads of decorations and gifts. All of my cousins and aunts from Mum and Dad's families would have been there. "All that effort," I whispered, "but it would have been on the wrong date. I wasn't two years old on the 10th of October. I was two years, one month and a few days. Does that make all of the love that went into making these memories mean any less?"

"I don't know. I don't think so."

"How can it not? What were they even celebrating? It wasn't my *birth* day?"

"There's more to a person than the day they were born. They were celebrating *you*, Sabina. That doesn't really change with the date of your birth."

"It's hard not to be cynical looking at these photos now," I admitted.

"She didn't have to do this, Bean. It tells you a lot about her intentions—they've told us that they never intended for you to know, but Meg obviously had other plans. There's hundreds of hours work in maintaining these books. She *wanted* you to find Liliana, and on some level I think she wanted you to be able to show her that you've been okay for all of this time. Isn't that exactly what you want too?"

"If Mum had told me about this twenty years ago, Liliana could *be* in some of those albums."

"I know. But maybe she can be in the next twenty years' worth of photos—and those years will include our baby. At least you will have that, and if you do, it'll be *Meg's* doing."

"You sound less angry with Mum after this morning."

"I'm still angry, Bean—God, what they're putting you through, and at this stage of our life? It's just awful. But at least she's trying. This is a step in the right direction. Until this morning I wasn't even sure Graeme and Meg were going to be a part of our life anymore."

"And now?"

"What do you think?"

"It's a step," I conceded. "It's not enough, but it's a step."

—

When the clock finally ticked over 8:59 a.m., I dialled Hilary's office.

"Adoption Information Re—"

"Hilary, it's Sabina. I found out her name. And the right date." I was breathless, and talking fast. Hilary broke off to give me space to speak. "She is—she was—Liliana Wyz-Wyzlecki, I think it would be pronounced. And I was born on the 3rd of September."

It suddenly struck me that I was a whole month older than I had realised. Which birth date would I celebrate now?

"So, your adoptive parents changed their minds about giving you some more information, then?"

"Mum did. Dad doesn't know."

"All right. I'll look into it. I'll try to call you back later today, Sabina."

Then, there was the second wait, and Ted finally seemed anxious too. I could tell because he had voluntarily started doing the dishes from the previous night's dinner. I, on the other hand, was sitting at the table talking about nothing much at all, nursing the phone. When it failed to ring, and several hours managed to trickle by, I moved to get dressed, and Ted changed out of his work clothes.

Almost as soon as I had taken my night shirt off, the phone rang. I answered it naked except for my underwear.

"Hello?"

"Hi, Sabina. It's Hilary again. I wanted to let you know, I found records for Liliana Wyzlecki at the home—I think we're onto something. There is no veto in place, in fact, she contacted us herself, almost twenty years ago, to request contact if you registered with us. It looks like..." I heard Hilary shuffle some papers, then she sighed just a little. "She called us on what would have been your real eighteenth birthday, actually."

"She did?"

I was relieved, and I was heartbroken. Liliana had been expecting me to contact her for twenty years. Oh, the longing and hurt that those years must have contained for her.

"So, I'm going to call her now, and if I can't get hold of her by phone, I'll have to send her a letter to let her know that you're looking to contact her. I'll just confirm that she's still open to hearing from you—it's been such a long time, I need to be sure her circumstances haven't changed. If she consents, I'll pass her contact details on to you. Hopefully she has email now, that makes things so much easier. It might happen quickly, it might take a while. It's really up to Liliana now, and you might need to be patient while she thinks this through. I'm just trying to set expectations, I know you must be excited. I will call you when I know something."

"Okay. Okay, that sounds good."

So I hung up the phone again, filled Ted in on the developments, and then heard the sound of my song echoing around our house as I dressed and finally found my appetite for breakfast.

# CHAPTER EIGHTEEN

## Lilly

## August 1973

Dear James,

It's been almost two months since we posted the first letter. I know you have it and I don't know what your silence actually means.

Why aren't you here? Why haven't your parents at least come? Were you too afraid to tell them? You've never let me down before and nothing has ever mattered like this before. Where are you?

Our baby will be here in less than a month. I am so big now—I just waddle slowly, my legs and back ache, and today Mrs. Baxter had to arrange me a chair for the laundry so I can sit down between loads of linen because I keep passing out.

There is no time left for you to dilly-dally or come to terms with this if you're sitting on your hands trying to figure out what to do.

If, somehow, you haven't understood, let me make it perfectly clear to you: we have a baby, and if you don't find a way to get me out of here, someone is going to take her away from us forever. I am not strong enough to survive losing this baby, James. I'm just not. I don't even want to be.

I'm going to give you one more week, and then as scared as I am to do it, I just have to try to escape. I have to get out of here. I can't stay here and let this happen to us.

I have never imagined a future without us together. But if

you have been receiving these letters and choosing not to come for me, I will *never, ever* forgive you. I want you to know that the place in my heart that was once full of love for you will be full of seething, furious hate.

If you do not come, and one day years from now we pass each other in the street, you'd better cross the road to get away from me. If you are knowingly leaving me here to face this alone, I hope that the guilt of it drives you slowly crazy. I hope that you realise that you cannot let our baby down and keep a shred of love or even respect from me.

You were my only hope. I trusted you. I was so sure that you would come. I can't understand how I could have been so wrong.

Please James…prove me wrong, I am begging you. Where *are* you?

Lilly

# CHAPTER NINETEEN

Sabina

April 2012

Several hours passed after I spoke with Hilary. Ted had put a load of laundry on, but I was so anxious that the sound of the washing machine was making me jumpy.

"Let's go out," Ted suggested. "Gardening? Shopping? The movies? What do you think will distract you best?"

"Let's go shopping," I said, thinking of my too-tight work clothes. "I'll just... let me just check my email before we go. Just in case."

I sat down at the computer. I was already thinking about dragging Ted around the mall—he'd patiently follow me around all day, and I knew he wouldn't complain once... not today, anyway. Maybe it was unkind to take him up on his offer. Maybe—

Every thought stopped when I realised that I already had an email in my inbox from Hilary. The subject line was: *Liliana Piper (Wyzlecki) and Sabina Wilson*. I called Ted and we stared at it together. After a moment, he sat his hand on my shoulder.

"Are you going to open it?" he asked softly.

"I can't," I whispered. I was physically frozen, my limbs had stopped responding to commands from my mind. "Why didn't she call? Hilary said she'd call after she spoke with Liliana. Is this to let me know that Liliana doesn't want to talk to me?"

On some level, I'd been so confident that there was a happy ending beyond all of this confusion, but of course it wasn't a given that my biological mother would want me to be part of her life. Perhaps it was too hard, or too late, or just too difficult. How could I judge her for that? I had no concept of how I had come to be, or even how we'd been separated.

The computer made the sound of a bell. Another email had entered my inbox.

From: *Lilly Piper*

I started to cry. Now I was shaking too hard to move the mouse, and I stood and stepped back away from it. I felt hot and sweaty and nauseous. Ted took my hand.

"Let me help, Bean."

I nodded, then nodded again and pointed to the chair, my throat too tight to speak. He sat, then clicked on Hilary's email first.

*Dear Liliana and Sabina,*

*I'm delighted to say that you are both very keen for contact. I am so pleased we are able to connect you. Having arranged some dozens of these reunions now, I encourage you to take it slowly, and keep your expectations of each other low. If I can help in any way as you re-establish your relationship, please let me know. I'll call you both in the next few days to see how you are feeling. Be kind to yourselves, and each other. Hilary*

"Are you ready for the next one?" Ted asked me, and I squeezed his shoulder because my voice wouldn't work at all.

*Dear Sabina,*

*I am so, so very glad that you have decided to make contact with me. I have been waiting for this moment for thirty-eight years. I want you to know that not a second has gone by where I have not held you close to me at least somewhere in my mind.*

*I just know you are a wonderful person, and I am so hoping this will mean a chance to get to know you.*

*You must have so many questions—I will try to guess what some of them are. I am married to your father, James, and we have two other children, Simon and Charlotte. You are an aunty to Dominic and Valentina, who are the most beautiful six-month-old twins, and to Neesa, who is twelve, and an equally beautiful, big-spirited pre-teen. Your father and I live on our family property,* Piper's Peace, *which is near the village of Molong in the central west of New South Wales. James is a farmer, and I am a history teacher.*

*I count you very much as a part of our family, and when you're ready, I would just so love to chat to you on the phone. Also, if you feel ready, but with no pressure to rush until you are, I'd love to see a photo of you. I have attached one of us all, taken a few days after the twins were born.*

*Thank you again for reaching out, Sabina. I feel a joy so big that I really can't find words for it.*

*All my love, always and always, Lilly*

Ted opened the image. There was a couple in the centre of the photo, each holding a tiny newborn baby and wearing an expression of pure delight. To their right, a tall blonde woman was embracing an older child.

I glanced quickly enough to surmise that an older couple were standing like bookends on either side of the group. I could not bring myself to look at them just yet.

"Ted," I whispered. "I have a sister and a brother."

"And you're an aunt."

"I'm an aunt," I echoed, and then I thought about this and I grinned. "I'm an *aunt*, Ted!"

"They look like you."

"They really do. Well, *they* don't." I pointed to two blonde women on the screen, then moved my finger towards the woman holding the newborn. "I guess that must be Simon's wife? The email doesn't say her name."

Ted nodded towards the other blonde.

"There is *no* way that glamorous woman just gave birth to twins... so I guess you're right."

"She's stunning."

"So are you," Ted said hastily. "But you sure have different... colouring."

"And builds, Ted. I *can* see her, you know." A bubble rose inside me and popped as a laugh. "I have a sister and she looks like a fashion model. I look more like Mum than I do her. How did that happen?"

"That must be your father, I guess she takes after that side," Ted said, and he moved his finger to the tall man on the left of the photo. I finally let my eyes wander past the younger family members.

He was thin, and beyond his high forehead was a patch of silver hair. He was tanned, actually quite a bit *too* tanned, in that weathered way that is so typical of Australian farmers. His grin was impossibly broad, displaying an undeniable pride and joy.

I liked him immediately, just on sight. There was something so open about his smile.

"What's his name again?" Ted asked, and when he moved to bring the email back onto screen, I squeezed his shoulder again.

"James Piper," I said. The name was already written onto my heart, there was no chance I'd forget it. "I guess that means that *she* is Liliana..."

I let my gaze focus on Liliana Wyzlecki—my mother, or at least, *one* of my mothers. I stared at her long after my vision had blurred and after the inevitable sobs started.

I cried for Liliana Piper, because she was standing in a photo with her beautiful, full family, and she was beaming a proud, delighted grin—but I could still see sadness in her eyes. I could see from my first glance at her that she, like me, had no way of hiding her emotions—this was not a woman who could contain a secret. Just like me, her inner feelings were written all over her face for the world to see.

And I really was the spitting image of Liliana. Her hair was shaped into a sensible bob, but it was thick and shiny and the same warm brown that mine had always been. We shared the same big brown eyes, the same chubby cheeks and the same broad smile. She was curvy like me, but physically stronger somehow—maybe she did some manual work on the farm. She was wearing a blue shirt, a red scarf and a pair of jeans, over a cheeky pair of bright red boots. I wondered if she liked to wear bright colours, just as I did. I wondered what else we would have in common.

I felt terrified, and overjoyed, and nervous and relieved all at the same time. I was just a bundle of anxious excitement. I had gained a family—a huge family by my standards—siblings to build friendships with, nieces and nephews to nurture. There would be complexities to a family with so many people, maybe a web of confused agendas and feelings, and I would have to weave my own life into that web if I was going to become a part of this group. That was daunting—Mum and Dad had proven complex enough.

I looked back to Lilly, and then over to James, and a sudden impatience gripped me. I gently pushed Ted's shoulder and when he rose, I took his place at the keyboard and began to type.

*Dear Lilly,*

*When we can meet?*

*Sabina*

Ted cleared his throat.

"That's where you want to *start* the conversation?"

I thought, remembering Hilary's comments about keeping our expectations low and taking things slowly, and I withdrew my hand from the keyboard.

"I just feel like I need to go meet her," I admitted. "Seriously, what am I going to learn via email? Or the phone? If I can't *see* her...I mean...I just won't know her until I meet her. Am I being hasty?"

"Hilary did say you should take it pretty slowly."

"That's easy for *Hilary* to say. I want answers. And if I was Liliana, and this was our baby, I would want her to drop everything and show me that she was okay."

Ted was silent for a long moment. I turned to glance up at him. "Well?"

"I think this really has to be your decision, Bean," he said quietly.

"Come on, Ted. Help me out here. I'm ready to hit the *send* button, the only reason I'm not is that you seem nervous."

"Of course I'm nervous. You're nervous too, or you should be. But if this is what you think we need to do, well, we may as well go for a drive this weekend."

I brought the photo back up onto the screen and stared at it for a moment. Were Ted and I the missing pieces of their puzzle, or were we extra parts that would never quite fit?

"We could meet somewhere in the middle. Or maybe we could invite them here first?"

"Bean, we can't even fit a sofa bed in here. Are you suggesting we invite them to come visit us and put them up in a hotel?"

"Good point," I sighed, and then I groaned with the frustration of it all. "I wish I could talk to Mum about this. It would all have been so much easier if I was dealing with it with their support when I was say...five. Or ten. Or when I turned sixteen, or even eighteen? Why now?"

"Judging by the way this has played out, you're pretty lucky you found out at all. And if you really want to talk to Megan, why don't you just give her a call?"

"Because I'm sick of begging her for information. And because they're so damned stubborn and it's not fair at all." I had a sudden moment of decisiveness and I sat up straight and drew in a deep breath. "You know what? I think we should offer to drive out and meet them, this weekend if they're free. But if we get there and it's awful you have to think of a reason for us to leave."

"Is '*this is really awkward and Sabina doesn't like you*' a good enough reason?" He grinned at me and I sighed impatiently.

"No, it's not. Do you think it will be like that?"

"I think it'll be a bit awkward, but I don't think it'll be awful, and I'm quite confident that you'll find *some* common ground. And if you don't, we never have to go back. Right?"

"Right."

"So we're doing this?"

"Let's do it," I said, and I sat my hand over the mouse and sent the email.

# CHAPTER TWENTY

## Lilly

## August 1973

Dear James,

I'm so sorry for doubting you, and for the horrible things that I said in my last letter. All that I had to go on was what seemed to be silence from you.

But now I know that you came for me.

When I came in for dinner last night, I heard that there had been some kind of trouble. The girls were all whispering about how, while we were at work in the afternoon, several people had to be removed from the home by security. I wondered if it was you, but that made no sense to me; I figured if it *had* been you and your parents, then surely they'd have just come for me and I'd be safe at home in the cottage by now.

Mrs. Baxter called me out the laundry today and she told me what's been going on. She didn't know either, at least, she *says* she didn't... and I suppose I have to trust her.

But now we understand that you and Ralph and Jean have been trying to get me released. We know you've been working with a lawyer and that you've been calling every day.

Mrs. Baxter said you've tried every possible angle, and that you've fought for us relentlessly. So we know that you came yesterday to try to take me home, and Mrs. Sullivan had the security guards drag you outside, and you caused quite the scene. And not just you, but your wonderful, feisty parents too.

And then she told me that none of it even matters in the end.

Yet again here I am feeling utterly stupid at how naïve I have been. I noticed that no one has ever tried to get me to sign any relinquishment paperwork, but I thought that was because they could see that I'd never do it, not in a million years. I was kind of proud of that, actually. I thought that they could see that I was strong.

Mrs. Baxter showed me my file today. I remember seeing the letters BFA marked on it on that terrible day when Tata admitted me. Today, I learned that BFA stands for *baby for adoption*, and it's a marker to the staff that the decision has been made.

It's just that in my case, the decision was made by Tata, not me, and because I am a minor, that's apparently more than enough.

Mrs. Baxter said that she took my file home on her lunch break and called your Dad from her own house so that Mrs. Sullivan wouldn't know. I wish that I was more surprised to hear that Tata has threatened you with the police if you cause any more trouble. Mrs. Baxter had to explain to me what statutory rape is and why they really could arrest you, and what that would mean for you.

I understand now that your hands are tied, just as mine are.

But James, I'm so proud of you. And I'm so grateful, truly I am, for how hard you've fought for us. The only thing worse than what is happening now would be to face it truly alone, and I *feel* your love for me and our baby through all of these wonderful attempts you've made to reach us.

I wanted to keep my chin up. I wanted to be positive. I wanted to hold onto hope.

Do you know what happens when all of the hope is gone? It feels just like death must. I am crying, all day and night. The colour is gone from the earth, and overnight, I see the world in shades of miserable grey. The other girls are trying to be kind to me, even Tania, who has brought me food to the room, but I don't want to waste energy on eating.

Every second that I'm awake I try only to remember. I feel a kick or a roll or a punch and I try to describe the way it feels to myself, with words in my mind that I can come back to. A baby can be taken, a memory can fade, but if I can hold onto those words, I'll have something of her with me. Sharp jabs. Violent rolls. Gentle wriggles. I will never, ever forget the gentle little wriggles.

I hug my belly and I cry and I still can't believe that even my body curled around her will not be enough to protect her.

Sometimes I think she has the hiccups. I feel these little jumps that come like the beat of a song. I want to smile at this, because it's so bloody adorable, but a few days ago when she was hiccupping I thought about how cute that is and then it made me realise how much I'm going to miss in her life and now every time I feel it I start to the panic of what's coming and—

Oh James. I can't do this. I just can't. I can't let her go. I *can't* not see her first smile and steps and every little moment that comes after.

How can I even continue to *be* if this is going to happen to us?

All that I am now is a bloated mess of fear and dread and loss, and once she is taken from me, there will be nothing left worth keeping.

Lilly

# CHAPTER TWENTY-ONE

## Sabina

### April 2012

Liliana replied to my email within three minutes.

I knew exactly how long it took, because I stayed right there at the computer, watching the clock in the corner of the screen.

*Dear Sabina,*

*I'm so glad that you're as anxious to meet us as we are to meet you!*

*Can we talk on the telephone and arrange a meeting? Please call me, I've put all of my other contact details below.*

*Love, Lilly*

I dialled straight away. My hands were shaking as I hit the keys on the phone, and then I held Ted's hand as I waited for her to answer. It didn't help allay my nerves one little bit that she greeted me with a sob.

"Is that you, S-sabina?"

"Yes? . . . . Hello! . . . It's me . . ." Was that a stutter I heard? I was crying too, and could barely form my own words.

She was laughing and crying, and I laughed and cried too. I was still in front of the computer, and I released Ted's hand to shrink my email and bring the photo of Liliana's family back into focus.

"Thank you so much for finding me," Liliana said. I could hear the smile in her voice, and I smiled too. "I am so glad that you did. Are you well? Are you happy? Where are you?"

"I'm well—I'm *very* well, I'm in Sydney—my husband and

I live in Leichardt, in Sydney. We're expecting our first baby at the end of the year."

"Oh, a *baby*!" she was crying again. This was how I'd wanted Mum to react—sheer, unbridled joy at the news of a new life. I fumbled for Ted's hand again and let the tears flow freely down my face. "That's just so wonderful, Sabina. Just so very wonderful."

"We want to meet you, if you want to meet us," I said. "We—I mean, my husband, Ted, and I—we'd really like to meet you and James."

"Yes. Absolutely. Please, please do. We can come to you? Or we could meet somewhere—or, *oh*! W-we'd love to show you the farm. Could you come to the farm? I know it's a long way, but we'd love you to visit."

"We can do that," I said. The excitement in her tone was infectious and it was mirrored in my voice when I spoke. "This weekend? Can we come this weekend?" When just a second passed before she responded, I tripped over my words trying to explain myself. "There's just so much I want to talk to you about—so many questions and so much I want to know—I don't want to rush things and I understand if you have plans, but if you don't—"

"Sabina, we would be honoured if you would visit us this weekend. You're coming from Sydney? It's probably too far to travel here and back in the one day. We have plenty of room, if you'd want to stay with us."

I opened my mouth, and looked at Ted, who shrugged at me and pointed to his ear to remind me that he couldn't actually hear her.

"We'd—we'd love that," I said, but it was her turn to read the hesitation in my voice, and she added hastily,

"Or, if that's too much too soon, there's a little hotel in the village near us. I could organise you a room."

I reminded myself that if things really did get too much out there, we'd always be able to find a way to leave. Besides which, in every step of this journey I'd been conscious of how *I'd* feel if I were in my birth mother's shoes. If this were *my* child reuniting with me after a lifelong absence, I'd want her under my roof. I'd want her to be bold and brave enough to be vulnerable as we set out building our relationship.

I'd want her near to me, if there had been such unimaginable distance.

"No, we'd love to stay with you. If you're comfortable with that, if you're sure that's okay."

"Of course. Of course it's okay, you're family—we'll be honoured to have you here." She was crying again. I released Ted's hand and clutched the receiver with both of mine, almost overwhelmed by the onslaught of her emotions.

"I can't wait to meet you, Liliana."

"Please, call me Lilly. And I can't wait to meet you too."

# CHAPTER TWENTY-TWO

Lilly

September 1973

Dear James,

Our baby came last night.

There is not much to tell you, and I don't have the energy to go into the detail. Maybe eventually we can talk and I can tell you more.

It was a long labour, and no one told me as much but I felt like both she and I were in trouble toward the end. Eventually, I couldn't even bring myself to try anymore, and just then Mrs. Baxter came in and helped. They gave me a lot of drugs over the days of the birth and all that I can remember is the pain, and the relief when finally there was someone in the room who was kind enough to take my hand. The baby came soon after that.

I only saw our girl for a few seconds, but in that time, I learned her by sight because I knew that there would never be the chance to know her by touch, or even to catch a waft of her sweet scent. All that I had was those seconds, and if sheer force of will ever could stop time, I'd have done it, I swear to you. I have never worked as hard as I did then, trying to imprint those moments into my mind.

First I saw the dark thickness of the hair on her head—surprisingly thick, stuck to her head in sticky swirls as if it might be curly. Next I saw her face—I think and I hope and I pray that I captured that little face in my memory; I tried to stamp it onto my eyelids, so that I can carry her with me and see her whenever I close my eyes. She had tiny, scrunched up features and she seemed furious that she'd been dragged out of the warmth of my body into the cold air. I love that and I was so proud of her—our baby has the *fight* about her to protest all of this, even in her first seconds. She had cherubic lips, and in that instant that I saw her, she was already rooting, searching hopelessly for my milk. Her chin was squished up and the sides of her face were bruised a bit, and she has a large, perfectly round belly...and she is indeed a girl, James.

We have a daughter, and as soon as that really sank in, I watched her disappear.

I had been so scared about what that moment would feel like—I knew it would be awful, but I'd underestimated the way that I'd love her the instant I saw her. I could never really have understood how much I had to lose until the moment it was being taken from me.

There has never been a purer being on this earth than our baby, James; never a purer emotion than the love I feel for her. I am not even angry that they have tainted that by taking her from me. I am too devastated to be angry, too broken to fight anymore, too lost to want to find my way home.

My arms are empty and that emptiness feels bigger than the earth itself.

The full depth of grief has swallowed me. Sometimes over the hours since, I have felt like I couldn't even breathe and it didn't matter a single bit because I don't even want to.

But James, in spite of all of this, I have not cried and I don't think I will—maybe never again. I stare at the roof and I think about a geography class once where we learned about those giant dams they build overseas. That's how big my grief feels, as big as the biggest dams in the world all joined up together and somehow held back only by the thinnest membrane. If I rip that membrane and let a tear or two out, what good will it do? Mere tear drops will not lessen the pressure of such an immense mass of grief—I will feel not an ounce of relief. There is just no point to tears when a pain is this big.

I finally feel something worse than unclean...after all they have said, and after all they have done to me, I finally feel *dirty*. Perhaps there is something fundamentally wrong with us that we'd wind up in this situation. Maybe they are right, and we deserve to be punished. Surely no one could inflict a pain like this on another person unless that person was truly deserving of suffering.

The nurses have told me that I have to stay here in the hospital a few days. Mrs. Sullivan will call Tata in to pick me up when I've had a chance to heal.

If they're really going to wait until I heal, I'll be in this bed until I die.

Every time I hear a baby crying I think it's her. I feel ashamed that I do not know my own daughter's cry. She needs me, and I'm right here but I can't go to her. I went for a walk earlier today, hoping that I would find a way to see her, but one of the midwives caught me and helped me back to bed. Her new family could already be here. The nurse said it would be unkind to all of us if our paths were to cross.

So now I can't bring myself to get out of bed at all, and I am lying here miserable and I don't even know what to wish for. Do I wish them good thoughts, those people who will take my daughter and make her their own? Do I wish evil for them, so that she might somehow find her way back to me? Am I supposed to be grateful to them?

All that I want is our baby in my arms. She was made to fit in *my* arms.

Maybe you would be allowed to visit me now, if you happen

to get this before they discharge me. And if you do come, they have me in the last room in the maternity ward corridor, the one with no windows, farthest away from the nursery.

But go to the nursery first. Stare at every baby and memorise them all, just in case she's still there.

Lilly

# CHAPTER TWENTY-THREE

Sabina

April 2012

I'd never been as nervous as I was that Friday. I'd taken the day off so we could leave early, and by 9:01 a.m. I was already regretting the decision.

There was no distracting myself. I sat at home and watched the clock, feeding my anxiety with junk food. I felt the same frustration an insomniac feels when sleep evades, except that instead of sleeping, I was trying to zone out in front of daytime television but I just couldn't convince my brain to *switch off.*

I had three outfits laid out on the bed—a funky red dress with a big black belt, sensible maternity trousers and a floral shirt, and a more casual set of elastic-waisted jeans and a long-sleeved shirt. I'd laid them out early in the day, then as I wandered the house like a ghost during talk show ad breaks, I'd walk to my door and stare at the outfits. The choice seemed life-changing. I didn't want to seem too out there; I didn't want to seem too conservative; I didn't want to seem too casual; I didn't want to seem too urban. Under all of those quiet thoughts was a much louder one—a horrifying one—which I didn't give voice to until Ted finally came home.

"You aren't wearing *that*, are you?" he said, when he stepped inside and saw me curled up on the couch in a tracksuit. I glanced down at myself defensively, then noticed the food stains on my chest. I sank into the couch even deeper.

"What if she d-doesn't like me, Ted?"

"Seriously? She's waited nearly forty years to meet you."

"Exactly! She's waited nearly forty years to meet me. What if I'm a disappointment?"

"Sabina, that's ridiculous."

"It must happen all of the time in these situations. I'll bet her expectations are *sky* high."

"She has waited a lifetime to meet you, honey. You could be a nose-picking serial killer and I'm sure she'd be at least glad to see you."

"I just want her to like me."

"She will, Bean. But if it's too uncomfortable, I am going to save you and make an excuse for us to leave and come home. I *promise* you. Please, go get dressed, we really need to get on the road."

I dragged myself off the couch, ignoring the shower of chip-crumbs that rained about my feet when I stood, and wrapped my arms around my husband.

"Thank you."

"That's what I'm here for."

"No, seriously Ted. I couldn't do this without you."

"Of course you could." He kissed the side of my head then turned me towards the bedroom. "Go get dressed, woman! You're going to make us late."

We left right on time, just after 2 p.m. That would, by Ted's exacting calculations, have us turning in James and Lilly's driveway just after 6 p.m., in time for my first meal with my biological parents.

I had packed a bag for two nights, and Ted carefully sat the box of photo albums in the car boot. I wasn't entirely sure if the timing was appropriate, but if it felt right, I'd give them to Lilly before we left.

I had never actually travelled to the west of the state before.

I'd been as far as the Blue Mountains that served as a physical barrier between the city and the state's rural side, but I'd never been past them. Ted knew the geography a little better, but he trusted the GPS—which is how we found ourselves driving down an isolated two-lane highway through dense bushland.

Initially, I was awed by the sights along the Bells Line of Road. There was lush greenery right to the very edge of the road, and immense views of the city and the valleys beyond to enjoy. I started to feel a little nervous when we passed a series of blind, sharp corners and found that the traffic ahead of us seemed to be backing up. Just after we came to an area where there was a high cliff-face above us on our left and a sheer drop on our right, traffic stopped flowing altogether.

After a while, I picked up my mobile phone to try to do a traffic issue search and figure out what the problem was ahead, and discovered that we were in a coverage dead spot. Ted tried to re-route the GPS, to see if we could avoid whatever the blockage was if we turned around, but we quickly realised that we'd need to go almost all of the way back to the city. Backtracking would add hours to the trip.

If I thought the earlier parts of the day had passed slowly, time seemed to freeze altogether now. Ted and I even managed to have a reasonably heated discussion about his choice of route, and I kept the argument going much longer than I otherwise would have, just for the distraction of the banter.

We'd been stationary for almost two hours when a policeman walked down the road, stopped at Ted's window, and informed us we'd have to turn around. The road would be closed overnight. A semi-trailer had been involved in an accident several kilometres ahead of us, and emergency services were trying to figure out how to clear the road.

We were silent for the first few moments, while the GPS

rerouted to the other main highway through the mountains. Our arrival time was now well after 9 p.m.

"I think we should just go home. We can reschedule for another weekend."

"You can't do that, Bean."

"It's an omen."

"Oh, rubbish. Do you have phone service, yet? You'd better call her and warn her."

I fiddled with my phone for a few moments, cursing my cowardice.

"Sabina…"

"I'm going to do it," I assured him. Then I sighed and dialled the number that I had learned by heart.

"Hello, you've got Lilly."

She was positively singing, and my heart sank like a stone.

"Hi, Lilly. It's Sabina."

"Oh sweetheart. Oh—" Her joy disappeared in a single breath. "Oh no. You've changed your mind."

"No, no," I hastened to reassure her. "No, we're just late—there was an accident and a traffic jam. We're going to get in really late tonight, we were thinking we'd stop at a hotel on the way instead. Maybe we could arrive for breakfast?"

I heard her breath catch and felt a pang of guilt, but a big part of me was relieved to put the reunion off for another night. We'd be fresher in the morning, plus it would mean only one night at the farm instead of the two we'd agreed to.

"Please come tonight." Her voice was small. "Please, Sabina."

"But it will be so late—maybe nine or even ten—"

"I understand if that's too much to ask." I could hear the tears in her voice now. "But if you could manage it, I'd so appreciate it. I know it's only one more day, one more sleep, one more sunrise . . . but I've waited . . ." Her breath caught. "Oh, I've waited so many."

It had been easy for me to forget how much this meant to her. To me, she was a curiosity. To her, I was a life-long dream.

And so I agreed that we would find a way to her homestead in the dark.

—

We could see silhouettes on the veranda, two tiny figures dwarfed by the vast emptiness of their property around them. Now I really was sick, my lunch was sitting ominously high in my throat. Ted stopped the car beneath a gnarled peppercorn tree.

"You ready?" Ted whispered.

"How could I be?" I whispered back.

We walked slowly down the path, towards the house. I was concentrating on my breathing, trying to push through the nerves and the excitement and exhaustion by focus alone. I quickly realised it was pointless. There would be no way to dampen these emotions, I was just going to have to live this. And then she broke away from the embrace of her partner and she ran down the stairs and across the lawn towards me, her step young and springy, like a child playing. As she neared, and I got my first glance of my first mother's face and recognised myself in it, I also saw her intention. She would have run through fire to embrace me. She had waited a lifetime to do it.

She almost bowled me over. Lilly was not a tall woman, but she was curvy and strong, and her arms enveloped me and then squeezed me tight. In the near darkness I smelt garlic and herbs and soap as she pressed her face hard into my neck. I heard her shuddering, deep inhalation, and then the sobs started.

I'd never heard someone cry like that. She clutched at me and she pulled at me and she drenched my shoulder in her tears. It was like she was washing me clean, marking me as her offspring.

I cried too, because you just can't stand within a storm like that, and not be moved. I hadn't even known about her a month earlier but I wept in sync with her. I wasn't crying for my own pain—I was crying for *her* and for what *we* might have shared.

After a while, the other figure from the porch slowly came towards us and I saw his face in the moonlight too. He quietly shook Ted's hand, introduced himself as James, and then tried to steer Lilly away from me. She'd have none of it, she couldn't even calm herself enough to speak, and instead she waved furiously at him and then, with a squeeze of a strong arm, directed me towards the house.

"I'm sorry." She was hoarse, and her breathing was ragged between the still-explosive sobs. "I'm so sorry."

"It's okay." I tried to offer comfort. "I can't even imagine..."

For all of the times in my life when words had failed me, this was by far the worst. What do you *say* to someone in that position? How *do* you even offer comfort, beyond platitudes? I felt like a bystander to a tragedy. I didn't yet fully grasp that I was one of the victims.

"I promised myself I'd hold it together. I promised myself, ever since you said you were coming," she laughed weakly. "But... not an hour went by when I didn't think of you, Sabina. Not a single hour. And thirty-eight years is a lot of hours."

—

My natural mother had baked all day for me.

She warned us that it would take some time for her to set the table up. She'd had the dishes waiting, either being kept warm or ready to be warmed, and while she did the work of preparing the feast, James gave Ted and me a tour of the house.

It wasn't messy, but it was full and cluttered in a way that Mum and Dad would never have tolerated in my childhood home. There was stuff everywhere; there were jars and canisters full of supplies on top of cupboards and the fridge and even the benches, and the spaces which weren't covered with such things instead housed little collectable figurines or knick-knacks. I could hear Mum tsk-tsking in my mind and motioning towards the benches to dismissively decry the stuff as "useless dust collectors." Not that there was much dust, but that was probably a testament to Lilly's cleaning effort, and I had a sneaking suspicion she'd been expending a whole lot of nervous energy over the days since I agreed to visit.

Every wall was like a mini-photographic exhibition with image after image of the family and grandchildren; some in frames, some just pinned right there into the wall. It struck me as I walked through the house behind James that in the Piper house, the décor *was* the photographs. There was no carefully selected artwork or cushions or rattan coffee tables like in Mum and Dad's house. This was a functional house, with sturdy furniture and hardy wooden floorboards—the life and flavour of it was generated entirely by mementos from family life.

How many times had I agonised over my own lack of flair for setting up our home? In the end, I too had opted for function over form. The decorative pieces in my house I had selected with Mum's assistance and never felt entirely sure of our choices. As much as I *wanted* a beautiful, stylish home like the one I'd grown up in, it had never been my forte.

Apparently it was just not in my blood.

"This was Charlotte's room growing up, and it had been my room too when I was a kid," James explained, pushing open a door to reveal a desk covered in paperwork and two armchairs. "It's kind of my office now. Lilly likes to read in there, it gets a lot of northern sun and there's a nice view of the front paddock."

We walked across a sitting room with heavy leather couches, and James opened the door to the outside, leading us onto a veranda with a swinging chair and an extensive series of small animal statues.

"Neesa used to pretend this was her zoo," James explained wryly. "These things seemed to breed for a while there, I think Lilly was buying them behind my back."

"I was not!" Lilly called from inside the house, but there was a laugh in her voice. This was clearly a well-loved game between them.

"Nee has kind of outgrown the game now, but sooner or later the twins will enjoy them so the concrete menagerie remains," James sighed.

The next bedroom had been freshly painted—very freshly, judging by the faintly lingering scent. The bottom half of the walls was a deep brown, the top half a more sober beige. There was an armchair and heavy wooden bed with an extensive array of pillows at its head.

The room looked suspiciously perfect—even the furniture seemed new. I wondered if Lilly had decorated in the four days between me agreeing to visit and my arrival. If the crazy, over-the-top spread in the kitchen was anything to go by it was a real possibility.

"This is beautiful," Ted said as he looked around the large room.

"It was Simon's when he was a kid, now it's our guest room, but we were thinking you two could take this room, this weekend, and of course if you ever want to visit again," James said, a little stiffly.

"Thank you, James," I said softly. His more gentle hopefulness was easier to bear than Lilly's over-the-top exuberance.

He showed us their bedroom and the bathroom, and then I finally realised how nervous he was when he lead the way into the laundry and then stopped dead.

"Not much to show you in here. I don't know why I brought you down here."

"We know where to go if we need to wash clothes while we're here," Ted said, I suppose trying to make polite conversation. James laughed.

The hallway looped around to the enormous kitchen and dining room. Ted whistled when he saw the spread of food over the dining table. Lilly had set up a porcelain dinner set and formal cutlery layout, but the rest of the table was covered in mismatched plates and bowls.

"Done," she said. "Are you ready to eat?"

There was a large, low feature light over the enormous table, the slightly yellowed shade throwing a warm light over the room and resulting in a surprisingly intimate feel. Ted and I exchanged a wide-eyed look over the sea of food before us. There were cakes and biscuits, slices and breads, soups and salads and a series of traditional Polish dishes that I'd never even heard of.

Lilly fussed about, loading up a plate for me to sample this and that, and James sat and silently watched her. I tried to make small talk, but for the most part, I was just watching them—her anxious busy-ness, and James' concerned silence. There were tears in his eyes from time to time, but he did not look at me, he stared only at Lilly. I wished I could read his thoughts.

"Try this one first," Lilly said, when she finally sat the plate before me. She pointed to a chunky dumpling, sitting in a little nest of bacon and onion. "That's a pierogi."

"Pierogi," I repeated it as if I'd never heard the word before, trying to roll my *r* the way she had. I glanced at Ted, and he nodded at me. We were both thinking of Mum's pathetic attempt at pierogi; burnt, chewy chunks of pastry wrapped around overcooked and under seasoned beef mince. Mum's efforts suddenly seemed almost insulting, compared to these tidy little parcels which had been fried with bacon and onion.

I picked up the fork and awkwardly chopped the dumpling, then speared one side of it and stuffed it into my mouth. It was delicious—salty and hearty, the pastry smooth and soft—together the tiny package was a satisfying surprise. I made sounds of delight and reached for the second half, and Lilly squeezed her hands together in front of her chest and squealed a little.

"I've always wanted to show you the food I grew up with. The original Sabina—*Sabinka*—she was my grandmother. She died in the war, so I never met her, but her pierogis were legendary. I can give you the recipe. I made you donuts too, the way my Tata used to at Easter time. See those there?" She pointed to an awkward, crispy donut on the side of my plate near the cakes. "I've had those every Easter of my entire life. Sometimes I raised the batter by parking the car in the sun and letting it sit in there. And that fish is *sledzi*, it's pickled in vinegar with onions and peppercorns—"

"Lilly," James spoke softly. "Honey, please sit down."

"I just need to get Ted a plate first. He's driven all that way. What's your heritage, Ted?"

"My family is ladled right out of the cultural melting pot, we're part-everything," Ted said, and he rose, and reached to gently take the plate from Lilly's hand. "I can serve myself, Lilly. Why don't you sit down and chat with Sabina?"

Her eyes were still red. Lilly looked at me, and they swam again. She reached to take the plate back from Ted, then wrung her hands together, and nodded at me. Finally she rounded the table to sit beside me.

"I can't believe you're really here," she whispered. I had a mouth full of donut and I mumbled something which hopefully expressed my happiness. "I had dreams like this sometimes. Only you're even more beautiful in real life than you were in my dreams."

"You're only saying that because I look just like you." I tried to make a joke when my mouth had cleared. She was eating me up with her eyes, savouring my presence. Of course she was. I'd expected her to be intense, given the situation. I just hadn't really expected to feel awkward about it, but sitting there as the object of adoration, for a woman that I did not really know, had left me surprisingly self-conscious.

"You really do look like me." She was still speaking in a slightly awed whisper. "I'd have known you for sure, if I passed you on the street. I always looked for you."

"This farm," Ted said suddenly, and I shot him a silent *thank you* with gratitude in my eyes. "How many generations has it been in this family?"

"Four," James said, leaning back in his chair. "My great grandfather combined a number of parcels to create the property we hold now. And next door, Lilly's brother Henri and his wife hold land that was in Lilly's mother's family for four generations too."

It seemed strange that I was sitting on a place that had been owned by my family for hundreds of years. I thought that some part of me at least should feel as if it had come home, but I felt nothing so profound, only exhausted and nervous and uncomfortable. And, blessedly, hungry.

"Did you come from big families?" I asked.

"I have one brother, he lives in Melbourne now," James told me.

"I have seven siblings," Lilly said softly.

"Wow."

They both laughed at my surprise.

"Will you two... do you think you'll have more than..." Lilly motioned now towards my stomach and I laughed.

"A few, hopefully," Ted answered for me. "Not *seven*. We've probably left it a little late for that."

"We've been travelling so much, until the last few years," I explained, although I'm sure I didn't need to defend myself. "Then we were setting ourselves up. The timing hasn't been right until now. You have three grandchildren though?"

I wanted to use different words, and as I planned the sentence, I intended to. It was at the very last instance that I self-edited. Instead of asking them if they had "three *other* grandchildren *already*," I just confirmed that they had "three grandchildren." It seemed a little presumptuous to refer to my unborn child as their grandchild.

"Simon and his wife Emmaline also took their time. He's three years younger than you and they've just had their twins this year. Charlotte, on the other hand..." James and Lilly shared a glance. "She married and divorced young. Neesa is twelve now, Charlotte is thirty-four. She told us she was pregnant the day she finished her apprenticeship. Then of course her husband left and she's been on her own for the most part ever since. I can't believe you're a teacher too." Lilly grinned at me, then drew in a satisfied breath. "It must be in the DNA. Who would have thought?"

"Not me," I laughed softly. "Mum and Dad convinced me to do a post-grad certificate in education, I had no intention of ever using it until I came back from overseas and realised that I needed to do more than just sing in bars one night a week."

It was only when I finished speaking that I realised that I'd referred to *Mum* and *Dad* as such. I waited for them to react, but Lilly pressed on with the conversation as if she hadn't heard me.

"I'm sure you must have my mother's voice, she never had any training but she sung all of the time. She used to walk around the farm singing. Usually we knew where she was by listening for her song."

"Were you close?" I asked, and a sadness settled in Lilly's eyes.

"Things were complicated with my parents," she murmured. "We didn't speak for many years once I finally left home. Just before she died, we made peace…but I so wish she could have heard you sing, she'd have been so proud."

"Are Charlotte and Simon musical?"

"Charlotte takes after me, she can't even play her iPod in tune," James chuckled. "Simon probably had some talent but no desire to develop it. Neesa, on the other hand…"

"Yes, Neesa is quite the singer. She's young, but she's got a real passion for it. They're all excited to meet you at dinner tomorrow."

"I'm excited to meet them too," I said. Excited, and petrified.

Somewhere in the house, a clock sounded a series of bells. We listened, each silently counting.

"That's eleven," James said, as if he couldn't quite believe it. "Lilly, we'd better let these two go to bed when they're done eating."

I saw Lilly's face fall, and I reached over to sit my hand over hers.

"We're here all weekend," I said softly, and I smiled at her. "We have so much to catch up on. Tomorrow, we can talk all day."

She smiled too, then she turned her hand over to grasp mine and entwined our fingers; locking us together.

"Come on," James rose. "I'll take your bags through to your room."

—

When the lights were out, and the house was silent, Ted and I were tucked up in the bed beside each other. I turned to him and whispered,

"She's so intense."

"No wonder."

"I know."

"How you doing with it all, Bean?"

"Good, good. I'm glad we're here. I'm hoping tomorrow is a bit less..."

"Awkward?"

"*Awkward.* I feel bad for even thinking it. She's so wonderful... but I feel a little shell-shocked."

"They seem like nice people."

"I have so many questions for her. I wanted to ask her even just the obvious ones tonight, but she seems too fragile."

"I know. But doesn't it make you wonder... God, what has that poor woman been through?"

I was still thinking about that question long after Ted had fallen asleep.

# CHAPTER TWENTY-FOUR

## Megan

## September 1973

I have always felt like life should just be *fair.* Don't you think that everything would make so much more sense if bad things happened to bad people, and good things happened to good people—if everyone got exactly what they deserved?

If life worked like that, I'd never even have heard of the Orange Maternity Home. I'd have been settled at Balmain at that stage of my life, busy caring for my own children. And if life worked like that, Lilly Wyzlecki would never have even met me. If we'd met in a just world, I'm sure we would have been great friends—each of us with our brood of children, each of us blissfully unaware of the alternate reality where a meeting between us would change the course of our lives.

I'd been at the maternity home for less than a month when she was admitted, and I'll never forget what she looked like that first day. Lilly was sixteen, but she seemed much younger, and even by the end of her pregnancy she never really looked pregnant. Maybe it was an optical illusion because she seemed so young, or maybe it was just a consequence of her heavier build, but even in the days before she gave birth I'd sometimes glance at her and just see a slightly overweight teenager, not a mother-to-be.

Lilly had huge brown eyes that displayed her every emotion like a projector onto a cinema screen. She could not be subtle or measured; she was just an open book. I saw the sweetness of her innocence in the early days at the home, and then I watched it dissolve by degrees. I was uncomfortable with every aspect of the home and upset for all of the other residents too, but Lilly was different from the outset. It was impossible to maintain any professional distance from her because every time I saw her, I was reminded that what was happening to her was wrong and unjust and that she in no way deserved it.

I *thought* that about all of the girls, but I *knew* it about Lilly.

No one should have the right to take the light out of someone else's eyes, but that's what we did to our residents. We stole the hope right out of them, and I watched the process in super-slow motion every time I made eye contact with Lilly. She was sweet and optimistic, intelligent and gentle—but then later she was confused and concerned, and later still she was devastated and terrified. And every shade of every feeling was right there on her face.

Her parents discovered her pregnancy late, and she was only with us for a few months. It was late on a Friday afternoon in early September when June Sullivan told me that they were going to induce her. Lilly seemed to have fallen into a severe depression and was refusing food most days, and June said that the doctors were concerned for the safety of the baby. They had no way of calculating an accurate due date for her, but based on the baby's size, they were pretty sure she was only a few weeks off a natural delivery date anyway.

When June told me the induction was imminent, I didn't realise she meant *that day.* When I got to work on Monday I was confused to hear that Lilly had been in labour for the entire weekend. I went to the delivery suite, but the midwives told me that things were very tense in the room and I shouldn't interrupt.

So, I stayed in the office that morning and I was sweating on news of the birth. June was always terribly lax with her paperwork and so I tried to complete records from past placements while I waited, but I could barely concentrate. Just before lunch the phone rang, and after a quiet conversation, June turned to me and shook her head.

"Not looking good for Liliana W."

"Not looking good?" I repeated blankly.

"Too lazy even to push, apparently. They're talking about taking her to theatre."

I left the office, ignoring the alarmed call June threw after me, and I ran across the road towards the delivery suites. As soon as I pushed open the swinging doors I could that she was in serious trouble.

They had tied her to the bed. Her wrists were caught in thick leather restraints, the edges bloodied and bruised from endless hours of straining to be free. Lilly was lying on her back, completely sunken into the mattress, and the obstetrician was between her legs with forceps. Several people were shouting at her to push, and there was a second doctor pushing at the bump of her belly.

Lilly's eyes were open but vacant—she was staring toward the window. Her lips were so dry that they had cracked, and there was a smudge of dried blood down her chin.

We'd shared some great chats during Lilly's time in the home. I'd come to admire her, and I felt certain that beneath all of the difficulty of her current situation, she was strong enough to go on and forge a great future for herself. I'd intended to remind her of that strength when she was adjusting to life without her baby. When I saw her on the bed, I knew that I couldn't wait that long.

I unstrapped her hands, leant over her on the bed and forced her to look at me. Her eyes were glazed—God only knows what drugs they'd pumped into her. I had learned that it was standard practice for the medical staff to sedate the maternity home girls during their labours. Easier on everyone, June had told me once, but whatever drug it was they gave those girls it didn't seem to make it easier on *them*. They were still in pain, just less able to protest or to ask for help—or to push, which meant forceps became standard practice and the girls had then to deal with the aftermath of a much more traumatic birth.

I shook Lilly a little bit, but when she failed to respond I shook her harder and then I shouted at her, until I felt she'd focussed sufficiently to be aware that I was there. I knew that she'd snapped out of her stupor enough to recognise me when those big brown eyes swam in tears.

"You can do this, Lilly," I told her, and she shook her head and moaned, and I squeezed her hand as hard as I could. She whimpered and I looked to the doctors at the foot of the bed. "Are you going to do the caesarean? Surely this has dragged on too long?"

"It *has* dragged on too long," one of the midwives muttered behind me. "The baby's heart rate is dipping, there's no time. We have to get it out now...or..."

I was suddenly aware of the beeping in the room, and of the unstable rhythm that was driving every action like the beat under a song. The heartbeat was too fast, and then it was too slow, and like everyone else in the room, I started to panic.

"Come on, Liliana! For God's sake, push!" the doctor shouted, and I grabbed Lilly's shoulders and pressed my face right up against hers.

"I can't do it," she whispered to me. I could hear from the rough edges to her voice that she'd been screaming, maybe for days. "I just can't."

"We'll do it together," I whispered back. I held her eye contact, and I took a breath in. "Push with me, okay, Lilly? Let's do it for a count of ten, together. You've got this. I *know* you have."

She nodded at me, and her hands fumbled for my shoulders.

We counted to ten together, over and over again, Lilly's hoarse voice a desperate cry at each number, but she did it—she bloody *did* it, even after all of those hours. She brought her baby into the world like that—her eyes locked on mine, her hands on my shoulders and mine on hers. It was a few minutes later that the baby slid free and the tension in the room eased with the sound of the baby's weak but determined protest at the cold air. Lilly collapsed onto the bed, but then she immediately pulled herself up, bolt upright into a sitting position.

I could almost see a shadow of joy cross her face as she stared at her baby. It was fleeting, but there was a definite hint of it there in the flash of light that I saw in her eyes. They took the baby straight out as they always did, and I wondered if Lilly realised how lucky she was that they'd been too distracted with the tension of the last moments of her labour to remember to block her view with a pillow, as they were supposed to.

Then she sank, all the way back down and into the pillows, and she no longer seemed too young to be pregnant and I felt sick with guilt at even thinking the words *luck* and *Lilly* in the same breath, given what was happening to her. Now Lilly seemed old and withered, dried out and worn, and she closed her eyes and I waited for her to cry.

"Good girl, Lilly," I whispered, but she turned her head away from me, back towards the window. I took her hand again, and she gave my fingers a weak squeeze, and then her hand went limp and I thought for a second she'd passed out. "Lilly?"

She shook her head a little, and I realised that she needed a moment to retreat into herself. I released her hand and stepped back from the bed, feeling awkward and uncomfortable. The mood in the room had shifted all the way back from panic to business-as-usual as the doctors prepared for the placenta and the nurses calmly discussed their weekend.

I backed out of the room, and as soon as I was in the corridor I realised that I felt almost sea-sick—nauseous from the shock of it all. There was no time to find a bathroom—I was lucky to find a rubbish bin, and I crouched over it and vomited again and again.

"Are you all right?" One of the junior nurses came to my aid, and when the moment had passed and I was leaning against the wall recovering, she nodded towards my stomach. "Are you…"

I shook my head, hastily—almost violently, and then I started to cry.

"Oh, I'm sorry—"

"Don't be," I said, too harshly, and then I felt bad all over again from the way the young nurse's face fell. "I'm sorry, it's been a rough morning. I'm okay now, thank you for helping me."

I pulled myself up and walked down toward the bathroom. I washed my face, then rinsed my mouth, and stared at myself in the mirror. So many times in my five months at the maternity home, I'd felt as though I had hit rock bottom, but surely there would be no worse day than this one.

I walked to the nursery, where the midwife was wrapping Lilly's baby. There were dark bruises on either side of the child's head, a strangely bright purple against her otherwise raspberry red skin.

"It's a girl?" I asked softly.

"Yes."

"Do you know why she was stuck?"

"She wasn't in the right position, she came out wrong side up, always makes things more difficult. Maybe if they'd let her go a few more weeks, until the baby was ready to be born, it would have been an easier arrival. It's done now, anyway. We can't very well put her back in."

"But she's okay?"

"She's fine, although I daresay another few minutes and the story might have ended differently."

I sighed and stared down at the baby. She was resting, quite peacefully, as if she'd already overcome the trauma of her birth and could now enjoy a nap. I didn't generally let myself touch the newborns, they seemed too small and fragile.

But there was something different about this baby. I felt almost as if I'd participated in her birth. I touched her cheek with the pad of my finger.

"Got a home for this one yet?" the midwife asked me briskly. I sighed and shook my head.

"We placed a few babies over the last few weeks, I don't have any families waiting."

"Off to an institution then? It doesn't seem right sometimes, we put these mothers through all of *that*, and the babe ends up without a family anyway."

"It doesn't seem right," I repeated, and then I felt all hot and sickly again so I withdrew my hand from the baby's face. "I'll come by later to see how they're getting on."

I walked outside, and the cold spring air hit me, easing the nausea and draining the heat from my cheeks.

I'd been at the home for five months, and for that entire time I'd been fighting with an ever-growing protest inside myself. Most nights, when I tumbled into bed, I could barely believe that I'd survived another day. At times I'd almost dissociated from the work I was doing. Maybe the only way I could continue was to compartmentalise my work and my private life, and to pretend altogether that I wasn't taking any part at all in what was happening in the maternity home.

Grae had trapped me, you see. In typical Graeme Baxter fashion, he'd waltzed in the door to our quaint home in Balmain after work one day, with a bottle of champagne and a devilish grin, and announced that he'd accepted a transfer to the finance department in the health service at Orange. That was shocking enough, but then he told me that as a bonus he'd convinced them to employ me too. He felt we needed a change of scenery after the sadness and struggle of the previous few years, and so he'd gone ahead and arranged one.

I didn't realise until I arrived for my first day at work that he'd forgotten to mention the part about my position being based in the maternity home, working with the adoption service. I'd just assumed I would be working in elder care, as I had been since I graduated university. We had just suffered the loss of our seventh pregnancy and there was no way... absolutely *no* way in hell that I'd have knowingly accepted a job working with miserably pregnant teenagers.

But I should have known. Grae had long since given up on the idea of a baby of our own. He had well and truly passed the limit of his tolerance for the waiting and the longing and the momentary joy before the pain started all over again, but I was so *sure* that we just needed more time. Miracles happened every day, I'd seen them myself in my fifteen odd years as a social worker at the nursing home. How many times had we called family and clergy to farewell a deathly elderly patient, only to have that patient up and walking the corridors within days or even hours? I had always felt so sure that sooner or later, we'd conceive and a pregnancy would stick somehow and all of the heartache would have been worthwhile.

Besides which, I was the one who had to struggle through the miscarriages, and if *I* was willing to keep going, who was *he* to suggest otherwise?

He was *Graeme*, that's who. My strong-willed, too-charming-for-his-own-good, increasingly arrogant husband. And after a few rounds of me pleading if we could *just give it one more shot* before looking into adoption, when his prompting and questioning and demanding became unbearable, I shifted my delaying tactics and told him that I just *loved* working and wanted to *hang in there* just a little longer before we committed to a ready-made baby. And perhaps there was some truth to all of that at the nursing home, where I felt that I was making a difference.

But then he manipulated me into a position where I had to stare my infertility in the face every single damned day. I was a fish out of water in the maternity home, working in a team of only two social workers, alongside June Sullivan who believed so passionately in our work. From my first day, I felt sure that I was walking the halls with a mortified expression on my face, and no amount of professionalism could hide my disdain.

It wasn't that I had anything against adoption. I could see that there were situations where it was a useful tool for helping young women who weren't ready for motherhood, helping babies who otherwise wouldn't have had a suitable home, and helping families who were infertile.

Of course, I did not think of myself as infertile, maybe just fertility challenged, and I felt quite certain that adoption was not for us... at least, not yet. I didn't just want a baby, I wanted *our* baby... I wanted the whole package—the morning sickness, the stretch marks, the birth, the bliss of looking down at my body and seeing our marriage extended in the most natural of ways. I wanted to raise our child without the complication of knowing that she had some other family out there... missing her and loving her and worst of all, missing *out* on her. Besides which, I was equally certain that any one of those girls in the home could raise their own child if they were given the right support. It felt beyond evil to convince them otherwise.

Grae, on the other hand, thought that this system of baby-farming was brilliant and he could never understand my struggle with it. At first, when I came home from work upset and conflicted, he found ways to be supportive. He'd give me back rubs and pour me wine and tell me to *hang in there*. He'd soliloquise on the virtues of adoption for teenage mothers, repeating all of the lies that I heard June tell every day...conveniently forgetting that I was seeing the human face of the theory and that I understood much better than he the actual reality of it.

When I was really upset, he'd remind me how generous the hospital was to find me a position so that we could move and have this *great opportunity*. He quickly became good friends with the general manager at the hospital, and reminded me again and again that the maternity home was a great source of pride to the upper echelons of the health service. When I first suggested I might need to resign, Graeme was so horrified about how offensive this might be to his colleagues that for a brief moment or two, I abandoned the idea altogether.

I was conflicted, and always uncertain about my own opinion, especially in something this serious, because Graeme was just not often wrong about things. Life had taught me, again and again, that when Grae and I disagreed, it was usually because he knew a little more about the subject than I did.

Three minutes into the next work day I was back to planning my resignation.

After a while, it seemed that my misery wore a bit thin on him, and he started avoiding me when I came home. He'd lock himself away in the study with his paperwork and if I came in to talk, he'd wave at me and insist that he was busy and couldn't it wait? I could see his frustration, but the situation was of his own doing, and as he slid into impatience, I was sliding into resentment.

And then, Lilly had her baby.

# CHAPTER TWENTY-FIVE

## Sabina

## April 2012

When I woke the next morning, Ted was gone, and the bed beside me was cold. I slipped out of bed, used the ensuite, and dressed. There were still nervous butterflies in my stomach, but I was hopeful that over the course of the day, we'd all relax a little.

As I stepped out of the bedroom, I could smell something delicious in the air and I felt an automatic hunger pang. I walked slowly down the hallway towards the source of the scent, noticing now a long series of family photos in matching black frames. I stopped and stared at one. A much younger Lilly and James sat on awkward, fabric-covered boxes against a too-blue background. Between them stood a very solidly built boy with a bowl haircut and a gappy grin, and a rake-thin little girl with spiral curls and a scowl.

I recognised Simon and Charlotte from Lilly's email. I walked further down the hall, watching the children age in each photo, and felt a strange sense of longing. I would have been in these photos. I'd have stood between them, because I'd have been the tallest, at least until Simon's pre-teen years. How would it have felt? Would I have scowled like Charlotte? Or would I have grinned like Simon?

More questions with no answers. But at least I was in in the Piper household, and there was a chance that some of my other questions might be answered that day.

"Good morning, sleepy head," Ted said, when I entered the living area. He was sitting at the breakfast bar, with a plate of hot food before him. Lilly was at the stove, flipping some kind of pancake, wearing a cotton nightgown and a dressing gown. She looked exhausted, but radiantly happy. When she saw me, her entire face brightened.

"Good morning, Sabina," she said through a grin. "Did you sleep well?"

"Like a log." I stretched. "Whatever you're cooking smells amazing."

"Potato pancakes, with bacon and eggs from a farm down the road," Ted told me with obvious delight. "Lilly is like the world's greatest cook. You've got to taste this."

I bit into the pancake and my eyes widened, then I pretend to push Ted off his chair to steal his plate. Lilly laughed, much harder than my joke deserved, and I saw the shining pride in her eyes.

"It's like a hash brown and a pancake had a baby together," I said.

"They're *placki ziemniaczane*," Lilly explained. "Potato pancakes. Another recipe from my father."

"Delicious!"

"I'll make you up a plate. James has already gone off to do a few things around the farm, he'll be back soon and we thought we'd show you around the place. We'll do a loop over to the Wyzlecki land—there's a track which leads you the full length of both properties."

We sat together at the breakfast bar, and for the next hour the three of us shared an easy, comfortable conversation about our lives. The details of a person—what job they have, or where they studied, even what they do for fun—those things don't actually matter, once you know them. Until you know those basic facts about someone, they are a stranger, and Lilly and I needed to trade the simple data about ourselves. We marvelled at the commonalities, and belatedly celebrated each other's milestones. Lilly was fascinated by our travels, I was impressed at her determination to achieve her degree even though the opportunity hadn't presented itself until she was nearly thirty.

"I was always going to be a history teacher," she told me. "I'd planned it since I was a little girl, I think because my father immigrated here after the second world war and he seemed so damaged by his experiences back in Poland. I was desperately curious to understand what had happened to him, but he never wanted to talk about it, so I had to do my own research. I remember being mortified by what I read and confused by why Tata wasn't more open with his story. I understand now the mental toll those kind of experiences must have taken on him, but I think because of my curiosity as a kid, I've always been passionate about teaching history to children. If we don't learn from the mistakes of the past, how can we stop them from happening again?"

"Is there a university near here?" Ted asked.

"There is at Orange now, but when my kids were in primary school, there was nothing close enough for me to study face-to-face. I finished high school by correspondence, then did most of my degree that way too."

"And you still teach?" I asked.

"Oh, heavens yes. Well, I qualified as a mature-aged student, so it's not like I've had a long and extensive career behind me! But still, I only teach three days a week and my plan is to keep doing that forever. Sometimes James wants me to retire and work with him here, but I think we'd end up divorced in a week if I had to go back to spending all of my days on this farm." She pulled up a stool opposite me at the breakfast bar and helped herself to some of the pancakes. "Besides which, I'm only fifty-four, you know. Far too young to retire, although I do only work part time so I can help Emmaline and Simon out with the twins on the other days."

"Of course," I said, and I felt stupid. "I keep thinking you're older because—" I stopped suddenly, my face flushing.

"I look older?" She was teasing me, and Ted laughed.

"No, no. Just because—" I cleared my throat. "Because Mum is."

"I was only s-sixteen when I had you," Lilly said, quite kindly, but then rose even though her breakfast was virtually untouched, and although her expression was calm the stutter gave her distress away. The conversation had been flowing so smoothly, and it seemed to me that even the mention of the adoption was a kind of stutter—an unexpected hiccup right there in the middle of the chat. I wanted to press her further, but even more than that, I desperately wanted the easy rhythm of our interaction to come back and solidify.

I changed the subject. When I spoke again, I worked very hard to keep my tone light-hearted, and I was pleased with how casual my next words sounded.

"You don't look fifty-four. What's your secret?"

Lilly smiled at me.

"It's all about good genes. You've obviously inherited the same ones, I can tell just by looking at you. You brown instead of burning, you don't get freckles and you stay that same light olive all year round, right?"

I thought of Mum's pasty white complexion and not for the first time wondered how on earth I'd missed the fact that we were genetic strangers.

"You're spot on."

"Charlotte has James' colouring, she fries in the sun and all she has to do is look at a glass of wine before her face flushes. But Simon and I…and you…" she smiled, and I realised we were again talking about something deeper, "We're the lucky ones."

—

Lilly informed me that the best way to see a farm is from the back of a ute. This was, apparently, James' work vehicle, an older style ute with a beaten-up tray. The back window was missing, which Lilly referred to as "air conditioning."

I thought she was joking about us travelling in the back, until she climbed up into the tray as if she were a playful ten-year-old.

"Is that safe?" I wrapped my arms around my middle, trying to remind her of my pregnancy. She gave me a confused smile.

"Of course it is," she said, then reached down and offered me her hand. When I hesitated still, her smile softened. "We really don't go very fast, Sabina. I promise, you're both safe up here with me."

I was still nervous, but I couldn't refuse her, not with that gentle, reassuring smile and the excitement shimmering in her eyes. I reached towards her and as soon as she had my hand, she all but dragged me up with her. She sat on a toolbox that had been fixed along one side of the tray, I automatically sat opposite. Ted winked at me and climbed into the front with James.

"Never ridden on the back of a ute before, hey?" Lilly surmised. I shook my head, then reached behind me to awkwardly clutch at the side of the tray as the ute lurched forward.

"Not many ute rides in the city."

"What was it like, growing up there? What school did you go to?"

"I went to a private primary school, then a performing arts high school."

"They were good schools?"

"They were great schools," I conceded. "I didn't even know how good I had it. The school I teach at now is a lovely little independent private school but it's got nothing on the fancy schools I went to. What about you, the school you teach at?"

"It's an average public high school. My kids went there too, it's about half an hour down the road in Molong. It's a nice school, but resources are always stretched and kids fall through the cracks. Even Charlotte very nearly did and I was teaching there by then."

We were silent for a few moments, as the ute wound its way down a bumpy dirt road, past a series of silos and a small group of mismatched sheds. I stared at the paddocks, endless seas of tiny plants sprouting in the dirt, punctuated by the height of rows of gum trees along the fence lines. I'd have roamed this land freely, if things had worked out differently. I'd have known what it was like to ride on the back of a ute, and to smell dust in the air all of the time, and I'd be used to dirt under my fingernails and no doubt have had callouses on my palms like the ones I'd felt on Lilly's when she'd pulled me up into the ute.

Then, James drove towards a fence, and I gasped as he drove into it. The fence flattened down so that the ute could pass straight over it. I watched the long lines of wire bounce back into place once we'd passed.

"Magic fences?"

"Who's got time for gates?" Lilly laughed.

We crossed the creek, a tiny trickle of water in a fairly deep valley. Lilly explained that when it rained heavily, which it seemed to less and less these days, the tiny creek would swell and had even been known to flood the paddocks around it. There were cattle grates on either side, bordering a single lane concrete bridge. We neared a homestead, much like the one we'd just left, with a wraparound veranda and an extensive chicken yard and veggie patch.

"Are your siblings still around here?" I asked Lilly quietly. "Other than Henri, I mean."

"They're all over the place. One lives in Sydney, one in Darwin, one of my brothers is living in Poland. The rest are in Orange or Molong, and Henri and his wife Sara are here."

"Do you have nieces and nephews?"

"Twenty-four of the little monsters, and most of them have spouses and kids now." She grimaced. "Family gatherings are a nightmare. We usually get together every year or so for something. I think we'll meet up at Christmas and I'll invite you… if you want to come, I mean."

"Of course. I'd really like that."

"Christmas in the Wyzlecki family is a bit of an affair. It's Polish tradition to do the Christmas Eve thing, we get together and eat all kinds of traditional foods, and some of the family take communion. What did you do for Christmas? Was it just you and…" She stopped, and the hesitation was painful to hear. "…your parents?"

"Just the three of us, yes, but we made a fuss," I said softly. "I woke up too early, pretty much every year until I turned thirteen or fourteen. I'd get up at 1 or 2 a.m., and Dad would put me back to bed, but of course I'd be too excited to sleep so he'd have to lie in bed with me and pat me until I drifted back off to sleep. Then I'd wake up again at five or six, and there'd be *no* getting me back to sleep after that, so instead they'd have to get up with me. Once I could read, they let me hand out the presents. And there were always too many presents—Mum is pretty disciplined in just about every area of her life, except when it came to gifts for me. I'd spend all morning opening gifts and then we'd usually go to one of the grandparent's places for lunch, then I'd spend all afternoon reorganising my room to fit in the presents." I was surveying the paddocks as I reminisced. When Lilly didn't comment, I dragged my attention back to her, and saw the strange expression on her face. It wasn't sadness, but it was something difficult, and I hesitated, unsure whether to retreat from the conversation or to press on. She had asked, after all, but it suddenly struck me how insensitive it was to rave about how wonderful my childhood had been without her.

"It sounds marvellous," she said eventually. "And did you go on holidays?"

"Oh, yes—pretty much every year. They dragged me all over the world. When I finished high school Mum took me to Europe, and we spent three weeks in Poland. I was only just eighteen and too spoiled to pay as much attention as I should have, but it was still wonderful."

"That's..." Lilly cleared her throat and stared at the floor of the ute. "Well, that's just wonderful for you."

"She even tried to make me pierogi for a while," I added softly. "They were horrible. Yours are much better."

I wasn't surprised when Lilly gently re-steered the conversation.

"Tell me about Ted, how did you two meet?"

The ute bounced along the road, looping around the homestead, and then over a ridge and down into a very long valley.

"We met at uni. At first we just kind of had shared friends, and then as we moved into our second year, we ended up as friends ourselves. We were both seeing other people then—well, I was seeing one person, Ted was bouncing around a bunch of beautiful girls."

Lilly laughed.

"He's a handsome lad."

"Oh, yes. And he knew it. It never occurred to me for a second that someone like Ted would have any interest in me. I knew he liked my company; we saw each other every few days and it was usually Ted who initiated the meetings. I just had a hard time imagining Ted settling down at all, let alone with someone as ordinary as me."

"You're hardly ordinary, Sabina."

"Oh, but I was," I laughed. "Ted tended to date these teeny-tiny stick figure women... which I am most definitely not. But for years and years we were just friends, until I finished working on the cruise ships and moved back to Sydney and then... it all fell into place for us." Lilly smiled at me, and I asked, "What about you and James?"

"James is two years older than me, and I'm pretty sure I only learned to walk so I could follow him around. There's no story of us falling in love—we just always were, and we always will be." Lilly smiled, then I saw her glance into the cab of the ute. "He drives me absolutely crazy most of the time. He barely speaks a word and then someone mentions dirt or seeds and he'll talk for hours. Seriously, who loves farming that much?"

"Ladies, we can hear you, you know," James pointed out, through the missing back window.

"I know." Lilly shrugged. "But you *do* go on, James."

"I have actually been politely waiting for you two to give the soppy gibber-jabber a rest so I could explain about these crops to Ted."

"What a gentleman." Lilly winked at me. "Go on, then."

As we continued through paddock after paddock of small plants, James talked, in far too much detail, about crop rotation and plant breeding and how much they'd increased the yields of their wheat crops in particular by following the science. Lilly rolled her eyes at me and I giggled, and soon struck up another conversation too. She shared her history with me via her memories of the farm.

These were the sites that should have been my birthright—the last dam Charlotte ever swam in, after she got a giant leech on her leg one hot summer day the year she turned twelve, the tree Simon fell out of and broke his leg, then the flat ground where James built a bonfire each year. Lilly told me about the big party they always threw when they finally lit it at the height of winter. Dozens of people would visit, and when the kids were at high school all of the teenagers from surrounding properties would come and camp.

"They went through this ridiculous phase, they'd dare each other to strip naked and run down the paddock."

"In winter?"

"Oh yes, it was usually freezing, or below, but that didn't stop them. They'd egg each other on for a few hours and then disappear one by one, and you'd see streaks of white flesh in the distant darkness and hear the shrieks as they ran. They were far enough away to maintain their modesty, but close enough that you could just about *feel* how cold they were. Bloody teenagers. Meanwhile all of the sensible adults would be sitting close to the fire toasting marshmallows or sausages and drinking hot chocolate."

"We didn't do *that* in the city either." I wrinkled my nose at her, and Lilly laughed that loud bark I was coming to love.

"I'm actually glad to hear that!"

# CHAPTER TWENTY-SIX

## Megan

### September 1973

It seems crazy, looking back now... but at the time, I really did think that I might have found a genius solution to everyone's problems.

The idea came to me in the middle of the night, as I tossed and turned and relived every second of those moments with Lilly in the birth suite earlier that day. I'd never seen someone suffer such anguish, both during the labour and after, and I was genuinely distraught for her... but the truth was, I was as unsettled about my own situation as I was about Lilly's. For the first time in my life, I was living out of sync with my own values. I was learning the hard way that happiness is repelled by inner turmoil.

I eventually took to staring at the ceiling wondering how on earth we'd both get through this period in our lives, and then in a single heartbeat, all of the pieces of the puzzle shifted into place and I started to wonder if I couldn't fix the entire mess in one fell swoop.

I knew that I desperately needed to find an out. Lilly desperately needed to find some more time, so that she and James could marry and set themselves up for parenthood. And Grae... well, Grae wanted me to consider adopting, and if that was all the leverage I had, then maybe I could work with it.

The lightbulb went on in my mind, and then all that was left to think about were the logistics. Eventually I fell into a fitful sleep, but I rose early and cooked Grae a full breakfast.

He was tucking into undercooked bacon and burnt eggs when I cleared my throat and threw my idea onto the table.

"We could do a trial adoption."

I saw his eyes light up a little, but he was wary.

"Is that a thing? Why would we do that?"

"Well... it's not really done very often..." The truth was, I'd made the phrase up on the fly. "... but there's this baby at the hospital that we don't have a home for, so she'll be going to the orphanage. We could take her for a few weeks."

"Why can't *we* just have her?"

I choked on my coffee.

"Grae, I told you, I'm not sure that I'm ready to adopt yet." The coffee stung my sinuses and my eyes watered, which I knew Grae misinterpreted as tears. His expression softened, but his words were firm.

"You've been telling me that for two years, Meg. We're not getting any younger. You said this baby doesn't have a home, why don't we just adopt it?"

"Well... eventually, I think her real parents will keep her. They're a wonderful couple... they're going to be terrific parents, but... they just need for us to buy them some time to get married and maybe to organise a few things before she comes home. We could really help them out if we brought the baby here for a while, and..." This was the tricky bit. I shrugged and tried to appear thoughtful. "Who knows? I think it'd help me get used to the idea."

"What about your job?"

"I'd have to resign, of course. A newborn needs a lot of care."

"But I thought you liked working?"

"I did. But you know this new job has been a struggle."

"So you'd leave your job just to look after this baby for a few weeks?"

"I'll find something else, or maybe we'll be ready to adopt our own by then." There was a natural lull in the conversation, and when I glanced at him, I could see that he wasn't convinced. "Please, Grae. I really want to do this."

"Can you even do that—just take a baby home? On a whim?"

"I can arrange it." At least, I was pretty sure that I could. "A few weeks won't make any difference at all. We'll just postpone registering the birth until her parents are ready to take her back. It will mean her official birthdate is out a little but given the alternative they won't mind."

Grae shrugged and went back to his breakfast, while I drank my coffee in silence, thinking about how perfect this solution would be for absolutely everyone. There were still some hurdles, but they were minor—maybe Lilly and James would have to apply to the court for a marriage licence because of her age, but I'd be very happy to do a reference for them, and maybe I could even convince the Captain at the Salvation Army citadel to do one too.

My problems, and Lilly's, seemed so very serious that I forgot that there was a third set of issues in play here. It was only when Grae looked up at me a few minutes later that I thought again about his part in all of this. There was a strange mistiness to his eyes and an intensity in his expression that I wasn't sure how to interpret. He reached across the table and took my hand into his and said softly,

"Meg, everything in our life seems perfect to me... except... there's this gaping hole in our family where our kids should be. If you think this really is a step towards a family of our own, then go ahead and do it. I was hoping when we took this job... I mean, I just kind of knew that if you worked with adoption for a while you'd come around."

I wish he could have seen the anguish in Lilly's face when

the nurse walked out of the room with her baby, or some of the other residents I'd heard about—young women who needed to be sedated because they screamed for their children and disrupted the whole ward, or the miserable cases where a birth mother returned begging for her child, weeks after it was placed.

I wish he'd been in the room when I presented new adoptive parents with their baby son, only to hear the father panic about the hint of darkness in the child's skin. I wish he'd heard the sad police chief on the other end of the phone, ringing as a courtesy to advise us that a child we placed for adoption last year had passed away in suspicious circumstances.

I'd seen delighted parents too, and children who would no doubt go on to gloriously successful and contented futures. But the truth about our service was that our adoptive parents generally had to pass only two tests before we placed a child: were they white, and were they married? If the answer to both questions happened to be yes, then they could pretty much take their pick.

If Grae thought my experiences at the maternity home had warmed me at all towards the idea of adoption, then he could not have been more wrong.

I didn't say any of that to him, though. I might have, at an earlier point in our marriage, before the doctor told us in those careful tones that we would probably never have a baby, and that the problems were *all* mine.

I'd likely have argued with Grae about every step in our married life that year—about the arrogance of planning a move without my input, or the insensitivity of lining me up a job that would involve dealing with pregnancy all *day*, every *damned* day. I might have resigned without his blessing for the sake of my own sanity, instead of questioning myself again and again because I felt so sure that he somehow knew better.

But I did not argue with him, and I did not correct him. Instead, I reminded myself as I always did that I was lucky that he was bearing with me, in spite of my barrenness, in spite of all of the pain of our losses.

A lesser man would have walked out long ago.

So I smiled and squeezed his hand, and went about tidying the kitchen so that I could bring the new baby home to a clean house.

# CHAPTER TWENTY-SEVEN

Sabina

April 2012

We had leftovers for lunch. Looking at Lilly's packed fridge, I had a feeling she could serve up leftovers for weeks from the oversized meal she'd cooked us the day before. I didn't miss the way her face lit up when I asked for the pierogi. Ted and James were engrossed in discussions about the timing of harvests and the impact reduced rainfall in recent years was having. Lilly and I made small talk about the recipes she'd prepared.

"Time for a grandpa nap, I'm afraid," James yawned, when he'd finished eating. He stretched back in his seat as I'd seen him do several times the night before and rubbed his round tummy. "Did Lilly tell you we need to head into town tonight to meet the others?"

"Oh no, I forgot." Lilly sat up straight suddenly. "I hope you don't mind. Simon and Emmaline are trying to get into a routine with the twins, they asked if we could head into Orange instead of them coming all the way out here. We'll have dinner at the bistro, so they can be home early."

"Of course," I said. "That's no problem."

"I might take a nap too," Ted said suddenly, and to my surprise. "That sunshine this morning has tired me out. Do you mind?"

I shook my head, and accepted the kiss he brushed against my lips as he left the room.

"He reminds me of James," Lilly murmured. "I'm so glad

you found yourself a good one, Sabina. They aren't always easy to come by."

"He found me," I laughed softly, and automatically started packing up the plates from lunch.

"Leave the dishes. Let's go sit out on the veranda. Do you want to see some photos?"

I cleared my throat.

"I'd love to. And would you... like to see some of mine?"

—

I brought my box of albums in from the car and found Lilly on the veranda, resting on a swinging chair. We sat side by side, and she lifted the first album from the box.

"I keep everything," she murmured. "You could probably see from the house, I'm a bit of a hoarder."

"It's a beautiful house," I protested, but I knew what she meant. Mum and Dad had lead a streamlined life—everything had a place, or its place was in the bin.

"I just like to be prepared. I like to plan ahead, it makes me feel peaceful," Lilly explained quietly. "I think it comes from my Tata. He used to terrify me with stories of not having even the most basic supplies when he lived in Poland. He never could stand to see waste... I guess I'm the same these days," she rubbed her stomach and grimaced at me, "I know I shouldn't but I'd much sooner eat something than put it in the bin." Lilly opened the top album to a page of aged baby photos. "So you'll see, I've kept the silliest mementoes, and it's all a bit of a mess. You'll have to bear with me."

"Is that Simon?" There were several photos of Lilly and a tiny baby on the first page, and a few with James too. They had obviously been taken soon after the birth—she had that worn-out look of satisfied excitement that new mothers often wear. But there was also an unmistakeable sadness in her gaze as she stared down the barrel of the camera.

"Yep, this is my boy. Developing photos was so expensive back then but I didn't dare miss a moment." There was an extraordinary amount of photos—not by today's standards, now that it cost virtually nothing to take a dozen photos and pick out only the best; but Lilly had taken that same approach in the film age. The album held photo after photo of baby Simon, and I watched him grow in slow motion, as she flicked through page after page.

"So many photos of the three of us together," she murmured, running her finger over a candid shot of her, James and Simon. "I was so scared I'd lose him somehow and I wouldn't have a recent photo with him."

The pain in that simple statement gripped me. I stared at a page of photos of my family and although they were posed in a natural triad, I could almost see the space I should have filled.

"What year was he born?"

"We married in '75, a few weeks after my eighteenth birthday, and I had Simon at the end of that year. I thought if I had a baby I'd stop missing you quite so much. And Simon was a wonderful, beautiful baby, as you can see...but that was just lunacy. You don't ever stop missing your child." She brushed impatiently at the tears on her cheeks and turned to a new page. "Here's Charlotte, she was born the year after Simon. She has my sister's hair, these wild and crazy ringlets from the time she was a few months old...although you wouldn't know it these days. Charlotte is built like James, even now, she's taller and skinny as a rake. You were unlucky in *that* gene lottery." Lilly winked at me, but a wink through tear-filled eyes is not heartening at all. Impulsively, I slid my arm around her waist and leant against her. Lilly drew in a shuddering breath and returned my embrace. We stared down at the page together, at the photos of the siblings I'd never known.

"...after Charlotte, we decided that was enough kids," Lilly continued unevenly. "I'd have have had more, if I'd ever found a way to deal with the constant anxiety...but I never really did. I love being a mum, but it's still the most terrifying aspect of my life."

She turned to the back page of the album, and there was a single photo, on the only decorated page of the book. There was pink cardboard, and a lace frame, and right in the middle was a faded Polaroid. Lilly was holding a newborn tightly in her arms. Her shoulders were bare. I could see blood and bruises on her wrists and the back of her hand. She was white and gaunt and even in the slightly perished photo I could see the shadows under her eyes, but she was beaming. There was no sadness to the Lilly in this photo, only joy and pride.

"That's me, isn't it?" I whispered. Lilly squeezed my shoulders.

"That is one of my most prized possessions in the whole world. I have a copy in our safe, and a copy at my brother's in case there was a fire, and a laminated copy in my wallet. But I put the original into this book with the other newborn photos, so that no one could *ever* forget that you were a part of our family." Her voice broke.

Staring down at myself in that photo was eerie, recognising my own form in the arms of the woman who knew me before anyone else—but who was also somehow a stranger. I fought and lost a battle against tears, and when I looked down at the page, through my blurred vision Lilly really could have been me. Soon I'd be sitting up in a hospital bed holding a newborn, soon I'd be the one beaming into a camera with exhausted joy.

But that was where the parallels would end.

"Mrs. Baxter took that photo," Lilly whispered.

"Can you tell me... about what happened?"

"What do you want to know?"

It seemed that we'd arrived at the moment that I'd been longing for since I learned about Lilly's existence. We were neck-deep in a conversation that had no filters and no hesitation; the truth was within my grasp.

"I really don't know anything," I admitted. "Just that you were very young."

"I turned sixteen just a few weeks before I was confined," Lilly confirmed. "James had just gone off to university, and it took me a while to realise I was pregnant. And then Tata bundled me up and dumped me in the maternity home. Do you know much about those places?"

"Only what I read on Wikipedia."

"It was not a nice place, and they were not nice people." She was tensing, her breaths becoming shallow and hurried. "I've been going to a support group for the last few years, for other victims of the forced adoption era. I sit sometimes with the women to help them record their stories, but until I started on that project, I'd almost blanked the worst of it out. The pressure and the lies, and the endless days of back-breaking work—God, it would have been a nightmare for a healthy adult, but pregnant teenagers? It seems inhumane through modern eyes. Then to remove the babies like that..."

She shook her head and looked down at the photo in the album again.

"In my case, I really did have no choice about you, you know," she whispered. "I was only sixteen. Tata had signed the relinquishment paperwork when he admitted me there. I had no say at all, neither did James, or even James' parents. We all tried, in our way, but nothing worked and so they took you."

"M-mum took me?" I wasn't even sure if it was insensitive

for me to call her that, and I suddenly decided that from that moment on I'd refer to Mum as Megan.

Lilly looked up at me, and her brown eyes searched mine. "What *do* you know, Sabina?"

"Not enough," I whispered. "I barely know anything at all."

"You know that she was a social worker at the hospital?"

"Yes."

"There were two of them, her and her boss, Mrs. Sullivan. Mrs. Sullivan was a vile, cruel monster with a God-complex. But Mrs. Baxter—Megan..." Lilly released me gently, and then sat back in the chair and rubbed her eyes for a minute. When she'd finished, she looked to her lap, back to the photo album. "She was kind to me—at least, while I was a resident. She was wonderful, actually. I never could remember much of the labour, but I remember her coming in and acting as labour coach when things got really nasty toward the end. But it was more than that. She broke the rules for me, a lot. She's probably the only reason I made it out of there sane at all."

"But?"

"But she tricked me," Lilly said, and she started to cry, her voice rising and then breaking. She sounded like a broken little girl. "I can only assume that the k-kindness was an act, part of some cruel game that she decided she would play with me, God only knows why." Lilly fumbled in the pocket of her jeans and withdrew a tissue, but she only held it in her hand, playing with it almost nervously. "I've spent nearly forty years trying to f-figure it out and I just can't make sense of it even now."

"But how? *How* did she trick you?"

"It looked like it was all over, and that I'd lost you," Lilly explained slowly. She was fighting to keep her tears mild, I could see the way that she held it back, forcing a stilted rhythm to her voice. "I knew that you were going to be taken, and then you *were* taken. I saw you only for a second or two before the nurses took you out of the room, and as terrible as that is, that would have been the end of it."

Lilly's face crumpled and she drew in several terse breaths through her nose, before she glanced at me again and whispered,

"But Mrs. Baxter came back the next day, and she brought you to me, and she had come up with this marvellous plan that would allow us to keep you. She quit her job, and she took you home, and once we were married she was going to give you back. I'd always liked her, but for a while after that, she was my hero."

There was rising static in my ears, the buzzing of dread. I felt like she was describing the mother I'd always known—but I knew that what came next would reveal a side to Mum that I did not want to know, as much as I *needed* to.

"What went wrong, Lilly?" I whispered, when the silence began to stretch.

"I don't know," Lilly said. With the admission, sadness overwhelmed her, and she started to sob. "All I know is that after a few weeks, she rang me and told me she was keeping you."

# CHAPTER TWENTY-EIGHT

Megan

September 1973

Telling Lilly about my plan was easy. It was like playing God, actually; I was handing someone a miracle at the time when they needed it most. She was sobbing from the moment I walked into the room pushing the little trolley that contained her baby, and that was before I even told her the best part.

"Mrs. Baxter! Oh, Mrs. Baxter..." She sobbed and cradled her baby and tried to hug me all at the same time, and I gave her a brief embrace but then stepped away to organise the camera. I had borrowed it back from Tania on the way to the hospital, and while her joy was still fresh I took a single photo of Lilly with her daughter. The radiant sparkle in Lilly's brown eyes was almost breathtaking.

That was motherhood, right there, evolving before me. It was hope out of total despair. *That* was what I wanted for myself, but even more importantly, hope was the very thing that I went into social work to achieve. I felt a burst of pride that had been entirely missing from my life for five months.

"I can't promise this is all going to work," I felt I should add, and I saw her try to brace herself a little. "There's the matter of your wedding, Lilly. You'll have to find some way to arrange that, but maybe the lawyer James engaged should be able to help. I think that because you're sixteen a judge can give consent if your father won't, and I'd be very happy to provide a reference or two if that will help."

“Okay, yes—I will write James as soon as you leave.” Her voice was always just a little lyrical, but when Lilly was excited or upset, she spoke in a song. She’d explained to me that it was a technique she’d figured out to manage her stutter, but like a lot of Lilly’s quirks and features, I found it to be utterly charming. “And are you sure you can arrange all of this? Will you just bring her to work with you?”

I shook my head, and inhaled deeply, savouring the moment. “No, I won’t be working after today. I’m going to resign.”

“You are? But Mrs. Baxter, that’s—I am so happy for you, but so sad for the girls in the home.”

“It’s the right thing to do, Lilly. It’s just taken me a while to figure out how to go about it. Your little girl is helping me out, too. And speaking of which, what exactly are we calling her?”

Lilly drew a sharp intake of breath, and gave me such a look of wonder and joy that I actually laughed. “She’s *your* daughter. You really should name her.”

“I wanted to name her after my grandmother, Sabina,” Lilly whispered, then she flashed me a teary grin. “These are happy tears, Mrs. Baxter. I never thought... I never even dared to hope I’d get to give her a name. I can’t thank you enough.”

“Thank me when we pull this off, okay?” I said, as gently as I could. “We’ve still got a long way to go yet.”

I left her with my phone number and instructions to call me when she’d spoken with James, and in return I promised I’d arrange for one of the midwives to post her next letter to him in case I didn’t make it back in before she was discharged.

I took baby Sabina back to the nursery, and made my way down the long hallways back to my office. I walked slowly, giving myself plenty of time to change my mind. Once I resigned, there was no turning back.

But I knew that I’d never want to turn back. What I wanted

was to help people... starting with Lilly. I smiled to myself as I opened the office door. June was on the phone, talking to the parent of a prospective resident, and when she hung up she gave me a curious glance.

"You're looking a lot happier than I expected today. I didn't realise you were sick yesterday, I heard you'd been ill in the maternity ward."

"It was just—well, I went in to check on the birth and it was quite overwhelming, she had a very difficult time of it." I took a deep breath, and spread my hands wide. "The truth is, I have been doing quite a lot of soul searching... well, Graeme and I have together. And we've decided that we are ready to adopt. I know Liliana's baby doesn't have a placement yet. I think we'd make a good home for her."

In my time at the maternity home, I'd noticed that June had two entirely different personas. The June who raised terror in the hearts of the residents was cold and hard, and absolutely ruthless in her pursuit of what she deemed to be *the best thing* for the babies. When our office door was shut, June was warm and friendly, reasonably patient with my struggles to settle into my role, and quite motherly towards me once she learned about my fertility issues.

I held my breath when I finished speaking, but I needn't have worried. June's face lit up and she clasped her hands together in delight.

"That's absolutely marvellous news, Megan. Congratulations. I'm so sorry to lose you, but I was hoping that you'd make this decision for yourself sooner or later."

# CHAPTER TWENTY-NINE

## Sabina

### April 2012

Lilly had shifted, and now sat with one foot tucked up under her body, the other dangling over the edge to the veranda floor. She was rocking the chair slowly and gently, each swing landing almost in time with the soft hiccups and sobs that she was still making. I'd taken her hand in the moments of painful silence as she tried to compose herself, and our fingers were entwined against the cushion.

"I want you to understand that we'd already done everything we could do, and once she took you, there was nothing left to try. I really hope you believe me, Sabina. There was nothing at all that I could do. As crazy as it sounds, they had more of a right to you than I did."

I was lost in my own thoughts, and almost to myself I whispered,

"Why would she do such a thing?"

"I was hoping you could tell me that."

"She hasn't told me anything, Lilly. Not really. She just told me that what she did was unforgiveable."

"She's dead right about that," Lilly murmured, then she wiped her eyes and blew her nose, and sighed an exhausted sigh before she continued. "After that, there's a pause of thirty-eight years in our story, until that call from the adoption information office. But of course, I didn't just forget about you once she took you. My life *did* go on, in so many ways, but there was a huge part of me stuck in limbo wondering what the hell had happened to you and if you were okay. I went through periods—months at a time—when it was like the sunshine had been sucked completely from the earth, usually when spring came and I'd realise that we lost another year of your life. A few times, James dragged me to doctors and they'd give me medication until the depression lifted, but it always came back. I saw counsellors and even a psychiatrist for a while, and over the years, they've become more sympathetic…but in those early years, no one at all seemed to understand why losing you had broken me so badly."

"God, Lilly. I'm so sorry."

"The worst thing is the hate," she choked. There was a tortured wildness in her eyes, and it would have been quite unnerving if her story wasn't so harrowing. Her trauma was difficult to watch, but it was absolutely understandable. "I felt they'd swapped a perfect seed formed in love with this seething, writhing *hate* and anger in me. It tainted every part of my life at some point. I just don't understand why she had to play with me like that. I had already lost you—why dangle you in front of my nose like that, and then take you away again? It's never made any sense."

"I really wish that I could explain it to you."

For a minute we sat without speaking. I listened to the shuddering sobs that still came from Lilly periodically, but I was thinking about Mum. I was livid—angrier with Mum than I'd ever been, and I'd had some furious moments over those recent weeks. But intermingled with that was a memory of the terror I'd felt when I first learned about her miscarriages, and how scared I'd been for my baby. I couldn't even begin to fathom what suffering through that, over and over again, would do to a person's mind.

Was it possible that something in Mum had just *broken*? I'd never seen her so unhinged as I had that day when she told me about her miscarriages. Had it just been too much, caring for a newborn when she'd wanted her own child so badly? I wondered if she'd thought about the chaos her decision would wreak, or if she'd acted purely on impulse. I could almost imagine her holding me, staring down at me with love and absolute adoration, and struggling with the knowledge that she would have to hand me back when she could so easily just keep me, and no one would ever know.

Or had it really been more sinister than that, as Lilly suspected? Had Mum planned it this way all along?

As soon as the thought crossed my mind, I battled with an automatic reflex to dismiss it. I wasn't sure I would ever believe that Mum would have made the choices she'd made out of malice. I wanted to hate her. I *was* still angry with her. But in spite of all of that, if I had ever known her at all, Mum was *not* the kind of person who would deliberately cause pain.

"So—it's your turn to talk...why did you find me now, Sabina?" Lilly asked. The softness returned, just a little. "After all these years, why were you ready now?"

"Oh..." I winced, and shook my head. "No, Lilly—I only just found out. About the adoption, I mean."

Lilly gasped, and then covered her mouth with her hand.

"They didn't even tell you?"

"No, they didn't. It all kind of erupted when I told them I'm pregnant," I said. "I don't think they intended telling me. They said they thought it would be easier on me if I didn't know."

She turned to stare out at the empty paddocks around her home. We sat in stillness for a while, as she digested this information, and then she turned to me and said flatly,

"The cruelty is just mindboggling. I registered with the agency so that you could find me the day that you became an adult. I literally waited by the phone for a few weeks after your birthday, I was so sure you'd call. And you didn't even know I existed?"

"I didn't even suspect," I admitted. I thought about Mum again, and I shivered a little. Regardless of how the adoption had come about, there was *no* avoiding the fact that she'd hidden it from me.

"But—didn't you get your birth certificate? How did you get a licence, or a job?"

"It lists them as my parents, it was forged somehow. Hilary told me it happened sometimes at those places..."

"I'm not even on your *birth certificate*?" she spoke with a wild panic, a desperate devastation in her eyes that just about broke my heart. I started to cry too then, as I shook my head. "They erased me. All of this time I thought you might be angry with me or blame me, but it's even worse than that. You didn't even know about me."

"I know about you now," I whispered.

"She has to pay, Sabina." Lilly was shaking now. "It can't be legal, what they've done. She just has to pay."

"Pay?" I repeated, and I couldn't contain my alarm. "But, Lilly..."

"The system was broken and messed up and treated us girls like disposable incubators. That's one thing, but this is another altogether. It was never legal to forge birth records. Do you have a copy of the certificate? We could go to the police. We have to do something—she can't just get away with this."

"Lilly—I d-don't know about that." Her panic was confusing, and I started to panic too. She was right, of course, Mum probably had broken the law if my birth certificate had indeed been forged. But that wasn't the whole picture. There were decades of love and laughter between *that* decision and *this* discussion. How on earth could I explain that to Lilly though, with that wild hate in her eyes, and the pain in her voice?

Surely Lilly was entitled to her vengeance. It looked very much like Mum had done a terrible, unforgivable thing to this woman, and maybe reporting her to the police would give Lilly some peace.

But... this was my mum we were discussing.

As angry as I was with Mum and Dad—and I *was* still furious—I was always going to be loyal to them, at least to some degree. Maybe I'd grow to really hate them, and maybe what they'd done really *was* unforgivable, but I could never forget the happy times. Could one side of the equation balance out the other, or was I destined to live with the ambiguity forever?

"Becoming a parent forces you to be selfless," Lilly whispered. She gestured towards my stomach. "You learn to adjust to a new reality where you're no longer your own first priority... you'll see all of this for yourself in a few months. Even if I ignore what they did to me and James, I can't fathom a parent deciding again and again to lie to a child about who they really were." Her voice rose again and then she broke off suddenly. She turned to me and finished flatly, "You must hate them too, surely?"

"I'm confused, Lilly," I admitted. "I'm so bloody confused I can barely even make myself a cup of tea these days." I cleared my throat again and picked at a piece of lint on my jeans so that I could avoid the distress on Lilly's face while I replied. "It's hard to believe now and I know this is probably going to be awful to hear but... but they were brilliant p-parents. I had the best upbringing a child could imagine—there was no hint of this darkness swirling around beneath it all. The first glimpse I got of that was when they told me about the adoption and it felt like it came out of nowhere. Wait until you see these albums... you'll see a childhood that could have been out of a storybook."

I stared at my thigh and waited for her to speak until the moment stretched just a little too long, and I finally found the courage to look at Lilly's face again. She was still staring at me, but it was like my confused statements had deflated her rage somehow. Now there was only confusion and hurt on her face. I wanted to say more—to explain more—but it felt like I'd run out of words. Instead, I offered her an apologetic half-shrug, and she sighed—a long, slow sigh, and turned away from me a little to face out towards the paddocks again. After another minute or two, the gentle rocking of the swing started up again, and she pulled me close for another hug.

Mum had dished out many motherly hugs in my time, but once I was an adult, we didn't really have much reason to touch. Lilly, on the other hand, seemed to offer a hug me every five minutes. She was just so different to Mum—softer, warmer, more passionate. More like me. I resolved then and there to become a woman and a mother who hugged. There was something so generous about the gesture.

"I planned it all out for when I met you," she said softly. "I kept my plans up to date, too. So when you were a kid, I pictured activities we'd do—colouring in, or going to the park... then when you were a teenager, we were going to go shopping or talk about boys... then when you were in your twenties, I planned to show you my photo albums—all of them one by one—then I'd talk to you about your plans for your life. And we're here now, doing all of the things I planned to do with you if we reunited when you were in your thirties... but I just never thought about the loudness of all of the emotion, you know... actually having you here with me." She sighed and rested her head against mine. "It's so full on, isn't it? And I never really stopped to think about the tension. I see the way you're looking at me, with just a little wariness in your eyes... I guess you don't know *me* at all. But I held on to the memory of you so tightly that it's like you've been here with me the whole time, and you are exactly as I'd expected and hoped...even if this meeting is even more difficult than I'd anticipated."

"I'm sorry, Lilly." I sat up and shrugged helplessly. "I can't imagine what this is like for you. If it's any consolation, I think you're wonderful, and I'm so, so glad that I've found you."

"Me too, Sabina. Why don't you show me these photos, hey?"

I opened the first one across our laps. Lilly stared down at the first page of photos.

"Oh, look at you," she whispered around a sob. She reached down and touched an image with her fingertip. "You were p-perfect."

She helped herself to the album then, lifting it onto her own lap as if it was actually my newborn body. I watched the emotions play out across her face as she looked from image to image. She touched each photo and let the pad of her finger linger on each word of each description. *Sabina, trying to roll over, January 1974. Sabina, sitting up, April 1974. Sabina, eating pears, April 1974.*

"Are they all like this?" Lilly asked me. "They're so organised."

"Pretty much," I said. "There are photos right up to my birthday this year in the newer albums. And...if you want them, you can keep them."

Lilly glanced at me and frowned.

"Are you sure? Don't you want them?"

"Mum has her own set," I whispered. "She made these for *you*."

Lilly froze. Her foot dragged limply against the deck as the echoing movements of the swing faded away. She had been staring at me, but now her gaze sank towards the ground, and her shoulders crumpled forward, and then a shudder ran through her as if I'd slapped her. She shook her head, then pressed her hand to her mouth. There was sheer wildness to Lilly's eyes for an instant, and I thought she was going to get up and leave, or worse still, to lose it completely all over again. In the split seconds after silence fell, I wondered if I should have waited to bring the albums out.

I rested my hand on her arm, trying to placate her.

"I'm sorry, Lilly. I really…I'm just so sorry."

She started crying again, just like she had when I arrived the night before; great, heaving sobs that originated somewhere in the core of her.

"I just wonder what she thinks about these," Lilly said, between sobs. "Does she think this makes everything okay?"

"I doubt it," I murmured, thinking of the guilt on Mum's face the day that she brought the albums to our house.

"It's a beautiful gesture. I'll look at these over and over again, you know. I'll memorise them, eventually I'll know them off by heart." Lilly wiped her cheeks and her nose. "But these weren't her moments to catalogue. As generous as she is to share them, they belonged to *me* in the first place."

# CHAPTER THIRTY

## Megan

## September 1973

I barely even looked at Sabina until I had her in my house.

As awful as it sounds, *she* was almost an afterthought. After all, she wasn't my baby. I was just minding her for a few weeks, a minor favour—a good deed for a friend. It was only when I found myself completely alone with her that I actually thought about what that would mean.

The midwives had loaned me a bassinet, and provided me with one of the little care packs they sent home with the new adoptive parents. There was formula and nappy cream and nappies, and I felt reasonably confident that I knew what to do with all of the supplies.

My calm went right out the window when I found myself standing in my own kitchen looking down at her. Responsibility rushed in at me, and it was instantly overwhelming.

She was lying on her back in the bassinette, with her little fists balled up beside her cheeks. The striped hospital blanket was tucked tightly around her, right up to her chin, where a purple bruise had formed after her birth. On either side of her head I could see the two deep scratches from the forceps that had assisted her delivery. She made a whistling sound when she breathed out.

It suddenly occurred to me that I had to keep this tiny bundle of humanity alive for several weeks at least, and a cold terror gripped me. The nurses had said she'd need a bottle, when was that? Would she cry? How would I know when she needed a nappy changed, or if she was sick? Would she sleep enough? Would I become too attached and find it impossible to hand her back when the time came? How would I protect myself against that? How would I protect Graeme?

I waited. I held my breath and braced myself for the adorable *newness* of her to grab at me. I loved babies... everyone loves babies, and in spite of her minor birth injuries, Sabina was beautiful from her very first hours. I had braced myself hard, but I needn't have. I felt no automatic emotional response whatsoever to Sabina as she lay there in my kitchen.

After a few minutes, I gently pushed the bassinet right to the middle of the table, and I went to make myself a cup of tea. No swell of emotion had risen, no resurgence of the desperate tide of longing for a baby of my own, and I suddenly acknowledged that *this* was what had scared me most about adoption. Surely for biological mothers there is some hormonal assistance in the bonding, and I knew that I would need that. I've never been an emotional person, certainly not an overly affectionate person, and my work had by then well and truly trained me to hold myself at arm's length even from highly emotive situations. I knew instinctively that even had Sabina been coming home forever with us, I'd have felt no different. I just wasn't programmed to parent someone else's child.

So I made my tea, and I sat beside the bassinet to drink it, then I read the instructions on the formula tin as I waited for her to wake up.

As I sipped my tea, I decided quite calmly that I would run these weeks with Sabina by the clock, with all of her necessary physical needs attended to in a timely fashion, and nothing more. There would be no pretence that I was parenting her, and certainly no fooling myself that this was any kind of trial for a real adoption. I was merely a baby-care nurse, here to do a job. That was a *much* smarter way to approach the situation anyway, rather than to be motivated by some hysterical emotion or desperation for my own baby, particularly given that I would have to pass her back to Lilly when she was ready.

I was going to pretend to be Sabina's attendant, not her mother. And as long as that was all that I expected of myself, we'd all come through this strange period in our lives unscathed.

I looked to the baby again, and then I sat back in my chair and let a grin cover my face. I felt proud and quite satisfied with my own cleverness—how, in just twenty-four hours, I'd completely turned things around for myself, and for Lilly and James.

Finally, I was back in a role I was comfortable with—helping people, supporting families, making a difference.

And maybe now that I was doing good again, life would be kind to me too, and my own family would be just around the corner.

# CHAPTER THIRTY-ONE

## Sabina

## April 2012

When Lilly was upset or anxious, she gravitated to the kitchen. We left the albums on the veranda and moved inside after a while, and I sat at the breakfast bar while she made tea and served us both some cake. We talked about the cake recipe to an unnatural level of detail. Lilly told me what brand of flour she used and how important it was to ensure the eggs were at room temperature. I asked her whether her oven was fan-assisted and what kind of cake tins she used. Every time the cake conversation seemed to stall, one of us would force a continuation—anything to avoid returning to the veranda, and the photo albums, and the confusion and the pain.

When the last of the cake was gone, and I felt like I was bursting at the seams from her giant portions, James wandered out from the bedroom.

"Cake? After *that* lunch?" he surmised, then grinned. "You're fitting right in already, Sabina."

I smiled at him and watched as he walked directly to Lilly. He seemed to review the expression on her face for a moment, then he suddenly embraced her.

"Can I get you a tea?" she asked him, but she was watching me over his shoulder.

"No, no—but thank you, my darling," he murmured, and then I heard him whisper, "Are you okay? You've been crying."

"It's just hard," she whispered back. "It's wonderful, but it's so hard."

I swallowed the lump in my throat. James turned back to me, but kept his arm around Lilly's waist. There was a twinkle in his eye, and I could tell he was going to make a joke to break the tension.

I suddenly realised why I'd never been able to keep a secret. Lilly and James were people who wore their every thought right there on their faces, and Megan and Grae had drilled into me the importance of honesty. I didn't stand a chance.

"What were you two ladies going to do next?" The twinkle in his eye grew bolder. "Do you want to see the crop where we're growing genetically modified—"

"James, *no,*" Lilly laughed, and she thumped him playfully. "*No more* farming chat. You'll scare Sabina away forever. I was just about to show her our wedding album. Did you want to sit outside with us?"

"I'd love to," James said, then he winked at me. "But if you *do* want farming chat, Sabina…you just say the word, okay?"

His presence was a comfort, even to me, because just by entering the room he'd shattered a lingering sense of tension from the discussions Lilly and I had been sharing. It was a very different conversation over the next few hours. Ted joined us after a while, and he and James sat on the step among all of the little concrete animals. Lilly and I stayed on the swinging chair, but now, she showed me photos of her wedding to James, and then we worked our way through all of the books of photos of Simon and Charlotte as children. We giggled together at dated hairstyles and outfits, and in a roundabout way I started to get to know my siblings.

I almost would have enjoyed myself, except for the heavy cloud that seemed to be hanging over my head. I wanted to enjoy the time with Lilly and this more casual trip down memory lane, but at the same time, I wanted to jump back into my car and drive to Mum's house. I wanted to corner her and to refuse to leave until she told me why she had kept me, rather than returning me to Lilly as she'd promised.

Everything seemed to hang on that decision, because *that* was the decision that created the lives that we'd all lived ever since. I needed to understand, and I could only hope that if Mum could explain herself it would go a way towards soothing the ache and anger in Lilly.

But in the meantime, I was there at the farm with my other family, and it was nearly time to meet my new siblings. As I dressed for dinner, I tried to steady myself and brighten my frame of mind. I desperately wanted to be positive at dinner—I needed Simon and Charlotte to like me.

When it was time to drive into Orange to meet them, James opened the garage to reveal his other car.

"We don't drive this one around the paddocks," he winked at Ted, and Ted laughed.

"I'll bet you don't. She's a beauty."

It was a dark grey, late model Mercedes, obviously lovingly maintained by James, who ran his hand along the roof as if he was caressing it. Lilly made sure that I could see her face, then rolled her eyes and slipped into the back seat.

"Oh no, you take the front," I protested, but she shook her head, closed the door with a slam and pointed to the front passenger's side. I reluctantly slid in, and Ted joined Lilly in the back.

"I want to chat with this handsome husband of yours. Besides which, someone is going to have to listen to James prattle on about the wonder car and I've heard it plenty of times already."

"She loves it too," James assured me, as he gingerly pointed the car towards the driveway. "We bought this car after a particularly bumper crop a few years ago."

And he did *prattle on*, as Lilly had said. He described to me in great detail all of the information about that model of car that I could ever have wanted to know, and I noticed myself drift off into my thoughts. I was thinking about James, and Lilly, and how wonderful their relationship was. The playful teasing, the open affection, the patience with one another... it all reminded me of my own marriage, and I was so glad for them that they'd not only made it work, but they'd built a lifetime together.

It was impossible to avoid comparing them to Mum and Dad. I felt fairly sure that my parents loved each other; they were sometimes affectionate and generally kind to one another. But in the brief period of time since learning about the adoption, I'd become so aware of what *wasn't* there in their relationship. There was no great sense of partnership, unlike Lilly and James, or even Ted and me. There was Dad, leading the ship, and Mum at the rear, propelling the thing. And that's how it had always been. Perhaps that was even part of what I had loved about Ted, that from the outset of our relationship, he wasn't looking for an accessory—he wanted a partner.

James was still talking about the car. Ted and Lilly were chatting about her school. And I suddenly started to wonder about Mum, and whether or not she was aware of how harsh Dad could be with her at times. I remembered him refusing her permission to join me when I visited the adoption information social workers, refusing to even allow her a voice, and I felt a pang of concern for her. Why did my intelligent, headstrong mother *put up* with that?

I hadn't really missed her until that moment. I had been so angry with her for keeping so many secrets, and then for making it so difficult to find out the truth about myself. Now, I wondered what else I was missing in all of this. How much of the structure of this lie had been my father's doing? Why was I so angry with Mum, when I'd finally seen for myself that she was sometimes only his pawn?

I wanted to call Mum and check in with her and make sure she was okay. She would be suffering terribly, and I knew she'd be fretting for me. And then I wanted to ask to speak to Dad, and to demand he explain himself and apologise, and just do better. Dad was a good man, I was sure of that. He had been a wonderful father to me, and I counted him as one of my best friends, so much so that I'd viewed him through a set of heavily tinted rose-coloured glasses for most of my life.

"Hey, Sabina, we're running a bit early—want to see where you were born?" James asked, and I froze, then turned back to Lilly, expecting to see horror on her face. She smiled a little, and shook her head.

"Its fine, Sabina, I was going to offer to take you past at some point too. I've been there plenty of times since, I've made my peace with that place."

"Are you sure? It seems like a lot to ask."

"I had Charlotte at the same hospital. There were some minor complications and I was transferred there from the little hospital over at Molong. But your birth was so difficult, so I always knew there was a possibility that things would be complicated and I'd have to come over to the Base hospital here. I'd prepared myself as well as I could." She snorted suddenly and then shot me a mischievous grin. "It helps that they built a whole new hospital and the old one is now a dilapidated shithole. It's hard to feel haunted by a place that looks like it would fall over if the wind blew too hard."

A few minutes later, James brought the car to a stop outside of the red brick building I recognised from the Wikipedia page. Lilly was right—it was totally derelict, the downstairs entrances were boarded up with particle board. The top floor looked like a ghoulish mouth—the entire line of windows damaged in some way; panes of fractured glass in a row like a macabre set of damaged teeth. Lilly stepped from the car without preamble and immediately walked over to a temporary security fence, then leant against it to peer inside.

I turned to James.

"Are you *sure* this is okay? It must be very difficult for you guys."

"We both have awful, awful memories of this place," James said with a sigh. "I got dragged out of here by security when Lilly was confined. She was here for months, and there was nothing I could do about it—and believe me, I tried. Lilly's dad had made sure that she was never leaving this place with you. So no, it's not pleasant to be here...but..." He nodded towards Lilly. "One of the remarkable things about my wife is that she never shies away from her past, no matter how ugly it is. She has this theory that you only kill the demons by bringing them to light. That's why we told the other kids about you as soon as they were old enough to understand. I'll be honest with you Sabina, she's walked through some very dark times over the years...but she has *always* spoken about you with me. We grieved every birthday and we missed you every Christmas, but if I happened to forget to honour you on some important occasion, she'd make sure I knew about it."

It was hard to believe that I hadn't known somehow about these wonderful people who had obviously held me so close to their hearts. I felt like their love for me was big enough that I should have felt it somehow, even across the vast distance of my not knowing about them at all. For a moment, I felt almost guilty at *not* having guessed, and although I tried to dismiss this thought, it was difficult to move past.

"Thank you, James," I murmured, then slipped from the car and joined Lilly where she had been waiting at the security fence.

"That was my room," she murmured, pointing to a window on the second floor. "That one right there, where both panes of glass have shattered."

"Was I born in there?"

"Oh no, the maternity ward is across the road, in the main hospital. But I lived in this home for several months before you were born, right from when my Tata found out about you."

We stared at the building in silence for several moments. Lilly silently slid her arm around my shoulders and pulled me close. There was a gentle wind blowing, just enough to rattle some of the windows. Dusk was falling; the light was fading fast. I had a feeling there would be some very vocal ghosts around this place after dark.

"Did you make friends with the other girls?" I tried to imagine what it was like for her, living in this near-prison with twenty other teenagers.

"Not really. My roommate was a strange kind of friend—although I didn't think of her like that at the time. She was an angry, angry young woman when we were in here," she smiled sadly. "She's actually the only one I'm still in touch with. I ran into her at the shops maybe ten years ago and we've become quite close."

"Has she found her child?"

"No. Well, she found him. But he doesn't want to know her."

"Oh..."

I wasn't sure how to respond to that, but after a minute, Lilly seemed to decide that she needed to elaborate.

"Her name is Tania. We don't know very much about her son at all, but it sounds like he wasn't placed with a great family and he's pretty messed up. Tania hopes that one day he'll be ready to reunite properly, but who knows if it'll ever happen. She's actually on the town council these days, and she runs a welfare agency, *and* she has formed a support group for other girls from rural homes like this one."

"She sounds amazing."

"She is," Lilly said. "Amazing and damaged, just like the rest of us in that support group. But at least we're not broken, and plenty of the girls who came through here were."

"Why haven't they demolished this place?"

"I think they will soon. And on that day..." She released me and linked her fingers through the chain again. "...I'm going to come here with my sledge hammer and do my part. See that door over there?" I looked to the wide front doors, now sealed up with chipboard. "They locked us in at night. Right on the dot of 10 p.m. a nurse would double deadlock that door. There were girls who tried to escape, but the police always brought them back. We were prisoners here, locked away to be punished for our crimes. There were physical locks, and procedural locks... but the worst part was the emotional lock. You can trap a person quite easily if you convince them they're unworthy of escape." Lilly sighed and rested her forehead against the chainlink, then glanced back at me. "Tania and I tried to get out once, just before you were born. It was years before I told even James about it, I felt too embarrassed because we failed almost immediately. We snuck out of bed after the nurses had done the head count for the night, but we only made it as far as the fire exit. The door was alarmed, we didn't even make it out of the building." Her face fell again and she stopped, her breathing laboured as she battled against the tears. "I tried, love. Between James and me, we tried *everything* to find a way to keep you."

"I believe you, Lilly," I whispered. "I can see how badly you wanted that."

"You know, I always thought of those months as the worst of my life...but I *do* have happy memories of my time here. I remember what it felt like to first fall in love with you, and how exciting those early weeks were when I was so sure that James was coming to take us both home. I'd been pretending I wasn't pregnant until they admitted me here, and then there was this period where I finally acknowledged to myself that I was going to be a mum and I still thought James would find a way to get us out." Lilly offered me a sad smile. "I was such an optimist back then."

"And...Megan..." I saw the way she tensed when I said Mum's name, but I desperately wanted to hear something positive about her, and I pressed on. "You were saying she was kind to you? When you were in here, I mean."

"Oh, yes. I have memories of her too when I was confined," Lilly whispered. "In fact just about any positive thing that happened inside of these walls involved Mrs. Baxter, and *all* of that is tainted now by what came after. She used to come and take me for walks so that I could get some fresh air, and she broke so many rules for me. Without Mrs. Baxter, James wouldn't have even known I was pregnant until after I was released. It was winter when I was here, freezing just like this all of the time, and she got me new clothes and an extra blanket, and one day she took me for a hot chocolate in the hospital cafeteria. She was kind, Sabina, but that's almost worse. Now I ask myself...was it her plan all along? I just wish I knew...I wish I understood what it was about *me* that made her do what she's done. Did I invite it somehow?"

# CHAPTER THIRTY-TWO

## Megan

## September 1973

When I heard the crunch of tyres on the gravel driveway just after noon, I was confused, and for a split second, a little paranoid. I did a quick mental check of my situation. Had I broken the law—were the police coming for me already?

But, no—although I felt a little guilty, the truth was that I'd not done a single thing wrong. I walked to the kitchen window and was relieved, and a little amused at myself, when I recognised Grae's car outside. I greeted him at the door with baby Sabina in my arms, and as he stepped out of his car, he paused and stared at us.

"Well," he said. "Isn't this just a sight? It suits you, Megan."

There was a softness to his voice and his expression, and a depth of longing that I recognised with a distinct sense of discomfort.

"Just practicing for when it's our turn," I said, the words higher and thinner than I'd anticipated. Grae brushed a kiss over my cheek, and when I moved to step out of the doorway to make room for him, he gently caught my elbow and steadied me, then stepped back to stare at me again.

"What are you—"

"Just let me savour this for a moment, Meg," he said, and when I shot him a look of pure impatience, he ignored it. He stared at me while he inhaled slowly, and a grin gradually spread over and transformed his face. I'd always felt, on some level, that Grae was just a little too good for me . . . just a bit too handsome, a bit too charming, a bit too clever. He'd aged rapidly over the last few years, but watching that smile transform his face I was startled to realise that the tension and wear faded away as he stared at me with the baby. "Let's go inside so I can take a look at her."

"I'll put her in the bassinet and make you some lunch," I said, but Grae shook his head.

"No, let me have a hold first." He extended his arms towards me, and I awkwardly passed him Sabina's sleeping form. She sat much more naturally in his arms, and he peered down at her with an expression of pure wonder. "My God, she's *adorable*."

"She's a baby," I said, and that same stiffness was in my voice. "They all look pretty much the same. Besides . . . you won't think she's so adorable tonight when she wants milk."

"Don't listen to cranky Meg, I'll get up to you," Grae whispered, and he reached down with a forefinger to gently touch her cheek. "What's her name?"

"Sabina."

"*Sabina*," he repeated softly. "What a beautiful name. It suits her perfectly."

I didn't want to see him with that gleam in his eye, or the joy on his face as he nursed the tiny child. I busied myself with some bread and deli meat from the fridge.

"So it went well at the hospital?" Grae asked.

"As well as could be expected. June was disappointed."

"Did she mention any chance of you coming back after we finish with the baby?"

I cleared my throat and shook my head.

"No, they'll have replaced me by then . . . I'll find something else, I told you that."

"I know. I was just asking." Sabina squirmed and gave a tiny grunt, and Grae effortlessly shifted her up to his shoulder and began to rub her back. "What stuff do we need to buy?"

"The hospital gave me most of it. I think we need more clothes, and some nappies and formula at some point. But I borrowed the bassinette from the hospital, so we don't really need anything else in the way of furniture."

Sabina grunted again, and I glanced back in time to see her give an almighty vomit down Grae's back. Shock registered on his face, then he winced and gingerly lowered her back into a reclining position against his forearm. I stared at him in wide-eyed shock.

"That feels like a lot of vomit," he said, then grimaced. "A *lot* of vomit. How much formula did you give her?"

"A whole bottle. She must have been so thirsty."

"Meg, I'm pretty sure new babies don't need that much milk."

"They don't?"

"No, they don't."

"How do *you* know that?"

"I was the oldest, remember. Mum fed Gilly with a bottle and I was twelve when she was born. I'm pretty sure it was no more than a few teaspoons at a time for the first few days."

"But...she kept drinking..."

"Maybe you should just call the ward, and get some tips," Grae suggested, quite gently. "I don't mind if she wants to vomit on me, but I don't want her to be uncomfortable if her tummy is too full."

So my first test of quasi-motherhood, something as simple as feeding Sabina a single bottle of milk, appeared to have been a complete failure. I ironed Grae a fresh shirt and trousers, while he held Sabina and ate his lunch, as if it was no big deal at all to him to be eating and nursing a newborn while his back was drenched in sick. Afterwards, he passed her back to me so I could change her jumpsuit, but in the time it took him to change his entire outfit I'd struggled to even get Sabina out of hers. Grae stepped in, and made it look like a simple operation. I hadn't realised how floppy new babies are, or how difficult it was to push limp limbs in and out of clothes.

"Don't worry, Sabina, you're in good hands…with me," Grae said, and he shot a wink my way.

"Lucky it's only for a few weeks," I muttered. I scooped the pile of messy clothing up carefully into my arms.

"Ah, you'll be a pro by then. You won't want to give her back." Grae rested Sabina back into the bassinet. "I better get back to work. I'll bring some formula and nappies home tonight to save you taking her out to the shops. You'll call the ward and check about how much milk next time?"

"They should have told me that when I picked her up."

"We've got lots to learn. But it's all good practice, right?" Grae grinned at me, then chased me across the room to swoop me into his arms. I dropped the soiled clothing and squealed as he dipped me backwards. My squeal faded into confused shock as he bent to kiss me tenderly.

"Grae!" I protested, and I pushed him away—after a moment or two. "What's gotten into you!?"

"I just think this is going to be *really* good for us," he said, and then he straightened his tie, planted a much more sedate kiss on my cheek, and headed for the door with a whistle.

# CHAPTER THIRTY-THREE

## Sabina

### April 2012

The sun was now completely behind the building and we were standing in shade. It was bitterly cold, and I wrapped my arms around myself and tried to stifle my automatic shiver.

"Their office was about here," Lilly said. She'd led the way along the street, to more boarded-up windows at the side of the building. "The social workers, I mean. Us girls didn't get to go in there much, I only saw the inside once or twice when I was down at the nurses station and the door was left open. But I know that there was always paperwork and folders stacked up, almost to the roof. I know now from the support group I'm in that Mrs. Sullivan was here for years and she did a terrible job with the paperwork. Dozens and dozens of families torn apart, with no proper paper trail between them so no hope of bringing them back together. I don't know what became of her and I hate to wish evil on another human being but..." Lilly let the words trail off, and she didn't need to finish the sentence. She cleared her throat then looped her arm through mine and almost dragged me around the corner. "That was the window to the kitchen. Behind it was the dining room, and a little rec room where we could watch television for a few hours at night. I didn't often go in there, mostly I stayed in my room and read books, but sometimes when I missed my siblings I'd sit in that room and try to pretend I was at home."

We crossed the road now, towards the main hospital. Its

footprint was an entire block, but it comprised a misshapen conglomeration of buildings in various materials and sizes. The tallest section was three storeys high, but all around it and clearly over many decades additions had been made. I glanced back to the car and saw that James was hanging back at a distance, but slowly following us.

"What did you do when you left?" I asked Lilly.

"I went home," Lilly whispered. "I didn't want to. I didn't have any choice. I stayed with my parents until I turned eighteen, and then as soon as I was an adult, I packed the same bag I took to the hospital with you and I walked across the paddocks and told Ralph and Jean that I was never going home."

"Ralph and Jean?"

"James' parents. They took me in, and James came home, and we married a few weeks later. I moved to Armidale with him while he finished his degree, and by then we had Simon so we all came back here to the farm. And you know the rest."

She stopped again, at the fences around the main building. It was getting dark rapidly now and it was difficult for me to see what she was pointing at.

"That was the entrance to the laundry. I spent all day, every day in there, except Sunday mornings when we walked to that damned church. And around here is the maternity ward..."

The doors and windows were now boarded up like the maternity home, with layers of weather-warped particle board. I was sure the effort to seal the building was to keep people *out*, but it looked a whole lot like someone was trying to trap the stain of the memories contained inside.

"The first time I heard your heartbeat was in a room just here," Lilly whispered. "I thought you were a boy, actually, and then I heard the sound of your heart and I just knew. Do you have a feeling what your baby's sex is?"

I shook my head.

"Not yet, anyway."

"I didn't with the other two, just with you. I never saw you on the ultrasound but I heard them talking about you and I knew you were healthy. That was early, just a month or two after I came here, and I thought I'd be able to keep you then if I just refused to sign you over. I was upset that day because they'd embarrassed me when they were doing the examination, but I remember having this gut feeling that you were a girl and I decided that if James would agree to it, I'd name you after my grandmother."

"You did mention her name last night but I've forgotten how you said it."

"*Sabinka*," Lilly murmured. "My father rarely spoke about his family, he lost most of them in the war and he was terribly traumatised by it—although, of course he'd never have admitted that. The one story he used to tell us was about one of his birthdays during the war. They were just barely surviving on rations at the time, and of course there were no gifts to be had. He was working in the fields with his brother and when he came home his mother had made them a huge feast of pierogis. He told me they were the best tasting pierogi he'd ever eaten, in *all* of his life...that even in all of the years since and with all of the prosperity here in Australia, he'd never tasted anything so good. He said that she'd made something magical for him out of absolutely nothing." Lilly finally seemed to acknowledge the cold, pulling her coat tighter around herself and digging her hands deep into her pockets. "I wanted to give you her name...partly because I thought it might appease Tata, I suppose, but mostly because that story was such a strength to me. Actually, it has been for my whole life. We come from a line of women who could make something out of nothing. That's worth remembering, isn't it?"

"Absolutely," I said softly. There was a flash of light behind us and I saw James bringing the car up close. We both turned around and he flashed the lights and waved to us.

"He's probably worrying that I'm going to freeze you half to death out here in the cold," Lilly murmured. "Are you okay?"

"I'm fine," I said. Although I was very much looking forward to returning to the heated car, I wouldn't have cut those moments short for anything. Even before I knew about Lilly herself, I'd dreamt of a visit to Orange to hear about my own birth. Even before I understood just how complicated things really were, I'd *always* wanted to better understand my origins.

"Just a few more minutes and we'd better go back to them. Just through there were the delivery rooms, and you were born in room one. There was a window in that room, and it led out to a courtyard in the centre of the hospital where a plum tree was growing. There were these tiny, beautiful little flower buds on the tree... I stared out at it while I was in labour, whenever I could manage to keep my eyes open. I thought it meant that spring really was on its way, some secret sign from the universe that things were going to be okay after all." Her voice started to waver, and she cleared her throat several times before she continued, "I kept worrying about this poor woman I could hear—she was screaming for help, but no one seemed to be coming for her and she sounded so desperate and in such pain. Then, as each dose of whatever they were drugging me would wear off, I'd realise that *I* had been the one screaming all along."

"Oh, Lilly..."

"I'd always wanted to study history, but after what happened with you... I was more determined than ever, and I didn't care how long it took. I didn't realise how widespread this kind of thing was at the time, or even how wrong it was... I don't think any of us did. But I wanted to be a person who brought history to the next generation, because if we don't learn about our history, how can we learn from it? And we have to learn from it, Sabina. We can't let these things ever happen again. We just can't."

"It wasn't fair," I choked. The thought of what Lilly had been through was almost overwhelming, even just hearing her recount it second-hand. I realised that at some point during the conversation I'd withdrawn my hands from the sleeves of my coat and had wrapped them tightly around my stomach and I knew that the gesture was not just a result of the cold. I almost felt guilty at my own fortune—to be born just late enough in history that such experiences were unthinkable, rather than the standard.

"Life isn't fair," she whispered. "But that doesn't mean it has to be cruel." She pulled her hands out of her pockets now and pulled me close for another hug. It occurred to me that in twenty-four hours, Lilly had given me more hugs than Mum had in my adult life. "I want you to know, Sabina—I don't feel any shame about what happened to us, only regret. That's why I want to show you these things and as we get to know each other, to really talk about what happened and bring it all out into the open, no matter how hard it is to do. When I let myself feel shame or guilt or regret, I feel powerless." She took a deep breath in, and her voice was strong and clear when she said, "They took almost everything from me, Sabina, but I won't ever feel powerless again."

The lights on the car flashed toward us again. It was almost completely dark now, and my ears and the tip of my nose were stinging from the cold.

"All right, all right," Lilly said, and she laughed a little and released me from the hug. "Let's go meet your siblings."

# CHAPTER THIRTY-FOUR

## Megan

## September 1973

We started trying for a baby as soon as we were married.

The world felt like our oyster back then. I thought I'd snagged the best guy in the world, and we had such grand plans. This was back before we fell into the drudgery of married life—back when I couldn't understand women who got frustrated with their husbands for not picking up the towels or making the bed. I loved to do those things for Graeme.

Through that first year I felt I was a child playing house. I shopped for trinkets and art and linen and Grae pretended to be interested in my purchases. I tried new recipes nearly every night and waited for that magic day when I'd suddenly be able to cook, and when that day never came, Grae usually pretended to like my meals anyway.

By the second year, he wasn't pretending quite as well, but I was still trying. And I was watching the months coming at me, faster and faster it seemed, and beginning to wonder why my period was always on time. At first, Grae did not want me to see the doctor about our lack of success in conceiving. He was so confident that our baby was just around the corner, supremely confident in his ability to get me pregnant. And I was so determined to please him that even as the warning sounds in my mind became louder and louder, I did not mention my concern to anyone at all.

By the third year, I was getting annoyed with the wet towels on the floor, and I'd occasionally only made half of the bed in a gesture of defiance. Grae complained incessantly about my cooking, but was not unhappy enough to take the task on himself. And I had taken to noting down when my period was due and making sure that we had not planned anything social for that evening, as I'd inevitably be locking myself away with a glass of merlot and a box of tissues.

Grae suggested we see a doctor well into that year. We were both nervous—I was wondering who was to blame, and praying it wasn't me. I wanted a baby more than anything—anything, except of course, Grae himself. If he happened to be infertile, I'd stay with him, but if *I* was infertile, I was sure that he would leave me. From our very first dinner together Grae talked about the children he wanted. Two sons and a daughter, he'd decided, probably in that order. And he wanted good, traditional Australian names: Bruce and Barry, and maybe our daughter would be Kylie. He'd even planned their sporting activities; the boys would play cricket and rugby league, and little Kylie would concentrate on her schooling and maybe learn an instrument.

Apparently Grae's sperm count was exceptionally high, so the first round of tests absolved him of blame. At first, they thought I was healthy too and the doctors seemed bewildered as to why we hadn't conceived. We tried some drugs, and I actually fell pregnant—I remember the breathtaking joy just like it was yesterday. It was only weeks though before the dream shattered. That first loss was the hardest, because I never even saw it coming.

Still, we dusted ourselves off, waited the long period of months the doctor recommended before we risked another pregnancy, and then I went back on the drugs and we hoped for the best.

And then we did all of that again, and again. If we weren't

failing to conceive, we were failing to stay pregnant—but there was always failure, seemingly at every turn. It took years before they put a label to my problem, *hostile uterus*, and even now, years and years later, I still don't even really know what that means. The day the doctor finally told us, though, we sat down at our kitchen table for dinner and I stared at my plate and told Graeme to leave.

He was still young, and in spite of his terrible domestic habits, quite a catch. I knew he would remarry quickly, and within a few years he'd have the family he dreamed of.

Graeme pushed aside his (burnt) roast dinner and reached for my hand on the table. He told me that he was in this for life, baby or no baby. And that was that.

Grae isn't really one to gush, but that night, I gave him an out, and he did not take it.

So then came two new dimensions to our relationship, dimensions which were equally unwelcome and confusing: gratitude and guilt. Maybe things had never really been equal, maybe I did all of the housework in spite of us both working, and maybe he tended to be bossy at times, but throwing into the mix the fact that I now felt incredibly lucky that he was staying with me, and guilty that he would never be a father because of me, I danced on a knife-edge every day. Every single time we disagreed about something, I would tense and wait for him to end the conversation with a shrug and a hasty exit, as if even an argument over the damp towels would be the straw that broke the camel's back.

No one used the word "adoption" for a long time. When Grae finally did, I shot him down the instant he said it. Every now and again, he'd raise the subject again, but even considering it felt like giving up to me—and I was nowhere near ready to give up.

I didn't just want a baby. I wanted *my* baby. I wanted the joy of the positive pregnancy test without the grief and misery that inevitably followed it for us.

If I couldn't have *my* baby, then maybe I didn't want a baby. Maybe I could live without one after all.

That was not the case for Graeme. He just wanted a baby.

He'd have begged, borrowed or stolen one, if that was at all possible.

And I'd have done almost anything for Graeme.

# CHAPTER THIRTY-FIVE

## Sabina

### April 2012

The Piper family met periodically for dinner at a bistro alongside a historic pub. Lilly explained the rationale as we walked to their reserved table.

"Simon and Emmaline live just a block away from here, so they can walk down with the twins in the pram. And the food is good, and the servings are huge. They reserve this area for us now whenever we need it." We took our seats and I picked up the menu. It was typical pub food; steaks and hamburgers and the like, and several roast dinner options on offer.

"You watch," Lilly murmured. "Charlotte will get the Caesar salad, Neesa the kid's chicken meal, Simon will get a medium rare scotch fillet, Emmaline will get the soup of the day, and James will order a Chicken Parmigiana."

"I go to a café, with Mum and Dad sometimes, for brunch," I said. "It's exactly like that. We all order the same thing every time. There's something really lovely about the consistency of it, don't you think?"

"I do think that," Lilly said, and she was surprisingly excited by my random observation. "I really do. That's why I make them come here. The menu never changes, and the décor never changes, but this is our place. The others don't get the beauty of that... not at all."

Ted took a seat beside me, and James sat beside Lilly. A young family with a twin pram approached us and my heart started to race. Simon was clearly my biological brother, there was no denying the genetic link. There was something breathtakingly exciting about seeing people who looked exactly like me.

"You must be Sabina," Simon said. His brown eyes were twinkling, and he'd extended his arms even as he approached me. I pushed back my chair and stepped back from the table just in time for him to envelope me in a hug. "It is just wonderful to meet you. I can't tell you how happy we all are that you've found us."

I was surprised by the hot tears that filled my eyes.

"I'm so happy to meet you too," I whispered, then I cleared my throat and smiled at his wife. "And you must be Emmaline?"

Emmaline was tiny and blonde, and both beautiful and exhausted. She shook my hand, then held it a moment too long with a squeeze.

"Welcome to the family, Sabina. We're so excited that you're here. This is Dominic, and Valentina, your slightly evil twin niece and nephew. As soon as they get bored of the pram I'll pull them out so you can say hello properly. If we time it just right they'll be able to smile at you before all of the screaming and hysteria starts."

I leant awkwardly to peer into the pram. Dominic and Valentina were rolled towards each other, reaching clumsily for each other's chubby hands.

"They look so innocent."

"Don't believe it," Simon snorted. "Em had three hours sleep last night, in four stretches. They are hell on pram wheels."

I chuckled, and he and Emmaline shook Ted's hand, then Simon invited his wife to sit while he retrieved us all some drinks from the bar.

I recognised Charlotte the moment she entered the bistro, her tween daughter in tow. There was no mistaking her, she was every bit as stunning in real life as she'd been in photographs, and I felt nervous again. I felt an immediate connection with the others—I could see myself in them, and they felt strangely familiar. But Charlotte was different, and that difference made her intimidating. Her long blonde hair was in a perfectly messy plait over her shoulder, she was wearing a full face of perfect makeup and a linen shift dress and heels. I glanced down at the jeans I'd worn, and wished I'd at least put some mascara on.

"Sabina," she said, making a beeline for me. "I'm Charlotte, this is my daughter Neesa."

"I'm so happy to meet you," I said. I waited for her to approach for a hug, but instead, she shook my hand. It was a brisk contact—long enough only for me to note the perfect crimson manicure of her fingers and how smooth her skin was.

"Here again, Mum?" she sighed, after kissing Emmaline on the side of the head and making appropriate noises toward Dominic and Valentina.

"It works for everyone, Lottie."

"Sabina will think we're savages after she sees the food."

"I'm easily pleased," I assured her.

"I like the chicken," Neesa interjected. She had Lilly's dark hair, just as Simon and I did, and the same big brown eyes. "And they always give me ice cream."

"I hear you like to sing, Neesa?"

"I *love* to sing." Neesa's enthusiasm was adorable. "Nan said you're a proper singer; that you went to uni and everything."

"And you're a teacher," Charlotte said. She was staring at me, her cool blue gaze uncomfortably intense. "Just like Mum."

"Well, yes... but I only teach music—I do classes with primary school children. I'm not a proper teacher." Charlotte was still staring at me, as if she hadn't heard a word I'd said, so I tried again to clarify, "My degree was in music, I did a post grad certificate in education."

"Interesting," Charlotte said, although her tone suggested that it was anything but. "Have you all had a nice day, getting to know one another?"

"It's been marvellous," Lilly said, and she gave me yet another one-armed hug.

"Lilly said you own a salon?" I tried to shift focus back to Charlotte.

"I do," Charlotte said. I waited, expecting her to elaborate. She flashed me a smile and rose. "Is Simon getting drinks? I think I need a wine."

"He's at the bar," Emmaline confirmed.

"Can I have a lemonade, Mum?" Neesa asked hopefully.

"Stay here with Nan and Papa, and be good," Charlotte instructed, then left the table. I glanced at Ted, and he raised his eyebrows at me. So I wasn't imaging it—Charlotte was decidedly chillier than the rest of the Wyzlecki family.

"This must be so weird for you," Emmaline said quietly.

"It's different," I admitted, "but I'm so glad to be here."

There was a grunt from within the pram, and I saw Emmaline immediately wince and shoot to her feet. She hushed the baby, rocking the pram gently, and after a moment I saw the relief in her face.

"I love them, but by God, I miss my sleep. Lilly told us you're expecting your first, Sabina?"

"I am."

"I hate to say this, Sabina...but evil newborns are genetic in this family. Most of our babies have reflux from birth." Lilly sighed. "Simon always slept like an angel, but Charlotte and Neesa were nightmares and so were my sisters. I always thought it was just the girls until Dominic was born."

Ted silently entwined our fingers and rested our hands on my thigh.

"Good times ahead, then?" he laughed softly.

"Lilly will help you," Emmaline assured us. "She has such a knack for babies."

I glanced at Lilly, and she beamed at me. I knew that we were both thinking the same thing—that I would indeed ask for and accept her help, and what a wonderful gift that would be to both of us. She would be a part of my newborn baby's life; even if, as predicted, that baby was a terrible sleeper and would turn my world upside down. For everything we'd missed, here was something magical about to happen, and we'd found each other just in time.

Charlotte and Simon returned to the table. She was carrying the tray of drinks, Simon a tray of empty champagne flutes, with a bottle of champagne tucked awkwardly under his arm. After they'd passed the drinks around, and Charlotte had taken her seat again, Simon remained standing. He quietly poured seven glasses of champagne, and then decanted some lemonade from Neesa's cup into the last flute. Once everyone had a glass in hand, he raised his towards me.

"It just seems right to stop for a minute before we do anything else, and to toast you, Sabina. There has been a hole in this family that is the exact shape of you and it's been there forever, but now you're back to us." Simon stopped, and pressed his fist against his mouth for a moment as he battled against the tears I could see in his eyes. After a moment, he then cleared his throat and laughed self-consciously. "Here's to the Piper family finally—*finally*—being complete. We can't wait to get to know you." He reached across the table and gently tipped his glass against mine, then added softly, "Welcome home, big sister."

The rest of the family—*my* new family—quietly echoed his words, but I held my glass and felt the gentle bumps of their glasses against mine. There was not a chance in hell that I could hold back my tears after that, and I looked around each of them, completely overwhelmed.

"T-thank you." I choked. Lilly pulled me close for a too-tight hug, and I flashed a very teary smile to James, who raised his glass silently towards me a second time with a grin.

"We need a photo!" Lilly cried, and she waved frantically to a waitress across the restaurant.

"Something wrong, Lilly?"

"No, sweetheart, everything is absolutely *right*," she laughed. Simon withdrew a camera from the bottom of the pram and gave the waitress a quick lesson on how to use it, and then he and Charlotte crept around to stand behind James and Lilly. There was some awkward shuffling of the twins, with Dominic soon seated with Emmaline and Neesa holding up Valentina as if she were a doll.

"A photo is a great idea," I said softly to Lilly.

"I've waited thirty-eight years for a real family photo," Lilly said. "This one's going to be enlarged so big I might have to get it made into wallpaper."

"Okay, three... two... one... cheese!" the waitress called.

A wave of chatter broke almost instantly, the babies were quickly returned to their pram and the adults picked up menus. Charlotte and Simon started debating whether or not Lilly's habitual preference for this particular bistro was ever going to pass.

But I lingered in the perfect moment, unwilling to let it pass. It had been captured in time by the camera but that just didn't seem enough. I stopped and let myself savour the welcome that Simon had given me, even though that meant that soon I was the only person at the table sitting in silence, fresh tears running unhindered down my face.

I consciously stopped and tried to remember everything

about it—the scents and the sights and the sounds of my first moments there with my family. I felt loved and wanted and accepted—truly and completely embraced.

It felt a lot like coming home.

—

Over dinner, I saw the dynamic of the Piper family at work. Simon was loud and jovial, cracking jokes with Ted and teasing me about my supposedly terrible taste in "fancy" beer. Charlotte was, for the most part, quieter, but when she spoke, a sharpness came and went in her tone, as if she was trying to hold back bitterness, and not always succeeding. Emmaline was sweet-natured and warm, and Neesa was just awestruck. Whenever I spoke to her, she'd giggle and blush.

"How do I become a real musician?" she asked me.

"I think the best thing you can do, other than loads of practice, is to listen to different styles of music. A lot of kids just listen to pop. Try to listen to some classical and to world music and older styles of rock and my favourite, which is jazz."

"I can do that." Neesa was staring at me, wide-eyed. She glanced to Charlotte. "Can you buy me some new music?"

Charlotte raised her eyebrow at me and offered a slightly sarcastic,

"*Thanks* for that."

Every time I looked to Lilly or James, they were silently watching us interact. I wondered how many times Lilly had pictured this moment in her mind, and whether it was playing out as she thought it would. There was no awkwardness at all here—it wasn't nearly as intimate as the chats between Lilly and I had been. There were more people to bounce questions off, and an easier small talk flowed. By the time we were finishing our meals, I found myself so engaged in the conversation that it felt completely natural.

Lilly started packing up the plates as we finished with them.

"Come on, Neesa," she said, gently scolding as she reached for her granddaughter's plate. "What's that doing there?"

Neesa had ordered her regular chicken meal, but she had left a small portion untouched.

"I'm not hungry, Nan," she said.

"Just have a few more bites." Lilly was insistent. "It's terrible manners to leave food on your plate, darling."

I glanced down at my plate. I'd eaten most of my risotto—it was delicious, a creamy mix of wild mushrooms and white wine. I'd enjoyed every bite, but I'd left sizeable corner of the serving anyway. I could hear Mum's voice echoing in my head, *restaurants always serve far too much food, you should never eat the whole serving.*

"But Nan..." Neesa was complaining for the first time all night.

"Hurry up, Neesa. Finish it up and you can order your ice cream." Neesa sighed and took another slow, reluctant mouthful. "Good girl."

I picked up my spoon and took another bite of my risotto, letting the creamy rice roll around my tongue. Those final bites were somehow the most delicious.

# CHAPTER THIRTY-SIX

## Megan

## September 1973

At first, it really was very easy.

In the first few days that Sabina was in our home, once I'd had some advice about newborn stomach volume, she just slept most of the time. I caught up on some reading and gardening, and enjoyed the early spring sunshine. I quickly got used to changing her nappies and keeping on top of the laundry.

And initially, I was actually amused by the sudden change in my husband. It wasn't that he'd been unhappy before Sabina arrived, but he was certainly much happier now. He came home for lunch and made it look easy to eat a messy salad sandwich with one hand while he nursed her with the other. He often got up to her when she cried at night, and every day he came home with something from the stores...generally toys, which I continually told him that she would not need while she was with us, but he just shrugged and said she could take them with her when she went to her real parents. Grae kept the house stocked with formula and nappies and had some kind of automatic instinct about caring for her. If she was unsettled, he somehow seemed to know why.

As the days stretched into a second week, I began to suspect that somehow, I was lacking that instinct. Sabina was awake more, and unsettled much more, and I found that those lazy hours to relax or even keep on top of the housework disappeared overnight. Grae could walk in and hear her crying and he'd go right to a bottle or her nappy or pick her up for a cuddle, but for me it was a process of painful elimination. Sometimes, when she was really upset, I'd get so flustered that I'd forget altogether about even the obvious things. Grae came home from work on Friday afternoon to find Sabina and I both sobbing, and within two minutes he had me settled with a glass of wine on the deck while Sabina greedily drank a bottle of milk in his arms. Apparently, I just plain forgot to give her lunch.

It wasn't that I didn't enjoy having her in our home. Emotions dawn slowly in me, and they build by degrees over time, but I've always been like that. I didn't fall in love with Graeme, so much as inch toward the edge of love, and then lower myself in gently over months and years. It was the same with Sabina. In those very early days I could quite easily hold myself at a distance, doing the job I'd committed to: acting as her professional and temporary nurse.

And there's no sugar coating it: they were difficult days. She was not an easy child to care for, she suffered terribly with reflux and I rode the waves of her pain with her. She'd go from screaming with hunger to screaming in pain in only a few minutes, and I could never really tell what it was she was looking for—was it more milk? Less? A burp? A nappy change?

Or...her mother?

Sometimes, I caught myself wondering if a child could even love me the way it should. Was it karma? Or some kind of universal truth? My body was not conducive to fertility, maybe that extended to how I would nurture—maybe Sabina saw the deficiency in me, and that's why she was so miserable? Graeme said it was because I got so upset around her, and in time I realised there was some truth to that. On the bad days it was like she was tied to me and I couldn't put her down, but the more upset I got, the more upset *she* got. We fed off each other, and as soon as Grae walked in the spell would break, and she'd be contented again. I could see the logic and rationality in all of that, but in the thick of it, it was impossible to stop myself from taking it personally.

I'd remind myself that this was only for a little longer, and I planned to spoil myself when Sabina finally went home. I intended endless sleep-ins, trips to the beauty salon, and reading... day after day of blissful reading in peace and quiet. I had to keep adding to that list though, because for a while it seemed like every new day was worse than the one before. Sabina soon slept and ate on her own schedule and day or night she was squirming and grunting as if she was in pain. I made a few frantic trips back to the hospital, where the midwives and doctors would check her over. Mild reflux, the doctor would say, and the midwives would tell me to hang in there and send me home.

I had no idea what sleep deprivation could do to a person's state of mind, but Sabina quickly taught me. I found myself walking around the house in a fog of exhaustion, barely meeting my own basic needs. The occasional flashes of tenderness I felt towards Sabina reminded me somewhat of Stockholm Syndrome—I was trapped with and by her, and that thought alone made it easier to resist any chance I might bond with her. It was with a kind of desperate longing that I looked forward to the day that Lilly would call to ask for Sabina. I couldn't wait until my life became mine again.

When the phone rang early one Monday morning and I recognised Lilly's voice on the line, I watched the fog recede and I stared towards a window, where the day instantly seemed to have brightened.

"Is she okay?" was Lilly's first question, delivered both with fluency and desperation.

"She's just fine," I assured her. "You're discharged?"

"They made me stay a while, the doctor wanted to make

sure my body was healing okay. But yes, I'm out n-now. I had to go home to my family." Her words were increasingly uneven. "It's horrible, Megan. I can't even look at Tata, I'm so angry with him. But the solicitor said our easiest shot at the marriage licence was for Tata to give his consent, so I had to come home and try to convince him."

"So, that's the plan, then? Have you talked to him yet?"

"I've tried, but he's still so mad at me, it didn't go very well. And James had to go back to university while we wait, he has exams coming up so couldn't miss any more school. But he's back in a few weeks and we're going to try to talk to Tata together then."

"Another few weeks?" I repeated, and glanced down at Sabina, who was finally asleep in my arms after a marathon night of wakefulness. The fog rushed back in at me, thicker than before, and my living room seemed to darken and shrink in around me.

"Is that still okay?" Lilly asked hesitantly. "I appreciate everything you're doing for us, Megan. I really…can't thank you enough, honestly. If it's too much…I mean, I can try to speed it up, we can apply to the court for a licence but the solicitor said that would take a while and without Tata's consent it might not work anyway."

"No, no it's fine." I cleared my throat. "You just call me when you're ready, and let me know if I can do anything to help the process along, okay?"

"Okay." I heard the smile leap back into Lilly's voice. "And is she well? Is she sleeping for you and growing and…is she okay?"

"She's doing beautifully," I said. "Actually I think I hear her waking up so I'd best go, good luck with everything and keep in touch, okay?"

I managed to hang up just as the sobs bubbled up, but they

were mine, not Sabina's. I was disappointed and confused, and so tired that even the effort required to get Sabina back to the bassinet in her room seemed beyond what I could manage.

I sank into a chair and looked around my living room through my veil of tears. There was a huge pile of clean nappies and baby clothes on the floor near to the laundry, and groceries by the door that I still hadn't unpacked from the previous day. Something about the chaos made me suddenly, irrationally furious and I felt the muscles in my arms contract as if I might squeeze the baby in punishment.

And then, of course, the tears came faster and harder because I realised that I was blaming an innocent child for the state of a house and none of that really mattered and none of it was her fault at all. What kind of monster did that make me?

It was my darkest moment, wedged tightly in a period of so many dark moments that I'd look back on it for years and wonder how we both survived. I was more than ever certain that I was not cut out to adopt a child. Surely *all* of this would be easier if I actually had a baby of my own, my own flesh and blood. Those fleeting glances of affection I had towards Sabina would surely be more steady and solid if this were *my* child. The instinct that I lacked would come naturally if only I'd been pregnant and given birth myself.

I'd love my baby, instantly and automatically. Maybe I was growing to love Sabina, but it was happening too slowly... she'd be surely back with Lilly before I even came to *like* her.

But, as difficult as it all was, I was stuck. What choice did I have? I had committed to helping Lilly and James, and I couldn't very well return the baby to the hospital and say it was too hard, I'd changed my mind. I had to stumble and fumble my way forward, and wait for Lilly to return to be a real mother to her daughter.

The most frightening part of the whole affair was that this was my first taste of motherhood, and it was not what I thought it would be. I expected it to be joyous and transformative.

I did not anticipate endless, monotonous days which blurred until life was both unenjoyable and unrecognisable.

# CHAPTER THIRTY-SEVEN

## Sabina

### April 2012

We were waiting for dessert when Dominic decided he was ready for his milk. The twins had been playing in the pram, coo-ing and kicking and content, but Dominic roused to protest his hunger in an instant, moving from near silence to a furious, demanding cry.

"Here we go," Simon sighed, and reached into the pram to withdraw him. "I suppose at least they let us eat this time, huh?"

"Sometimes we have to take turns eating," Emmaline explained to me, as she bent down to pick Valentina up. Lilly immediately reached forward and Emmaline grinned as she passed her daughter across the table. "Don't get me wrong, we adore them..."

"So you keep saying," I laughed.

"If we just keep telling ourselves that..." Simon grinned at me. He was fumbling now in their nappy bag with his free hand, and withdrew two small bottles of milk, which he sat on the table. Then he adjusted his son in his arms, and offered him a dummy. The baby sucked it greedily, and Simon glanced at me. "Want to hold your nephew while I go get these heated up? You probably need the practice."

"I *do* need the practice. And I'd love to." I accepted the squirming baby into my arms and peered down at him. "Hi, Dominic."

Ted rested his chin on my shoulder, staring down at the baby with obvious longing.

"See, you're a natural," he said softly. I smiled a little nervously and offered my finger to Dominic, who gripped it tightly in his fist. Then he spat the dummy out and tried to manoeuvre my finger into his mouth.

"Whoa, no," I laughed, trying to pull my finger away, but he would not be deterred. He was grunting now and craning his neck to reach. The grunts quickly turned into outraged cries. Beside us, Valentina was starting to grizzle too.

"Oh, you are cranky children," Lilly gently scolded, then she reached down to nuzzle Valentina's cheek. "Delicious, but cranky."

Simon returned with the bottles, which he automatically handed to Lilly and I, and he sat back beside Ted and resumed a conversation about seed harvesting. I watched Lilly test the milk on the inside of her wrist and did likewise.

"What am I testing for?" I asked.

"It should be lukewarm, you shouldn't really feel it," she told me quietly.

I moved the bottle towards Dominic's mouth, and he lifted his head to grab it, obviously impatient with my unpractised technique. He gulped down the milk much quicker than I expected, and then I again copied Lilly, lifting him onto my shoulder and gently patting his back until he gave a big, satisfying belch.

"They'll be getting tired now and they'll probably start yelling again, we'd better head home," Emmaline said, but she seemed reluctant to go.

"Oh, please stay for dessert," Lilly pleaded. "We can hold them and keep them quiet, can't we, Bean?"

The casual use of the nickname left me feeling warm and *known*. Loads of friends had called me variations of Bean and Beanie over my lifetime, and Ted never really used my full name, but there was something particularly special about the way Lilly said it. She wrapped the word in softness and familiarity, as if she'd been infusing the sound in maternal longing for decades.

"Speak for yourself, Lilly," I murmured. "I'm just copying you and hoping Dominic doesn't realise that I don't know what I'm doing."

"You're doing just fine," she said firmly.

The desserts arrived. Neesa's appetite had suddenly returned, just in time for her ice cream. I sat Dominic on my lap and dodged his determined attempts to hijack my spoonful of tiramisu. Valentina's energy faded first, and soon not even the tiny tastes of Lilly's ice cream she was managing were enough to placate her. Lilly lifted her onto her shoulder again and began to rock gently, and then I heard her humming a tune under her breath. I glanced at her, and smiled at the image of it, Lilly in all of her maternal perfection, enjoying her granddaughter.

Dominic let out a squeal on my lap, and I jumped, having forgotten for a moment that he was even there. Ted reached down and lifted him away from me, passing him back to his father.

"Maybe we should go," Emmaline said softly. Lilly passed Valentina back too, and as she did so, she leant close to me.

"It'll be your turn soon," she whispered. "You'll visit us with your baby, won't you?"

"Of course," I promised. "Of *course* I will."

# CHAPTER THIRTY-EIGHT

## Megan

### September 1973

In those early weeks, I rarely left the house. The prematurely grey roots of my hair began to grow out, but I didn't notice, because I no longer had time to fix it or even shower most days. Whenever we did venture out, it was usually just when we were desperate for groceries. Those outings were inevitably an exercise in humiliation and panic.

Sabina was most settled a few hours after a feed, just before the hunger started again. I timed it with military precision and I sprinted through the aisles, throwing groceries into my trolley with little care or attention to what I was purchasing. Inevitably she was screaming by the time we reached the checkout and people stared at us. I was sure they were wondering how someone so clueless managed to get a baby. I was sure they were concerned for her welfare, and maybe they should have been. I was too tired to be rational most of the time. My thoughts spiralled often and I struggled to control the trajectory.

Sometimes, darkness would settle over me and I would pace the hallway with her in my arms, thinking things that were too dark to even acknowledge. Each time those moments passed I found myself terrified that Lilly and James wouldn't hasten enough and that I'd lose my mind completely before I could hand Sabina back.

Grae said it might have been easier if we'd had time to prepare; just a little time to read up about newborns. Or if we lived somewhere warmer, or if my mother was here to help, or even if I had a friend that I could turn to just to give me advice.

I could snap myself out of the darkest moments only by reminding myself that things *would* get better...because Sabina would soon be with her real mother, instead of me. I felt there would be an instant change in her, and she'd go from an unsettled baby to a happy one in a single instant, if someone could just provide her with the right care.

I'd hear Sabina cry in the middle of the night and feel a furious resentment that my sleep was so constantly being broken. I hated that if I ignored her, Grae would swing his legs over the edge of the bed and tiptoe to her room, and I'd hear him whispering cheerily to her as he prepared her bottle. It was only guilt that kept me from ignoring her every single time she cried at night—after all, he still had forty hours of work to do each week, he needed his sleep.

I was torn between wanting to let him help, and feeling like it was my job to handle all of her care on my own, besides which I was increasingly concerned that Grae was enjoying this temporary arrangement rather too much. The spare room had once contained only a borrowed bassinet, but was rapidly morphing into a little girl's room. Grae was loading it gradually with toys and items that Sabina wouldn't need for years, and whenever I protested, he'd shrug and remind me that it was nice to send her off to her family with a few special items to remember us by.

Our life had become a fragile chaos; with me counting down the hours until we could pass Sabina back to her real family, and Grae clearly dreading that day more and more. Some days, he greeted me at both lunch time and after work with a hesitant, *Did Lilly call today*? And I'd watch him visibly relax when I mumbled my disappointed *no* in response.

During those long days at home alone, I planned to sit him

down once Sabina was gone and to tell him once and for all that I just could *not* adopt. This experiment had been a miserable failure. I had warmed to her somewhat, but not nearly enough given the time and effort I'd put in, besides which—it was just too hard. This entire experience was an ominous precursor to our own inevitably failed adoption down the track.

I had decided that we would simply have to find a way to have a baby of our own. Maybe we could seek out a new specialist, maybe a younger doctor with some fresh ideas, maybe we could visit a university clinic and see a professor.

There had to be a way.

# CHAPTER THIRTY-NINE

Sabina

April 2012

It was a very late night.

Lilly and I sat up talking outside until it just grew too cold, and then we moved back into the dining room and we looked through the photo albums Mum had prepared for us. This time, the conversation flowed, and it was easy. I had wanted for Lilly to see the beauty of my childhood; here was my chance, and I ran with it.

I filled in the blanks for Lilly, explaining where I'd been and what I'd been doing when each photo was taken. I relived the birthday at Disney World, the day I finally graduated from speech therapy and Mum surprised me with a trip to a concert at the Opera House, and the day we moved into that big house in Balmain.

It was a rapid-fire synopsis of my life. Every significant moment had been captured in some kind of photo or memento, and me telling Lilly my story was as close as she could ever come to being a part of it. I shared the details as I recalled them, like the tastes of the awful cakes Mum had made me until I turned ten and I finally insisted she buy them, and the smell of the lavender in Mum's sitting room.

And when I remembered moments that weren't captured by a photo, I just shared the emotion—in *this* moment I was happy, in *that* moment overwhelmed, but in *all* of these, I was *loved*.

I had relived each of those memories, only recently, when

I learned about the adoption, but I had remembered them through a lens of confusion, and I had viewed each incident with suspicion and a sense of shame. At the dining table with Lilly that night, I corrected that perspective. It may have been birthed in pain and deceit, but I had grown up in a family which truly did revolve around me, and I'd had two parents who had given me a wonderful, blessed life.

I saw Lilly change too, as the hours wore on. She listened intently, but as we talked, the intensity was gradually fading from her gaze. She was living what she'd missed, decades too late, and it would never be what it might have been, but I was *there* now. We would make the most of it, even the catch-up of the years we'd spent apart.

I certainly didn't intend for that time to be a testimony on Mum and Dad's behalf, but even as the hours wore on, I was aware that I was proving to Lilly just how well I'd been cared for. Every now and again I'd think back on her threat earlier that day to take my birth certificate to the police. There had been such fury and anger on her face in that earlier discussion, but even by the time that I'd turned the page on the last album, Lilly looked like a different person.

She was a woman on her way towards peace.

When we'd finished with the albums we shared another sneaky piece of cake with yet another cup of tea. Our yawns were so frequent that they seemed to run into one another, and I knew we'd have to sleep soon, but I didn't want to break the spell of the wonderful evening. Lilly seemed similarly torn.

"We really need to go to bed," she said softly, and she glanced at me. "Pregnant women need their sleep."

"I'm exhausted. But it's been such a great day, I don't want it to end."

"You won't leave early tomorrow, will you?"

"No, we were thinking about going around lunchtime."

She sighed a contented sigh, and I thought about how lovely Lilly Piper was to look at. She'd seemed weathered when I first arrived, but now I could see that the lines on her face were not just from a lifetime of sadness, but a lifetime of really experiencing life. Lilly truly was an open book, just like me.

"One more lovely breakfast with you, then," she murmured with a smile.

I shook my head with fierce determination.

"Not one more. One more this weekend, but one more of many, Lilly."

"I hope so," she whispered.

"I *know* so," I whispered back.

—

When I crawled into bed beside Ted, the alarm clock on the bedside table said 4:03 a.m. I fell into a very deep, dreamless sleep, and when I woke the next morning, the sun was beaming through the windows. When I turned to the clock, I was startled to see it was almost 11 a.m.

I could hear laughter from the living areas, and so I dressed quickly and all but skipped down the hallway. The first person I saw when I stepped into the dining room was Neesa, sitting with her earphones in, staring at the table as she concentrated. She didn't look up when I entered the room.

"Kids these days, hey?" I greeted Charlotte and Lilly, who were sitting opposite, flicking through the photo albums I'd given Lilly the previous afternoon. "Did Ted go home without me?"

"He's out helping James in the paddocks," Lilly told me. "And Neesa is listening to jazz."

I grimaced and bent down low to catch Neesa's gaze. Her eyes widened when she saw me and she pulled the earbuds from her ears.

"Aunty Sabina, your music is *so* good."

*Aunty Sabina*. I beamed at her.

"Breakfast, sweetheart?" Lilly was already rising.

"Oh, don't go to any trouble, Lilly—"

"You can tell that you're new here," Charlotte grinned at me, as Lilly waved her hand and headed for the kitchen. "This is what she does, it's no trouble to her."

"I'll just whip something up," she threw over her shoulder as she left the room.

"Neesa, pop those headphones back in for a moment," Charlotte said suddenly, and I glanced at her in surprise. She grimaced and leant forward towards me. "I'm really sorry about last night, Sabina. I wasn't as welcoming as I should have been. I wanted to come out today to apologise and to let you know that I'm really so excited to get to know you, and so very glad that you're back—especially for Mum."

"You didn't have to do that, Charlotte," I said.

"I didn't want us to get off on the wrong foot, and I know I nearly did that last night. The truth is... I've been a little freaked out since Mum said you'd contacted her."

"I can understand that."

"I know it's scary for you too, but for me..." She shrugged her svelte shoulders. "Well, I grew up in a family of five. There was Mum and Dad, and Simon and Charlotte, and the ghost of a little girl named Sabina, who was perfect in every way."

I didn't know what to say to that. She pulled her hair over her shoulder and began to plait it. Her fingers worked fast, winding and unwinding. I wondered if it was her profession or a lifelong nervous tic that made her braid so quickly.

"I always thought that Mum and Dad assumed you were perfect just because they'd never seen you grow up and they'd never seen otherwise. I was so jealous of you, and sometimes I was glad that you weren't here because I felt so sure that I'd never be able to compete. And then last night, I went with the best intentions in the world, to welcome you and get to know you—and I walked into that bistro and it was like I was a kid again, like the ghost had resurfaced. And lo and behold—" she smiled sadly, "it turns out that you are perfect after all."

"Not even close," I assured her, thinking of how much I'd struggled over the weeks since I learned about the adoption.

"You're like a snapshot of my mother forty years ago. You have her smile, and her curves, and those bright brown eyes, and you're even a teacher, for heaven's sakes. And it's ridiculous but the worst thing for me was, you have that freak-of-nature shiny hair that I always wanted." Charlotte smiled sadly. "Did you know that I'm a September baby too? I was born four years and four days after you—she fell pregnant with me straight after they had Simon. It was like she was still trying to replace you."

"I'm really sorry, Charlotte."

"She used to get so sad just before my birthday," Charlotte murmured. "I was maybe eight or nine when they finally explained. Mum was such an overprotective parent—and I'm so much more adventurous by nature than Simon ever was... so I was constantly getting in trouble. Until they explained what had happened with you, I really thought she was miserable for my birthday every year because I was such a terrible child and she wished she'd never had me."

I thought about how intimidated I'd been when I saw her, but we were more alike than she knew. I was sad for Charlotte, of course, but I was suddenly so excited. I had a sister—an insecure, neurotic sister, just like me.

I reached across the table and placed my hand over hers. Just then, Lilly entered the room, with a plate piled high with hot breakfast food, and gave a silly grin at the sight of us.

"Look at that, my girls are bonding," she said, sliding the plate in front of me. "This has just been the most marvellous weekend."

"I could give you some killer highlights, you know," Charlotte said suddenly. I reached up to touch my hair self-consciously.

"I've never coloured my hair," I admitted. "Do you really think so?"

"Trust me," she smiled. "I know hair. Brighten up a few strands here and there and those awesome eyes will pop. Next time you come, we'll stop by my salon and I'll give you the star treatment."

"She's really very good," Lilly assured me. I grinned and nodded.

"I'd like that."

—

When the time came to say goodbye, the weekend suddenly seemed to have been too short. As we loaded our bags back into the car, I turned to James, feeling quite panicky that I'd spent so much of the weekend with Lilly, and so little with him.

"I didn't really get to talk to you much," I said. It suddenly felt like this was an unforgiveable oversight.

"This weekend was about my Lilly," he said, quite gently. "There will be more weekends, more dinners, more chats. The next time you visit, bring me some of that beer you make, and it will be our turn to sit out on the swinging chair and shoot the breeze, and Ted and Lilly can sit in front of the big screen and watch movies."

"Sounds fine," Lilly said, "as long as they're historical documentaries. You will come back soon, won't you?"

"We absolutely will," I promised her. "It's been wonderful." She embraced me, and I felt gentle sobs rattle her strong arms around my back. "I'll be back, Lilly. I promise."

"I know," she whispered into my hair. "I know you will. The truth is...I'm crying because I'm happy. I'm crying because I know I'll see you again, and I can call you whenever I want to, and I can look at photos of you and of *us* and I don't have to wonder anymore. You're going home, but this is a beginning, not an ending." She pulled away a little and met my gaze. "I wanted to tell you, Sabina...when we were talking last night, something became quite clear to me. When I think back to losing you, I think about it as if I am still sixteen years old. All of my emotions and thoughts about losing you are loud—and everything seems black and white...all angry, all hurt, all unfair. But talking to you this weekend...the truth is, I see myself in you, but I also see Mrs. Baxter in you, the good Mrs. Baxter anyway...the woman who showed me such kindness in the home."

"Thank you, Lilly."

"For the first time ever, I think I am starting to look back at what happened with adult eyes. I'm still angry, of course, and I'm still hurt and I want answers and it should never have been allowed to happen...nothing of that time in the maternity home was *okay*. But the truth is, it's not black and white. I just don't know how we would ever have managed if we'd been allowed to take you home, or even if we would have. If she'd handed you back, would someone *else* have just taken you? And even if we had kept you...well, we would have made it work, but there would have been no private schools or overseas holidays for you, just two very young, very terrified parents."

"That would have been enough," I whispered. "Wouldn't it?"

"Of course it would. Children don't need things, they need love. But... I really don't know how we would have provided for you without James leaving university, and if he had left university... life would have been so much more difficult for us all. Of course I'd have preferred that life," she smiled sadly, and offered me a shrug, "but it would have been a very different outcome for every one of us."

I nodded sadly. I thought about the wonderful hours we'd shared overnight, and how I'd seen the change in Lilly even as we talked. Maybe she would never forgive my parents, and maybe they didn't deserve forgiveness, but at least Lilly seemed closer to finding peace for herself. A sudden thought struck me, and although I was hesitant to raise it again, I had to ask.

"Yesterday, Lilly, you were talking a-about the birth certificate and maybe going to the police..."

"Ah, Sabina. I was angry. If I'd ever understood how they went about this, I'd have found a way to stir up some trouble for them. But I watched you when we were talking yesterday and I could see as soon as I said it that the only thing I'd achieve in going to the police would be to hurt you... and to drag out the misery for all of us. I have to let go of the bitterness now. I have to look forward, and so do you. We can't change anything that happened, but we can mine the good out of how it all panned out and build a better future from it. For ourselves, and..." She reached down and gently touched my belly, and she smiled at me, "... for this little one."

I glanced to Ted, who was standing beside me. I thought of that *other* Sabina I'd wondered about, and the very different life she'd have led. Most likely, I would never have met this man, and I'd never have been pregnant with *this* baby.

I'd have grown up right there on the farm, and although it would have been wonderful... that just wasn't what happened for me.

Lilly was right. The past was important—but it was also gone. *This* was the life I had, and it was a pretty bloody good one at that.

"You're very wise, Lilly," I whispered, and although he'd surely have no idea what I was thinking, Ted suddenly shot me a smile and I knew that he was proud of me.

"Thank you," Lilly murmured, and I heard another one of those contented, happy sighs I was coming to associate with her.

*That's my mother*, I thought, and a sudden impulse overtook me. I threw my arms around her neck. She immediately wound her arms around my back and squeezed.

"Sabina Wilson-*Piper*," she whispered, "you are every bit as wonderful as I'd ever imagined you'd be."

I saw her sneaky tears as we waved goodbye and drove away, but all I could manage was a smile.

"Are you glad I didn't let you talk me into heading back home on Friday night?" Ted asked.

"It was equal parts heartbreaking and wonderful," I conceded. I took one last glance at the endless paddocks and sparse gum trees, and a last deep lungful of the country air. "But now that we've survived it, I feel better than I have since I found out."

"So what's next?"

I was already fumbling in my bag, looking for my phone.

"I'm a woman on a mission now, Ted."

Mum answered on the second ring.

"Sabina? Love!" She was simultaneously delighted and concerned at my call. "Is everything all right?"

"I need to speak to you. This evening. By yourself," I said.

"Dad won't—"

"Lie to him."

"But—"

"Come to my place, about six tonight, please."

Mum sighed, a nervous, uneasy sigh, and I softened my voice.

"I don't need to interrogate you, Mum, I really don't. I just want to fill in the final piece of the puzzle, and then we can finally start to move on. I know that's what you want too. I'll see you at six, okay?"

"Okay." I heard the resignation in her whisper. When I hung up, Ted glanced at me.

"If it was that easy, we could have done it weeks ago."

"You see, my darling husband, something very important has changed." I smiled sadly at him. "Now, there's only one question left to ask."

—

When the doorbell rang that evening, Ted automatically answered it. He opened the door and greeted Mum with a gentle hello, then he shot me a confused glance and I saw Dad appear in the doorway behind her. I looked at Mum in alarm, but she only offered me a calm smile, as if she didn't notice my confusion. While Dad and Ted shook hands, Mum sat her hand bag by the door, and carefully unwound her scarf then hung it on the coat hook.

Ted had planned to leave Mum and me alone to give us some space to talk. Now though, Dad was here, and I was relieved when my husband lingered, taking his place right next to me on the couch. Mum and Dad sat directly opposite me, and I realised we were inadvertently sitting in the very same positions we'd taken weeks earlier. That night, they seemed to break my life into pieces. What would come out of tonight?

"I didn't think you were coming, Dad," I said quietly.

"I didn't know *where* I was going until we got here," he said, and he shot Mum a furious glance. She stared right ahead at me, but when a moment passed and no one spoke, I felt my optimism about this meeting begin to slip.

"Please don't do this to me again. *Please* don't make me beg. It's time."

Dad gave Mum an irritated glance and then a heavy sigh, and then he said,

"We keep telling you—"

"No," Mum spoke, and the word was short and harsh. "Grae, this is *my* turn to speak. You are *not* here to talk. You're here because we were in this together, and we're damn well going to *face* it together."

We all looked to Mum, because there it was. There in her words was the harsh tone I'd heard every single time I'd stepped over the line. It was the sharp gaze that she'd used freely on my boyfriends, the pursed lips she'd shot towards unsupportive teachers, the frustrated lecture she'd delivered time after time when I couldn't be bothered putting the effort into a task.

I knew that aspect of my mother so well—it was the strength of her character. But not once, in my entire life, had I seen her direct it at Dad.

"It was *not* for the best." She was shaking and pale, but this time, she trembled with the passion of her conviction, not because she was weak. Suddenly, my mum was beautiful again to me, and the tears in my eyes were of pride, not confusion or pain. "We should have told you the truth when you were a child. We didn't, because we were scared. We never intended to keep you, Sabina. It was an impulse, and although I'm so very glad that we've had you in our lives... there's no denying that we went about it in the wrong way. We have both lived for all of these years terrified of what the consequences might be, and we let that fear overrule what was best for you."

Dad looked like someone had detonated a warhead on his lap. He gaped at her and I waited for the returning thunder to come. He would not need to raise his voice, he would respond with a sharp word or two, and Mum would surely shrink.

But Dad did not deliver some stinging rebuke. He fell silent, in fact, and I could barely believe what I was seeing.

"I won't speak for Dad—but I knew from the very beginning that you needed to know. I let you down. I was too scared to stand up to Dad, and *I let you down*." Mum's breath caught on a sob. "I never wanted you to know what I did to Lilly. I never wanted you to understand how weak I really am... how selfish we really were. But above all, I should have had the courage to do what was best for you. *I failed you*."

"But—" Dad tried to speak at last, but Mum immediately silenced him with a fierce wave of her hand and a glare.

"Grae, shut up! This is Sabina's moment."

I saw Dad's struggle. He was trying desperately to hide it, but he was battling—watching the control slip right through his fingertips. There was an unbridled fury in his eyes as he stared toward Mum. I knew that I was watching a paradigm shift in their marriage that was so profound that it would change everything for them. I was hurting—for myself, for Lilly, for Mum... and for Dad.

For all of his flaws, I could not deny the lifetime of love and devotion he'd given to me.

"Dad," I choked, "you are *always* going to be my dad. I love you so, so much. Nothing you can say tonight is going to change that."

He closed his eyes and blindly fumbled to take Mum's hand. She carefully wound their fingers together and sat their hands on her thigh, and Dad turned towards her and opened his eyes.

Mum and Dad stared at each other, with such rawness and

pain that I suddenly felt like an intruder in my own home. I'd wondered at the way they communicated with just a glance, and in the weeks since they'd told me about the adoption, it had felt like those messages were encrypted. Now I could read their expressions crystal clear—*it's time.* After a moment, Mum gave a subtle nod, and then turned back to me and offered me a watery smile.

"You always looked so like her, you know. And now here you are, and you're pregnant too, and you've got that same beautiful glow about you. That's why I finally found the courage to tell you. I convinced Dad we *had* to tell you because I'd scared you about my own history with pregnancies... but that was just an excuse." She shook her head, as if even after all of those years, she still could not believe what she had done. "I took your whole life from her, Sabina. I couldn't take her grandchild too."

Mum was speaking softly but her words came without resistance. She was ready to be true to herself—to be the open, honest woman who had drilled into me the importance of truth and integrity. I *did* know my mother, in spite of these secrets, and that realisation confirmed the suspicion that had been growing in my heart over the past few days.

"You always intended to give me back to her, didn't you Mum?"

"I just wanted to help," Mum whispered, and she started to cry.

"Can you tell me where it all went wrong?"

Mum took a deep breath in, and after a long, slow exhale, she finally gave me the one thing that had always been missing in my life.

My mum gave me the truth.

# CHAPTER FORTY

## Megan

### October 1973

The fragile balance between my plans and Grae's dreams came to a sudden end one lunchtime when Sabina was just over a month old.

Grae did as he always had since Sabina had come into our lives; he rushed home for lunch right on noon, and as soon as he was inside he'd brush a kiss against my cheek before immediately seeking the baby out. Whether she was asleep or awake he'd pick her up and deliver his cheerful greeting before he settled to eat his lunch with her in his arms. This time, he sat at the kitchen table with Sabina resting in the crook of one elbow, then he reached into his pocket with his other hand and sat a folded paper on the table between us.

"June came to see me at my office today."

"June?" I repeated. "June Sullivan?"

I was seated opposite him trying to inhale my tenth cup of coffee of the day, hoping it would keep me awake long enough to at least wash and dry a load of nappies.

"Meg, do you have any idea why June thinks we're keeping this baby?"

Of course I had an idea. I'd told her as much. I shifted a little in my seat, as if the vinyl cushion had suddenly become uncomfortable, then offered him a mild smile over my coffee cup as I said,

"You must have misunderstood."

"I didn't misunderstand her."

"You must have." I sat the cup down, but maintained my smile as I pushed my chair back. "I better get those nappies on—"

"No, Meg. Stay here, we need to talk about this. Did June know that we were just minding Sabina temporarily?" I cleared my throat. I'd never really been much of a crier, but sleep deprivation had wreaked havoc on my emotions. Tears were building, and I was silent as I fought to dispel them. I sat with my hands on my lap, chair pushed slightly back from the table, staring at my knees while I rallied against the weakness of my resolve. "You don't need to answer me, Meg. I know the answer. So you lied to me?"

"I didn't lie," I whispered eventually. "I just didn't explain it very well."

"June filled out the birth registration paperwork for you, to help things along. She thought you might be busy with the baby and you might have forgotten that you said you'd take care of it. You were supposed to register her within four weeks of her birth."

"*Lilly* will do it. And soon."

"Meg. It's the tenth of October. June said that we really can't leave it any longer or someone might notice."

"But…there's still time. How many weeks old is the baby now?" I had completely lost track of time. It felt as though Sabina had been in our house forever, but somehow, each day also felt so very long. Had it been a few days, or a few years? I could barely tell.

"*Five*, Meg. She's five weeks old."

"I will try to call Lilly and see—"

"Wait," Grae said. I hadn't heard him use such a terse tone in weeks, not since Sabina came into our lives and the strange happiness had come over him. The sharpness of it startled me. "June's prepared the paperwork already. She thought it might have been asking too much of you, leaving it to you to handle the whole lot."

"But Grae...Lilly *has* to do it, they have to pick her middle name and—"

"Meg...listen to me...Lilly has nothing to do with this anymore. June's filled the paperwork in...for us."

"I don't understand."

"She said that sometimes for special families she fixes the paperwork." At my blank look, he spoke carefully, stressing the syllables. "She simplifies it."

I looked at the paper on the table and shuddered against a sudden, rising sense of dread. I had seen June falsify birth records twice in my time working with her. The first was when we placed a baby with one of her friends, the second time when a local politician had decided to adopt.

Even at the time I knew the consequences of this. In an ordinary adoption, there was an original birth certificate listing the biological parents of the child—locked away, yes, but they existed. What June was proposing meant removing any record of Lilly and James from Sabina's history.

The thought of it made me feel physically sick.

"But...Lilly..."

"June told me that you're putting off the registration *because* of Lilly. She said that you two had become far too close, and you might be struggling with the idea of registering the birth to her then having to file for an amendment to the certificate down the track."

My heart had started dancing a slightly frantic tango. I could feel the sweat building on my palms.

*No, no, no.*

"Did you...you didn't *tell* June, did you? That we're giving Sabina back to them?"

"I'm not an idiot, Megan. Although you obviously thought you could play me for one."

"I just wanted to help, Grae." Tears were rolling down my cheeks and onto my blouse.

"In all of this time, you forgot to mention to me that this *Lilly* is a sixteen-year-old kid. The way you talked about it, they were a stable, sensible couple who'd just missed the formality of the wedding ceremony. I was starting to wonder what was taking so long. Are they even legally allowed to get married?"

"They're working on it," I whispered. Grae's heavy exhalation condemned me.

"Did it occur to you that you've played God here, Meg?" I thought about the day in Lilly's hospital room when I had thought as much myself, and how proud I'd felt about that. "There are reasons we don't send babies home with sixteen-year-olds. How did you expect her to cope?"

"She's going to marry James."

"She's sixteen, for Christ's sakes, Megan! Married or not, do you seriously think the right thing to do is to give this baby to a *child* to raise?"

"Grae, she's a smart kid, she really is." My tears were as irritating to me as Sabina's were in the depth of the night; I was *furious* with myself. I just wanted to clear the emotional confusion so that I could explain my plan calmly to him. There was a logic to it, if I could just calm myself down enough explain it, he'd see that. Why, oh why, did I have to face this conversation now, when I was so exhausted that I could barely remember my own name?

"But she is a kid." There was no denying how frustrated Graeme was, probably as frustrated as I, although our points of view were diametrically opposed. His face was red, and there were beads of sweat on his forehead and cheeks. I marvelled at the way his arm around Sabina remained relaxed, as he shielded her from the force of his emotion. Why couldn't I do that?

He took a deep breath, then looked down to Sabina. She was staring up at him, wide awake and curious.

"Her eyes are changing colour," he said suddenly. The frustration was gone from his voice; in an instant, he was speaking with tenderness again.

"Are you sure?"

"Haven't you noticed? They were bright blue but I think maybe they're darkening."

"No, I haven't." I barely looked at her, compared to Grae. I fed her and I clothed her and I changed her nappies. I didn't talk to her, and no way on earth would I allow myself to gaze down at her lovingly like Graeme did every time she came into his field of vision. And that was surely a good thing—because I couldn't imagine the pain of truly connecting with that tiny little whirlwind and having to pass her back.

"That paperwork," Grae said, and he picked it up with his spare hand again and tossed it towards me. "It could mean that Sabina is ours. Really ours. No one would *ever* know any different. You never wanted to adopt, Meg—well, this is barely adoption, no one would ever even know. My family, your family, the courts, Sabina herself. To the entire world, she'll be ours. Do you really believe that some teenager can provide a better life for her than we can, just because they're biologically related?"

"But... this isn't even working, Graeme." I was panicked at the mere suggestion. "I'm terrible at this. She hates me. Why the hell would you want to make this a permanent arrangement?"

Graeme shifted Sabina so that she was resting along his forearms, her tiny head cradled in his palms. He stared down at her, and I saw then…at last I really understood what I'd done. I'd missed a lot of things in the weeks that had passed me by in a blur—the change in Sabina's eye colour apparently, but also the depth of love in my husband's eyes.

As distant and frustrated as I felt by Sabina, Graeme was equally besotted, and that was entirely *my* fault. I had put us in this situation, a pressure cooker of tears and emotion and twenty-four-hour baby care, and of course he had bonded with her. He had done what came naturally. *I* was the odd one out, with my frigid distance and my exhausted resentment.

"I'm thirty-five years old, Megan," he whispered. "We've been trying to have a baby of our own for fourteen years. Every time we fall pregnant, I wait for the moment I'm going to have to watch you die a little bit, right in front of me. We've given it our best shot, Meg…we really have…but I'm not doing it anymore."

"What are you saying?" Cold fear had gripped my gut. At first, I thought he was talking about our marriage. Had Sabina shown him that he wanted a baby, even more than he wanted me? I'd been waiting for that axe to fall for years. He looked away from Sabina, to me, and I felt overwhelmed with relief at the gentleness in his gaze. He still held affection for me.

"I'm going to be sterilised. I am giving up on the idea of a pregnancy, Meg."

"No—but, *no*! Grae, we can do this, we just have to keep trying—maybe next time…"

"*No.*"

He didn't need to roar the word. He stared right into my eyes and delivered it quickly but with a force of emotion behind it that stopped me in my tracks.

The tears that spilt this time were different. These weren't exhausted, embarrassed tears at having my manipulative plan found out. These were tears that came from the very core of me.

Grae was taking from me the one thing in my life that I'd kept going for.

"Sometimes you have to let go of one dream to pick up another one."

"It's not the same for me, Graeme. It's just not. I need to *do* this... I want to carry our baby, to make you a *real* father—"

"Meg," he sighed, and shook his head, then looked down to Sabina again. "Can't you see? I *am* a real father." His voice broke and we sat there in ragged silence, now we were both battling to bring our emotions under control. When he spoke again, he was pleading with me. "Life has handed us this baby for a reason, and I love her already. I'm not letting her go—not to some foolish kids; too young to get married, far too young to provide her with the life that she deserves. Can you really ask that of me, after all we've been through together? I know this is hard on you, Megan, and God—I understand how much you've wanted to have a child and I've tried to be supportive. But this is the end of the road."

"Grae..."

"I'm putting my foot down, and I'm doing this for all of us—for me, for you, and for Sabina."

"She needs to go home to Lilly," I choked.

"She *is* home."

"I promised Lilly—"

"Even Lilly will see that this is for the best in time." Grae stood abruptly, and turned away from me. I saw the rise of his shoulders as he lifted Sabina close to his face and kissed her gently. He walked to the door, then turned back to me. "I don't want to be cruel, Megan. I really don't... but I need you to think about something. For fourteen years we've fought for a baby. For fourteen long years *your* body has been all that stood between us and a family. You can't control that, but you can control *this*. We have a chance here to raise this beautiful little girl as our own." He stared directly at me. "Are you really going to take that from me too?"

—

The neatly folded paperwork sat on my kitchen table for four days. We ate meals beside it and I wiped the table several times a day but did not touch it, I wiped around it, as if even brushing against it would be dangerous.

I thought about a lot of things during those four days. I thought about Graeme and how much I loved him, and how much marriage to *me* had cost him. I thought our lost babies had drained and wounded me. I thought they were exhausting and devastating and depressing to suffer through. I'd never much thought about the toll they took on Graeme.

He could have walked away, and he didn't.

I wondered what he would do this time, if I refused to sign the paperwork, and insisted on handing Sabina back. Would this be the final straw? Would he leave me now, and render me utterly barren for once and for all? He hadn't said as much, but there had been an undeniably deadly intent to that difficult conversation at the kitchen table.

On the fourth day, I stopped looking at the paperwork and thinking about what would happen if I didn't sign, and instead, I picked up Sabina and I walked outside into the garden with her. I lay a blanket down on the grass and I sat on one side of it, then I rested her on her back on the other.

She was awake, and content for once, that precious state of emotion she usually reserved for Graeme. I sat apart from her on the other edge of the blanket, but I stared at her and I asked myself if I could even bring myself to do this. What kind of a future could I offer Sabina? What kind of person would she grow to be, with a mother like me?

Sabina waved her fists and kicked her feet a little, and she stared up at the sky as the shadows of clouds overhead passed across her face. I remembered Grae's remarks about her eyes. I bent low to investigate and realised that her eyes really were changing, morphing from baby-blue to something darker... brown, like Lilly's?

And mine. Maybe Sabina's eyes would be brown like mine.

Sabina suddenly met my gaze, and then for the first time in her entire life, a smile broke over her tiny face. Her eyes brightened and her mouth opened and her cheeks turned upwards and for a moment we both froze just like that.

It was the first moment of real connection I felt with Sabina, and it was almost as if some essential part of her reached in and hooked deeply into some part of me. There were weeks and months and probably years of exhaustion and tears and self-doubt left ahead of me, but in one single smile, she managed to persuade me that I really *could* do this... that there was untapped love for her inside of me, and if I just gave her the chance, she'd draw it right out.

Then her smile faded away, but her gaze was locked on my face, and I couldn't look away from her either. There were tears raining down from my eyes all over her and I tried to push them away as they rolled onto my cheeks but soon gave up, there were too many and they were flowing too hard and fast. It was like a dam had burst within me, and I was crying for all of the babies I'd loved and lost already, and for this baby that I really could take, and the fact that she would never really be mine. After a while, I picked her up and I cuddled her close to me, and I breathed in her scent and delighted in the softness of her cheek against mine, just as I'd seen Graeme do and just as I'd been too afraid to do myself.

I finally looked at the paperwork that afternoon. Grae had already signed the line designated for *father*, and in June's careful handwriting I was listed as Sabina Baxter's mother. It was a beautiful sight to behold—that paper may have been a lie, but it said that I was a mum. I wanted to frame it somewhere prominent and tell every person I'd ever met.

There was a careful space left for a middle name, and the date.

Just a few more lines of black ink on a page, and history would never even know the difference; June had even had one of her less than honourable doctors certify that he'd seen me give birth.

Sabina had gone to sleep in her bassinet for once. I was feeling tender after our sudden moment of connection in the garden and it was good to have the distance from her while I thought about our situation.

It was even better to have empty arms when I walked to the phone.

I didn't even have Lilly's phone number. It was an oversight on my part—but the plan to take Sabina for her had formed so quickly that I hadn't even had a chance to scribble it down before I resigned. It wasn't difficult to find, though. There was only one listing for *Wyzlecki* in the entire district.

"Hello?" The voice that answered was young and male.

"Is Liliana home?"

"Yes. Who's speaking?"

I panicked, and stammered rather like Lilly when I said,

"T-this is a teacher from school. I'm—Mrs. Baxter."

"Lilly doesn't go to school."

"I know that," I said, and offered a thin laugh. "But she used to be in my class."

I heard the sound of the receiver dropping, and then in the

distance heard the boy calling for Lilly. A few minutes later, she came to the phone.

"Hello?"

"Lilly, it's Megan. I mean, it's Mrs. Baxter."

"Oh...hello! Is everything okay?"

I'd almost forgotten about the breathless, naïve quality to Lilly's voice. Over the phone, she sounded younger still than she seemed in person. I tried to steel myself against the sickly guilt in my gut.

"Everything is fine, Lilly. She's fine. But...how are you and James going? Are we any closer?"

I could hear movement on the other end of the phone, then the sound of a sliding door closing. When Lilly spoke again, she was whispering,

"Not yet. Tata won't even let us talk to each other, and he won't let me send letters and if James is sending them, I'm not getting them. I really don't know what to do."

I'd hoped that she'd tell me that there was a plan, that they were days away from a marriage licence, that the solution was within arm's reach. If they'd been ready, the decision would have been made for me, and I would have politely wound up the phone call and readied myself to break my own heart, and to break Graeme's with it.

Instead, the directionless optimism in Lilly's voice was like a knife twisting in my gut. I slowly sat in the chair beside the phone table and closed my eyes.

I had the fate of two families in the palm of my hand, and the power to change more lives with one decision than I could bear to really contemplate.

"And you're not even going to school anymore?" I whispered.

"Tata was worried people would find out what...about...

you know," she whispered back. "He said he might send me to boarding school in the city next year but . . . I don't know if he means it. I'm working on the farm with him and Henri."

"Lilly—" I was going to explain to Lilly a few practical things—about birth registration requirements, and my marriage, and my husband and Sabina and the nature of love and bonding. Then I realised that not a single thing I could say would justify to Liliana Wyzlecki what was about to happen.

I knew, you see. Even in the moment, I knew that it was not justifiable, and I knew that it was unforgiveable.

I did it anyway.

"We can't go on this way forever, Lilly," I whispered instead.

"I know . . . I *know*. But . . . I don't know what else to do." I could hear the tension and the terror rising. "C-can't you take care of her any more, Megan?"

"That's not what I'm saying." I could barely form the words. "I'll . . . we'll . . . I promise you I'll take *very* good care of her." A sudden sob interrupted my words and I pressed my hand over my mouth. "I promise, Lilly."

"Are you going to keep her?" She was suddenly weeping too, and I couldn't bear it. She'd trusted me with the most important thing in her life, and I was taking it from her.

"I think so," I choked. "I don't think I have much choice, Lilly. Grae loves her, and we have to do the paperwork now, plus—it's not good for anyone to go on like this."

"Please, Megan. Please just give us a few more weeks, maybe a month or two—"

"I *can't*." I could barely speak. I knew I had to end the conversation. There was no good to come out of this chat. "We all have to get on with our lives. I am so, so sorry."

I should have hung up. Instead, I listened to the desperate

gasps of breath as Lilly struggled to control her own panic. We were both silent for a moment, and then when Lilly spoke again, she sounded as if she was choking.

"You said you'd help me," she said. Her voice was rising, getting stronger and louder with each word until she was shouting. I knew her family would hear her and I knew she had been whispering for fear of that. She was beyond rationality, and all because of the hurt that *I* was causing her. "You said you'd *help* us, but you're the worst of all of them. You just wanted my baby for yourself, didn't you? You couldn't have one of your own, so you tricked me into giving you mine!"

I hung up then, frantically fumbling with the phone, desperate to distance myself immediately from the pain that I'd caused her.

It was a retreat into denial. I *could* hang up the phone, I could cut her off. And out of all of the unfairness, it struck me that *this* was the worst part.

Lilly had been powerless in the hospital, and I had watched that struggle and been sickened by it. It seemed but a heartbeat later that now *I* was the one rendering her powerless...offering her daughter and then snatching her back...hanging up the telephone right in the middle of her speech, cutting off her right of reply.

Lilly was right.

I really was the worst of all of them.

—

When Grae came home for lunch, the paperwork was still on the table, but I'd signed and dated it and left the page open for him to see. He had repeated his usual routine and had Sabina in the crook of his arm.

He reached forward for the papers with his other hand and brought it close to read it, as if he couldn't quite believe what he was seeing.

"Please take it to June on your way back to work so that she can finalise things."

I waited for him to protest at the middle name I'd chosen. Instead, Grae dropped the paper back onto the table. Then he lifted Sabina and rested her in the corner where his neck and shoulder met. He swayed a little, and he closed his eyes, and I watched the endless shades of joy breaking over him. I was watching the man that I loved becoming a father as surely as if I were present at the birth of his child. *Here* was my reward for the terrible thing that I'd agreed to do.

When he opened his eyes, I met his gaze, and the thoughts that passed between us were not given words. It would be almost forty years before we'd raise the subject of the adoption again—the paperwork denied those frightful early weeks, and we were content to play along, even in the intimacy of our own relationship. We didn't need to speak about it; we both knew that we were now complicit in the deception together.

Grae did not realise it yet, but I knew that we would be guilty together too. The guilt and shame of it all was the shared price that we would privately pay to create *this* family.

I knew that every time Sabina cried and I felt irritation at the sound, somewhere else in the universe Lilly would be longing with all of her heart to hear that same cry. I knew that there'd be a million more smiles over the years and that every time I enjoyed one I'd be committing another act of theft. I knew that Grae would love Sabina with all of his heart, but that James would have done that too, and however big our love for her grew to be—their loss would always dwarf it.

"We will have to move back to Sydney," I said, after a while.

"I'm not going to be able to do this on my own...I think the past few weeks have shown that. I'll need my family to help. Plus...I don't want any complications arising...and if we stay out here...we're just...it's just too close to them. There's just too much potential for messy run-ins."

Grae looked at me at last. Then he smiled, and at least in that moment, all of the years of longing and pain had been wiped clean from his face. He was that charming young man I'd married, and I loved him so deeply that there were no limits on what I'd do for his happiness.

"You'll see, Megan," Grae said, after a while. "You'll see that this is for the best. For all of us."

# EPILOGUE

## 21 March 2013

Mama Lilly and Papa James were running late.

Mum was sitting beside me shaking so hard that my chair was shaking too. I took her hand, more to hold her still than to calm her. Every now and again, I heard a little squeak from deep in her throat a whimper of sorts. Mum was as unsettled and anxious as I'd ever seen her.

Around us, hundreds of people were taking their seats. The Great Hall of Parliament House was full, the space both bursting with people and laden with grief. The event hadn't even started yet, and already I'd seen countless people sobbing.

I kept glancing at my watch, because Mama could *not* miss this. She'd texted me a few minutes earlier to say that they were still trying to find a parking space, and I'd have run out and given her mine if there'd been a way to do it without leaving Mama and Mum to reunite without me here to support them both.

"Please take your seats," some nameless suit spoke softly into the microphone, and I released Mum to stand and look around for Mama. I saw her slip through the door just before it was closed. She was wearing a beautiful pink and purple dress, the colours bright and striking, and a pair of hot pink sandals that I'd helped her select on one of our monthly weekends with her. Mama was running—Papa coming in several steps behind her as he often did. She saw me and waved, and then she beamed.

This was my mama's day.

Her footsteps slowed as she approached us, her gaze fixed

on Mum. It had been Mama's insistence that Mum should be here, and I'd actually tried to talk her out of it at first. I couldn't quite believe that they wanted to meet at all, but today hardly seemed the day.

This was the day that the Prime Minister was going to apologise for the hurt and damage caused by forced adoption policies.

But Mama had been adamant that Mum should attend, and I'd already learned not to mess with Liliana Wyzlecki when she set her mind on something. She and Mum had crossed paths electronically over the past six months—both working to collate stories of other families affected by forced adoption. Mum had also joined forces with the lobby group who had worked towards this apology, and in recent months had returned to full time work supporting and reuniting affected families.

Mama felt that Mum should be at the apology too. She said that she'd earned it. That was nice in theory, but I was nervous about them coming face-to-face. Mama had come a long way in a short time, but I was terrified that she was asking too much of herself.

Mum rose as Mama approached, and so I did too. Mama hugged me, and then Papa too, and finally they both stood in front of Mum. It was my turn to shake, this time with adrenaline.

"I'm so sorry—" Mum started to say, but Lilly shook her head. Her lips were compressed into a tight line and there was such a tension in the way that she held herself that I was suddenly sure that I had been right all along and that this was a terrible, terrible mistake. I wondered if she was going to launch herself at Mum and physically injure her.

Lilly did raise her arms, but as I hastily moved to intervene, she pulled my mum into one of her those overwhelming embraces that I'd come to love so much. Mum was stiff at first, but no one could resist the all-encompassing warmth of Mama

Lilly's hugs. My mothers stood like that, both sobbing, until almost everyone else in the Great Hall had taken their seat.

When they finally sat, they took the seats on either side of me. Mama sat very close to me and took my left hand between both of hers. Mum took my right hand, and I was right there in the middle...just as I always had been, I suppose.

I had wondered what good this apology would do for us all. Could anything undo the damage done, could any mere words achieve healing that would not come through time alone? There was an astounding energy to the room though, and from the minute the Prime Minister took the stage, I understood why so many people had fought for so long to see this happen.

It was just as Lilly had said to me. It's by bringing the ghosts to light that we lay them to rest.

In that crowd of officials and dignitaries and other affected families I listened, and I cried, and I thought about the childhood I'd had, and the childhood I *would* have had. Then my thoughts turned to my precious son Hugo, just a few months old and safe back at the hotel with Ted and Dad. It was my first full day away from him, and it would have been easy to fret about the small things. Had Ted given him enough milk? Was he remembering to change his nappy?

Then I'd tune back into what was happening around me and the context of it would make me dizzy. Hugo would be waiting for me, and in just another few hours, I would take him back into my arms. I promised myself that I would always remember to be grateful for the privilege of parenting him.

I would be a warm mother like Lilly—generous with my hugs and my emotions. I would wear bright clothes and I would beam at people and I would cook up a storm at the slightest invitation to do so.

But I would also be a strong mother like Megan—fierce

when I needed to be, and endlessly supportive. I would drag Hugo to speech therapy if he needed it, and I would gently bully him towards hard work if he'd inherited my tendency to avoid it.

I had the best of both worlds now, and because of that, *Hugo* would have the best of both worlds in *his* mother.

As the Prime Minister closed out her speech, we rose automatically for a standing ovation. I looked to Mama, who was clapping and cheering and weeping and beaming. Every now and again she'd stop all of that and pull me close for a hug, then she'd go right back to it. For my Mama, nothing could undo the damage caused by forced adoption, but our reunion and now the government's apology were vital steps in the right direction.

Mum was clapping too in her much more reserved fashion, her guilt and shame etched onto her face. No amount of tireless charity work was going to redeem my mum, although the work leading to this apology was at least a start towards her finding peace with herself.

As messy as it was, this was my family now—birthed in good intentions gone astray and the heartbreaking decision that had changed all of our lives. As much as we could, we would let the past rest behind us as we worked to build the future together.

Mama and Mum might never be friends, but for me and for Hugo, they *would* be family.

And because of that we had a second chance, together.

# LETTER FROM KELLY

Thank you so much for reading *The Secret Daughter*. I hope that Sabina, Lilly and Megan's story touched your heart. Although this is a work of fiction, forced adoption was unfortunately a very real part of recent history in many parts of the world. You can find more information about former forced adoption practices in Australia at the National Archive of Australia's Forced Adoption History Project online.

If you enjoyed this book, I'd be so grateful if you'd take the time to write a review. I really appreciate getting feedback, and your review will help other readers find my books.

Finally, if you'd like to receive an email when my next book is released, you can sign up to my mailing list at:

www.kellyrimmer.com/email

I'll only send emails when I have a new book to share and I won't share your email address with anyone else.

Kelly

# *The Secret Daughter*

## Reading Group Guide

# WRITING *THE SECRET DAUGHTER*

Hello! Thanks so much for reading *The Secret Daughter*. I wrote this book in 2014. I'd published my first novel the year before I wrote it and was, for the very first time, writing to a deadline—while holding down a day job and parenting two small children. It was an exciting, nerve-wracking time, and given how busy I was, I set out to write about something easy...something that wouldn't break my heart...something light. That was my plan right up until I saw an article in my Facebook feed about the Australian prime minister's apology to victims of forced adoption. Soon, I found myself spending hours reading through hundreds of personal submissions to the Australian Senate Inquiry into Forced Adoption and, later, the Forced Adoptions History Project (you can find it here: http://forcedadoptions.naa.gov.au/content/forced-adoptions-history-project). I was horrified at my own ignorance about forced adoption and obsessed with better educating myself on the subject. But as I read those real-life stories, this fictional one took shape in my mind, and it nagged at me until I agreed to write it. Sabina, Lilly and Megan's story was soon born.

I decided to set the story near my own hometown of Orange, New South Wales—about three and a half hours west of Sydney, in the rural area known as the "Central West." It's a region of rolling hills and flat plains, of rural cities and tiny villages, all surrounded by wheat and sheep farms and dusty eucalyptus-rich bushlands.

I loved the idea of Sabina living out her childhood in the inner city with Graeme and Megan, then discovering Lilly and James' farming lifestyle through eyes more accustomed to the cityscape. You might have noticed other contrasts—Megan's more formal nature versus Lilly's emotional, physically affectionate personality... Megan's pride in her home versus Lilly's more functional décor. Every single mother is unique both in her strengths and in her weaknesses. For someone like Sabina, wondering what might have been, those differences would be glaringly obvious.

When I was halfway through writing the first draft, I had the opportunity to travel to the United States. My children were three and five years old at the time, and I'd never spent more than a night away from them, so finding myself on the other side of the planet for more than two weeks came as quite a shock to my system. Of course, in the scheme of things, it was the blink of an eye, and I was able to video chat with my children reasonably frequently. But I wrote a lot during that trip, and I reflected on how distance can make a mother's mind play tricks. I'd speak to my children when the time zones allowed, be reassured that they were just fine, and take myself to bed, only to wake up shaking in fear, convinced that something might have happened to them in the minutes or hours since we spoke. There was something uniquely stressful for me in knowing that I didn't actually have a full picture of their welfare, even though it was for a short period of time, even though they were almost certainly just fine. I started to imagine how permanent distance, such as the one Lilly faced from Sabina, might wreak havoc on a mother's mind. I remain awed by women who survive separation from children they love dearly, and in some ways, I see Lilly is the hero of this story. She faced an almost unimaginable trauma, and not only survived but also found a way to both help others survive too...and then, of course, to ultimately find the grace and generosity to offer forgiveness to Megan.

I wanted to write about Megan and Graeme as a couple who faced infertility in a time before the advanced treatment options available today, but I soon realised that it's not just medical science that's come a long way over those decades—the same can be said for the dynamics of what's considered a "normal marriage." Some readers have told me they see Graeme as the villain of this story, and perhaps they are right. He is controlling and demanding, and he consistently works to withhold the truth about Sabina's history. But equality in a marriage is a new concept, and Graeme would have been raised at a time when a different kind of masculinity was idealized. That doesn't excuse his behaviour, but I hope it helps to explain why I wrote him the way that I did. When I planned Graeme, I thought that for such a man the underlying shame in his life would be crippling. He's ashamed of his inability to give Megan the baby she so desperately wanted, and then even after he manipulates his way into parenthood, he finds himself trapped by the shame of the truth for forty years. When Megan finally finds her voice and stands up to him, they have an opportunity to redefine the dynamic in their relationship, and when the truth is exposed, Graeme is liberated from his shame in the same way Lilly, Sabina and Megan are liberated from secrecy and lies. I like to imagine him and Megan working toward a new happiness in their later years, spending time with their grandson Hugo and rebuilding their relationship with Sabina.

As for Sabina herself, she's just the kind of character I love to write. She's flawed and she has challenges, and she doesn't always get it right. But beneath it all, she's strong enough to know what she wants and courageous enough to pursue her desires despite her anxiety and her fears. And I wanted to pair her with a partner who would be both a sounding board and an endless support, someone she loved dearly, but who was also her closest friend.

*The Secret Daughter* was published digitally in 2015 and, to my surprise, quickly found momentum and even a place on the *USA Today* bestseller list...and the emails started coming. I've lost count of the numbers over the years since then, but I've been honoured to have women from all over the globe share their stories with me because of this book. This story is about Australian forced adoption, but the term *forced adoption* covers many practices, both institutional and personal. One woman told me about her experiences in a maternity home in her teens and about the baby she'd never even laid eyes upon because it was taken from her so quickly. More than sixty years later, her email to me was the first time she'd ever "spoken" of her experience. Can you imagine living with a trauma like that for sixty years, unable to give voice to it? One woman told me about having her baby literally dragged from her arms, and I wept at a party as I read her email on my phone. Not one but two of my own friends told me about their own experiences of forced adoption—I'd had no idea anyone I knew had personal experience of the subject until this book was published.

I've heard about women who were reunited with their children as adults, only to find that the wounds were simply too deep and the relationship they'd dreamed of never took hold. I heard from a son who sought after his birth mother for years, only to locate her just after her death. I heard from women who were reunited with their children as adults and who went on to forge a uniquely close bond. I hold all of these stories in my heart as gifts from readers; they are the greatest honour of my career.

# QUESTIONS FOR READERS

1. *The Secret Daughter* is narrated by Sabina, Lilly and Megan. Do you think these characters were reliable narrators? Was there a particular narrator you connected with more? Are there any other characters you would have liked to "hear" tell part of the story?
2. Who was your favorite character? Why? Were there any characters you disliked?
3. Lilly's thoughts on Megan evolve dramatically over the story—from admiration and gratitude to a deep-set hatred, and finally, to forgiveness. What are the catalysts for these shifts? Do you think her thoughts about Megan are healthy?
4. Do you think Megan and Graeme made the right decisions? If not, where did they go "wrong"?
5. Do you think Megan and Graeme were good parents to Sabina? What makes a "good" family?
6. Did you think Megan's relationship with Graeme was realistic? Given the period when this book is set, do you think she could/should have done anything further to assert herself in that relationship?
7. Is there a villain in this novel? Why/why not?
8. Did the story end as you expected it to?
9. Were you aware of forced adoption in Australia before reading this book?
10. Do you think there are ever circumstances where forced adoption is morally right?

# ABOUT THE AUTHOR

Kelly Rimmer is the *USA Today* bestselling author of contemporary fiction novels including *Me Without You*, *The Secret Daughter*, *When I Lost You*, *A Mother's Confession*, *Before I Let You Go*, and her most recent release, *The Things We Cannot Say*. She lives in rural Australia with her family.

You can learn more at:

KellyRimmer.com
Twitter @KelRimmerwrites
Facebook.com/KellyMRimmer